THE ROGUE PRINCESS

THE FOUR KINGDOMS AND BEYOND

THE FOUR KINGDOMS

The Princess Companion: A Retelling of The Princess and the Pea (Book One)

The Princess Fugitive: A Reimagining of Little Red Riding Hood (Book Two)

The Coronation Ball: A Four Kingdoms Cinderella Novelette

Happily Every Afters: A Reimagining of Snow White and Rose Red (Novella)

The Princess Pact: A Twist on Rumpelstiltskin (Book Three)

A Midwinter's Wedding: A Retelling of The Frog Prince (Novella)

The Princess Game: A Reimagining of Sleeping Beauty (Book Four)

The Princess Search: A Retelling of The Ugly Duckling (Book Five)

BEYOND THE FOUR KINGDOMS

A Dance of Silver and Shadow: A Retelling of The Twelve Dancing Princesses (Book One)

A Tale of Beauty and Beast: A Retelling of Beauty and the Beast (Book Two)

A Crown of Snow and Ice: A Retelling of The Snow Queen (Book Three)

A Dream of Ebony and White: A Retelling of Snow White (Book Four)

A Captive of Wing and Feather: A Retelling of Swan Lake (Book Five)

A Princess of Wind and Wave: A Retelling of The Little Mermaid (Book Six)

THE ROGUE PRINCESS

A RETELLING OF PUSS IN BOOTS

MELANIE CELLIER

LUMINANT PUBLICATIONS

Luminant Publications
PO Box 305
Greenacres, South Australia 5086

melanie@melaniecellier.com
http://www.melaniecellier.com

Cover Design by Karri Klawiter
Editing by Mary Novak and Laura Cifelli
Proofreading by Deborah Grace White

For my sister-in-law, Karyn,
one of the most caring, thoughtful, and creative people I know

ROYAL FAMILY TREES

RETURN TO THE FOUR KINGDOMS

KINGDOM OF ARDASIRA

Sultan Kalmir—Sultana Nadira

Parents of

Prince Zain (Zaid)—Cassandra of Eldon

KINGDOM OF KURALAN

Sultan Khalil—Sultana Rabia

Parents of

Prince Tarek (Rek)—Zaria of Kuralan

Princess Adara—Navid of Kuralan

Prince Xavier

Prince Xander

THE FOUR KINGDOMS

KINGDOM OF LANOVER

King Leonardo—Queen Viktoria

Parents of

Prince Frederic—Evangeline (Evie) of Lanover
    Parents of
    Prince Leo
    Princess Beatrice

Princess Clarisse—Charles of Rangmere
    Parents of
    Princess Isabella
    Prince Danton

Prince Cassian—Tillara (Tillie) of the Nomadic Desert Traders
    Parents of
    Prince Luca
    Princess Iris
    Princess Violet

Prince Raphael—Princess Marie of Northhelm
    Parents of
    Prince Benjamin
    Prince Emmett

Princess Celeste—Prince William of Northhelm
    Parents of
    Princess Danielle

Princess Cordelia—Ferdinand of Northhelm
    Parents of
    Princess Arabella
    Prince Andrew

Princess Celine—Prince Oliver of Eldon
   Parents of
   Prince Oscar
   Prince Otto

Four Kingdoms
Northhelm
Rangmeros
Rangmere
Kuralan
Arcadia
Arcadie
Northgate
The Great Desert
Karema
Lanare
Lanoren
Seekala
Ardasira
Inverne
Banishment Island

PART I
BEYOND THE DESERT

PROLOGUE

I stared at the stranger standing in front of me, my mind blank. I couldn't process his words.

When I didn't speak, he repeated himself, his face growing concerned.

"Kalila? Did you hear me?" he asked when I still said nothing.

"It's Kali." The words came out clear, despite the strange numbness of my lips.

He nodded once before hesitating and peering at me again. "Did you hear what I said?"

"You said my father is dead. *Our* father."

This stranger claimed to be my brother—a claim I couldn't deny given his face. I had heard people reference the strong resemblance between my brother and our mother—just as they always said the same about me—but I'd been so young when Bernard left. I hadn't had the chance to see it for myself. My memories of him were too hazy.

But I could see it now. This had to be the Bernard who had left so long ago.

His expression cleared at my words, the concern replaced with relief. He must have been wondering if I was witless.

I felt witless, my thoughts stolen by the shock of his news.

"I know he'd slowed down since the accident, given the damage to his leg," I said, still struggling to grasp his meaning. "But…dead? The leg was getting better!"

"The wound had become badly infected." Bernard grimaced. "The actual injury had improved, but the infection got into his blood. There was nothing the doctors could do. So Father wrote to me. I came as quickly as I could."

My brain whirled as I tried to imagine my father secretly meeting with doctors at the mill or when I was out shopping. How could he keep something like this from me? In the confusing mess of thoughts, I latched on to something of little relevance.

"Our mother died, too. You didn't come back then." I sounded accusatory, but I let my words stand, hanging in the air between us.

Bernard shifted uncomfortably. "Yes. But that was two years ago."

"And Father was still alive." I didn't need to say any more. We both knew it was all the explanation necessary.

Mother had often spoken of my older brother, but only when Father was absent. Father and Bernard had clashed badly, their constant conflicts growing more frequent as he neared adulthood. According to Mother, they were too alike. I didn't know anything about that, though—my ten-years-older brother had left home at fifteen when I was still a young child.

I tried to call up the memories I did have. All I could recollect was a tall lad—almost an adult in my eyes—who used to throw me in the air while I squealed with laughter. And I remembered crying after he left. That memory was clearest of all.

"She died, and you didn't come." I knew Father had written to inform him of our loss, and I'd looked for him, sure he would return. But he hadn't even written back. "And yet somehow you're here now."

Bernard had turned up at the house early that morning, but I'd barely managed a glimpse of him before Father hustled me out of the house for the day, saying he needed to speak to my brother. I'd spent the hours shopping with Zaria, my closest friend, trying to distract myself from the all-consuming curiosity over the unexpected appearance of my supposed brother.

I'd had a good excuse to shop, though. Zaria would be officially betrothed to the crown prince of Kuralan within days—an event that was to be marked with a large celebration at the palace. My first palace function naturally necessitated a new outfit, and Father had handed over an entire purse of gold without a grumble.

It had been far more than I needed to purchase a single outfit, and most of the coins remained in the pouch. I hadn't protested at the excess, though, since Father rarely gave me anything to spend on myself. I had kept careful hold of the extra, intending to return the coins when he asked for them.

And now he would never ask.

"He knew." Horror leached into my tone. "He knew how close he was to the end."

"Yes." Bernard shifted his weight awkwardly. "In his letter, he told me he was dying and asked me to return swiftly. I think he was barely holding on for my arrival. I was shocked to hear he'd hidden it from you."

"Father didn't like uncomfortable conversations or grief." I'd learned that after Mother's death. "But why did he want to speak to *you*?"

I didn't care how rude I sounded. My brother had earned any rudeness.

He cleared his throat. "Because of the mill, of course."

"The mill?" I stared at him, wondering why nothing made sense anymore. "I don't understand."

"Surely you must know the terms of the lease?"

I shook my head. I knew the lease had been a source of frustration to Father, but I had never read the actual document.

"You at least know that His Majesty owns all the mills in Karema?"

"Of course. Everyone knows that."

He nodded. "The terms of the lease allow for it to be passed between generations of the same family—as long as it's passed directly to a trained, adult relative without any break in the mill's operation."

"You? You're trained as a miller?"

He laughed. "Of course. I've been learning about milling since I was old enough to walk. I might have left Karema, but I wasn't fool enough to throw away years of training. Father arranged for me to transfer my apprenticeship to another miller in a town near the Great Desert."

I gaped at him. "*Father* did?"

"Well, I think Mother was the one behind it. But it was the mill where Father did his own apprenticeship. Where he met Mother. He still knew the old miller, and..." He trailed off, looking away from me. "I'd have come back if I'd known she was sick." His voice sounded thick, but he kept his face turned away. "But there didn't seem any point after...It wasn't as if she was here to..."

"I was here," I said, my voice small.

He said nothing.

No surprise stirred inside me. Why would my brother—a staid miller, like our father—make such an effort for a sister he didn't know? One who had nothing to offer him or the mill.

The silence lengthened between us as I tried to come to terms with my new reality.

"So you're taking over the lease," I said eventually, hoping that if I spoke the words aloud, they might start to make sense. "You'll be the new miller here."

Father had always seemed so solid and sturdy, a fixture who

would be there forever, never changing. Any concept of a future after his death had been nebulous. But if I had ever thought about the matter, I had always been reassured by the fact we owned our small house near the mill as well as many of the tools father used. If I sold Father's tools, the proceeds could easily support me and the house for some time. I hadn't imagined Bernard coming back and making a claim on any of it.

But now…

"I suppose you'll be using his tools," I said, remembering the single bag Bernard had arrived with.

He nodded, his face alive with awkwardness at the topic.

"I was only an assistant miller back in Maddox. I don't have any tools of my own, so Father has left me all of his. He wrote it all down before…If you want to see…"

I shook my head swiftly. Part of me wanted to rage and protest—to declare it couldn't be true. But the weight of the purse in my pocket held me silent. I should have questioned Father when he gave it to me after all. There was only one reason he would have handed over his savings in coin to me. Only one reason he would have sent for his son—or Bernard would have agreed to come. But if Bernard was to be the new miller, did that mean…

"And the house?" I asked, the final word coming out on a squeak.

His discomfort grew. "Of course you're welcome to continue living here for as long as you like."

Live with the brother who was now a stranger—in the home of my dead parents, no less? I usually had a lively imagination, but it failed me now.

Bernard hadn't mentioned a wife, so he must be single still, but his fortunes had just changed drastically. He was a senior miller in the capital city with a lifetime lease on a royal mill. He wouldn't remain single for long, and the house wasn't that big.

I gasped a breath, shaking my head. Were the walls moving,

the room around me growing smaller? If I didn't get outside soon, I would start to suffocate. There was no way I could stay here, confined as I had always been but without even the comfort of familiarity.

I had always yearned for adventure, but the burning desire to be gone from this place had a new urgency now.

Bernard cleared his throat, his uncomfortable expression somehow deepening.

"Is there perhaps someone—" He cleared his throat again. "A young man…"

"Oh." I looked away, feeling my cheeks heat. Was that what he was thinking? That I was likely to leave for my own household before he brought a wife home to his?

"Father mentioned his disappointment that—" He broke off and rubbed the back of his neck. "But fathers don't always know what's in their daughters' hearts. I believe he provided you with a dow—" He faltered and fell silent as several things finally came into clarity.

Father had hinted often enough that I should take an interest in one of his apprentices or assistants, but I had never taken him seriously. Why hadn't he explained his true concern? If I had married one of the millers of his training, he could have passed the mill to his son-in-law.

But would understanding the lease have made a difference? It didn't take even a second's thought to know the answer to that. The fear and grief coursing through me now did nothing to lessen the certainty I had always felt inside. I had no desire to be a miller's wife, growing old in the same home I was born in.

While I knew better than to talk about my desire for travel and distant adventures in front of Father—such talk had been reserved for my mother—he had known my true nature. And since I had inherited it from her, he had accepted it begrudgingly. Our mother had given up her roving life as a desert nomad for love of our father, and he had loved her back too dearly to force her daughter into a life of security and monotony.

My hand went to the purse in my pocket, resting over it. Father must have held out as long as possible before calling for Bernard, hoping until the end that I would choose a miller husband. My brother thought I had refused to do so because I had someone else in mind—but that, at the end, our father had decided to give me my dowry anyway. Bernard saw the coins as the tacit approval Father had refused to speak, and he wanted me to know he wouldn't cause any trouble over my choice, now that our father was gone.

The coins pressed against my fingers. Father had never been one for deep conversation or for indulging hopes and dreams, but he had always known my true desire. And he had given the purse to me directly, rather than entrusting it to Bernard as my dowry. Was Bernard partially right, then? Had it been given as unspoken acceptance of a life decision Father had always opposed?

Had Father handed me, not a dowry, but my freedom?

Slowly my back straightened, my hand dropping to my side.

"There's no one here for me," I said, my voice surprisingly steady. "But don't worry, I won't be a burden to you." He opened his mouth—no doubt to protest—but I continued. "I'm going to Mother's people."

"Mother's people?" He gave me a piercing look.

I expected him to respond with surprise, perhaps to remind me that our mother's people had all been killed or driven off long ago. Desert nomad tribes had once existed beyond the borders of Ardasira and Kuralan, living on the fringes of the Great Desert which bordered both kingdoms to the west. But the tribes had been hunted by someone wanting to steal their secrets, and the only survivors had disappeared into the depths of the uncrossable desert.

Mother had survived because by the time her tribesmen were

hunted and attacked, she had already left her tribe and blended into the settled population far from the Great Desert.

Even as a child, I had never had contact with that side of my family. Mother was sure some of them were still alive—whispering to me at night about the existence of other kingdoms beyond the sand. But I hadn't been sure if it was anything more than a fairy story until our neighboring kingdom of Ardasira announced the arrival of a girl claiming to come from a kingdom across the Great Desert. Mother had been delighted, sure it was the first step to renewing contact with the peoples on the west of the desert.

But it wasn't until eighteen months later that the Ardasirans found a nomad survivor who knew the secret of the crossing. Mother had never known the route of oases that allowed caravans to cross the desert and reach those kingdoms. But the information came too late for her—she died before the first delegation crossed the sand.

She never had the chance to take me in search of her remaining relatives, although she hadn't wavered in her belief they had survived the crossing. She had often told me the tales about the time before, when the land to the west was a garden empire, and the land that was now Ardasira and Kuralan was merely uninhabited fringes. Everyone knew the story of the three brothers, and the treachery of the youngest brother which had caused the gardens to turn to sand and sent the people fleeing east.

Of course many had believed the stories to be no more than legend—at least until the recent discovery of the youngest brother's fabled treasure caves. And few knew about the extra part of the story told by the desert nomads. Their story claimed half of their own people had gone west instead of east, toward the fledgling kingdoms located on that side of the empire. But the separated people had refused to stay thus, learning to know the desert and eventually to find a path across, keeping the knowledge protected for generations.

Mother had always longed to make the crossing, and I had dreamed of doing it with her. But when the way was at last rediscovered, I was too immersed in grief to care. I hadn't even once asked Father to take me in her stead. It had seemed a waste of time, given his inevitable refusal, and in the fog of that time, the whole idea seemed impossibly out of reach.

But this time was different. This grief was different. I was older now, and the last tie holding me here had just been severed. I had a pocketful of gold, and I refused to let opposition from my brother hold me back a second time.

But there was nothing of either shock or disapproval in Bernard's face at my announcement. He must know that finding the remnants of our mother's people would involve making the desert crossing, but his expression was one of satisfaction. He looked as if a guessed-at prediction had proven correct, and he didn't even comment on a young woman traveling alone into unknown lands.

"You'll want to start at Maddox," he said matter-of-factly. "It's a border town, so it's one of the closest to the Great Desert. It's as good a place as any to begin."

"Maddox?" I stared at him, remembering he had mentioned it already. "Your old town?"

He nodded. "I hired a room there, in the home of a family who lived near the mill. I've already paid to the end of the month, so it will still be mine for a few weeks. You can go there. I had to leave in a hurry and travel quickly, so I only brought one bag." He gave me an odd look I couldn't interpret, something almost like humor reflecting in his eyes. "Everything I left behind is yours now—to take, leave, or sell as you choose."

Sell? growled a voice that wasn't entirely human, although I couldn't explain how I knew that.

I spun, staring around the living space of my home. There wasn't anyone in sight.

"Puss?" Bernard sounded equal parts shocked and exasperated. "I told you to wait in Maddox!"

An enormous cat, unlike any I had seen before, strolled out from behind the sofa. He had ginger fur, unmarked except for large white sock markings that extended most of the way up his two back legs, giving the unnerving impression he was wearing high boots.

And you thought I would listen? the cat asked in a tone of mild curiosity.

I stared at him as he jumped onto the sofa and sat stiffly upright, his tail wrapped neatly around him. It made no sense that a cat was talking, and yet I felt utterly certain the words had come from him.

He turned to stare straight at me. *I am not a possession.*

"I didn't mean she should sell *you*," Bernard sputtered.

Puss turned his piercing stare on my brother. *You left nothing else of value in Maddox. Your sister need not bother herself with that... place.*

I stared from the cat to Bernard. "What's wrong with Maddox?"

"Absolutely nothing," Bernard ground out through his teeth, while at the same moment, Puss said, *What's right with Maddox?*

A strange giddy feeling rose up in me, strong enough to overwhelm even the grief and shock. I had no idea what was going on with this strange animal, but he carried around him the taste of the unknown and the hint of adventure—and every part of me responded.

Puss looked me up and down and then turned back to Bernard. *Why have you been hiding her from me? The other miller's child?*

"Hiding her from you?" Bernard shook his head. "You really have lost it this time. I haven't been hiding anything from you.

How could I when you barged in out of nowhere and insisted on living in my only room?"

I had to live somewhere. Puss somehow made the words sound reasonable. *But certainly you were hiding her from me. That's why I had to follow you. And, of course, I was proved correct.*

"The other miller's child?" I asked, trying to make sense of their conversation. "What do you mean? Were you looking for my father's children?"

I was following my instructions. Somehow the cat's meow made the words feel icy in my ears. *But those godmothers went too far this time, sending me to the wrong one. Who knows how much of my time could have been wasted if I hadn't had the sense to follow Bernard here?*

"The godmothers?" I stared at him. "Who are they?"

You call them wise women in this kingdom.

"Wise women?" I blinked, finally making sense of his existence. "Do you mean that you come from the Palace of Light? From the High King himself?"

Of course. I am an enchanted cat from the Palace of Light. How could I talk otherwise? Please don't tell me you're as hopeless as your brother!

I eyed Bernard doubtfully. "I haven't seen my brother in ten years, so I couldn't answer that question."

"See!" Bernard glared at Puss. "I wasn't hiding her. I just had no reason to mention her."

That is a matter of irrelevance, Puss said, as if he hadn't been the one to bring up the topic. *What matters is that she intends to do her duty.*

"My duty?"

Panic filled me. Surely the sense of impending adventure rising inside me couldn't be in error. Surely this enchanted cat hadn't come all this way to repeat the same message given by everyone else around me—that I should do my duty, settle down, and live a life of service to my community.

You will come with me across the Sea of Sand?

My thoughts flipped upside down, swirling in confusion for the second time.

"Go with you? Across the Great Desert? To the new kingdoms?"

I am thinking we can start with Lanover, he meowed as if choosing a kingdom at random.

"You don't have to listen to him." Bernard fixed me with an earnest look. "It doesn't matter how much he says about duty or miller's children, neither of us owe him anything. You don't have to go anywhere."

"But…I want to go somewhere! Anywhere, in fact."

Puss gave a satisfied smile, as if I had just offered him a plate of cream and a bowl of fish.

I stared at him, my brow wrinkling. "But why do you need a miller's child to go across the desert with you? We're not exactly known for our adventurous qualities. Is there something you need there?"

Not a miller's child. The miller's child.

"My father wasn't the only miller in the city of Karema, let alone in all Kuralan," I said slowly, forcing myself to speak, even while I wanted to grasp this opportunity with eyes closed.

Do I look like a fool to you? Puss asked coldly.

"Don't bother pressing him with questions." Bernard gave a long-suffering sigh. "He doesn't answer them well." He sent Puss a pointed look. "He doesn't listen well either. I don't know how many times I've told him that even his exalted origins aren't enough to convince me. I have no interest or intention in ever setting a single foot onto that sand."

I stared at him. "Don't you care about our mother's heritage or her people? Some of them might still be alive across the desert."

Bernard shrugged. "Of course I hope they may be, but it's not as if I've ever met them. I'm more interested in the inheritance of our father—it's a great deal more relevant to my life."

I shook my head, unable to understand such thinking. Did he have no curiosity? No desire at all for something greater?

Puss didn't even turn to look at him, his attention focused on me.

You are no longer of consequence. Kali will accompany me. Will you not, Kali?

I swallowed, looking at Bernard and then back at Puss. "Yes… if you're sure you want me."

I had been ready to set off with nothing but the gold in my pocket. Puss might be full of mysteries, but how could I turn down a traveling companion from the Palace of Light?

Very well, then. It is settled. Puss jumped down from the sofa and sauntered toward the half-open door that led to the kitchen. *We will leave in the morning.*

Deafening silence accompanied his departure. Had that really just happened? Had my whole life been upturned in the space of a single day? I would stay only to bury my father the next day, and then I would leave Karema behind.

Duty. The word echoed through my head. What nonsense was the cat talking when he spoke of it being my duty to set off in such a way. Could it possibly be so?

I shook my head, mistrusting the allure of the idea—how could going off on a reckless adventure be my duty? It was impossible. And yet, knowing that didn't change my decision. Puss seemed to need me, and that would be duty enough for now, at least.

"Very well, then," Bernard said, sounding bemused. "I suppose that's all settled. I'll have the mill, and you'll have the cat." A slow smile spread across his face, a glint appearing in his eye. "I'll look forward to your return and to hearing how grateful you are for my generous gift."

CHAPTER 1

"Generous, my foot," I grumbled as I glared at my companion. "Bernard will hear all about my *gratitude* when I return, that's for sure."

The fluffy ginger monstrosity beside me merely flicked his tail, unaffected by my sour mood. His head was down and his posture menacing as he stalked through the light undergrowth, his form only visible above the green because of his unusual size. Everyone we met commented they had never seen a cat so large. Of course, they soon discovered his size was the least remarkable of his unusual characteristics.

I don't know what you're so irritated about, he meowed. *Did you want the traders to make a fuss about you leaving alone? I thought you wanted adventures over here in Lanover? Wasn't that the whole point of joining the caravan to get across the desert?*

"It's not that we left the caravan!" I sighed. There was little point arguing with someone who always managed to get the last word. "I always knew I would be leaving Caravan Golura at the edge of the desert. They don't bring the camels west."

He made a low rumbly noise and stopped, giving up on his hunt with a shake of his furry head. *Humans. So unreasonable.*

I glared at him as he sat on his hind legs, his tail wrapping around his legs in the now familiar way. As I considered his pale orange fur, the glare slipped away, replaced by a laugh.

"As always, you're quite right, Puss. I'm being most unreasonable. It's just a little insulting to have everyone entrust me to the care of a cat."

Whatever do you mean? Who could be more suitable than a cat? He turned his head to stare at me, narrowing his eyes slightly in an expression that should have been impossible for an animal. *You can't have thought they would entrust* my *care to* you?

"The thought might have crossed my mind," I said in my humblest voice.

Nonsense. What could you do for a cat? He shook his head, his fur swishing. *Let alone an enchanted creature from the Palace of Light. I can see why my friend had such a hard time here for all those years.*

"I hope I never meet this friend of yours," I muttered. "He sounds almost as insufferable as you."

Puss's occasional mentions of a horse named Arvin were the only hints he ever dropped about his original home. I suspected Arvin had a lot to do with Puss's current sojourn among humans, but Puss didn't like direct questions about himself, and always refused to answer them.

You may relax, Puss said, standing back up. *I will certainly take sufficient care of you.* His tone turned sour. *I waited long enough for the miller's child I was promised.*

I dared to reach across and ruffle the top of his head between his ears. He whipped his head away, turning the full force of his glare on me. I just smiled back at him.

"You shouldn't have wasted so much time on my brother. No one could have convinced him to set off across the Sea of Sand."

That much I worked out on my own. His tail whipped back and forth as he glowered into the distance.

"And yet you stayed in Maddox, trying to convince him." I kept my curious gaze pinned on him, but he didn't turn again.

I had my reasons.

I sighed. It had been overly hopeful to think I might actually get an answer. We'd been together for months, but he never responded to the topic of why he had been promised a miller's child to accompany him across the Great Desert from Kuralan to the newly discovered Four Kingdoms on the other side.

We had ended up going to my brother's room in Maddox, after all, since he was right about the town's useful location. It had taken time to organize the crossing, but eventually we had joined Caravan Golura which was returning after a trading expedition. No one was foolish enough to set off into the desert without an escort of desert nomads to guide them through the series of oases that made the crossing possible.

Trading caravan, I reminded myself, using the name used by the portion of desert dwellers who had made their home on the western fringe of the desert all those generations ago. Instead of keeping to traditional tribes, like my mother's people on the eastern side of the desert, they had organized themselves into formal caravans.

Their ancestors had likely been inspired by the Four Kingdom's established network of regular trading caravans—ones that used horses and weren't bound to any specific geographic area. The trade from these traveling merchants was so necessary to the economic health of the kingdoms that the traders had their own governing council and treaties—ones that granted them the same authority as a kingdom, although they owned no land. With the lure of inclusion in their council, I could see why the western desert dwellers had formed formal trading caravans.

With the opening of the desert crossing, lots of people wanted to travel to the new kingdoms—more than were accepted for passage with one of the caravans. But I managed to secure a place with Caravan Golura for two reasons: my mother and my cat.

My mother's desert nomad heritage gave me instant acceptance with the desert traders, but I suspected Puss might have been enough on his own. It had certainly been amusing to see their faces of astonishment the first time they heard him talk. He generated enormous interest among them, and they even offered us both a permanent place in the caravan. But Puss was resolute in refusing, and despite the allure of spending more time with my mother's people, I also stood firm. I couldn't give up on further exploration so soon.

Because of their camel trains, the desert traders limited themselves to traveling up and down the western edge of the desert, crossing only into the eastern fringes of Lanover. The only large city visited by the caravans was the southernmost Lanoverian city of Largo which perched between the jungle, sea, and desert.

I hoped I would make it to Largo at some point, but I wasn't willing to travel south through the desert to reach it. We had traveled directly west across the desert, reaching the northern section of Lanover, just south of the capital of Lanare, and the traders were now turning south. But as soon as we reached the edge of the desert, I was itching to be off into the new kingdom. I had seen enough sand to satisfy me for a long time.

I still had a journey ahead to reach the capital, though, since it was located on the western side of the kingdom, near the coast, not the desert. Thankfully this section of Lanover was densely populated with many towns and villages along the way. And thanks to Caravan Golura's acceptance of me as distant kin, I had been able to work my way across the desert, assisting with the camels in exchange for my passage. As a result, my purse of gold was still largely intact. I would have plenty of funds, as long as I didn't start spending extravagantly.

Don't worry about your coin, Puss said, seeming to read my mind, as he did all too often—although he insisted it wasn't a special ability, just the wisdom that came with great experience. *I am an excellent hunter and can easily supply our food needs while on the road.*

I gave him a horrified look. "I am not eating mouse!"

Naturally not. I cannot expect a human to have a refined palate.

I choked. "Mouse is a…refined palate?"

I will provide you with rabbits and other small game. I'm sure you can trade some of them for other foods. He gave me an assessing look. *You've proven yourself reasonably adaptable for a human, so I assume you can also forage for leaves.* His lips curled in disgust at the last word.

A laugh bubbled out of me, and I had to resist the urge to ruffle his fur.

"I will certainly take care of my plant needs," I told him gravely when I recovered myself.

He looked at me suspiciously but said nothing.

"Will we make it to the closest town before dark?" I asked, thinking aloud. "Or should we look for somewhere to camp for the night?"

I squinted ahead, as if the road before us would give some hint. But it had been empty since we left the desert. We were heading for Tarka, the easternmost town of this region, so the only thing behind us was the desert. Regular travelers had no use for the road beyond Tarka, its existence purely due to the desert trader caravans.

Apparently caravans frequently took their camels as far as the closest town in order to meet with one of the caravans of regular traveling merchants to exchange wares. It was the main reason so many towns existed in such close proximity to the desert. But we were alone on this occasion because Caravan Golura had been in Kuralan collecting wares for customers in Largo. They didn't intend to make any northern stops.

We can make it tonight. Puss stood back up, but I hesitated, giving him a bemused look.

"How are you so sure? I thought you'd never been in the Four Kingdoms before."

What difference does that make? A ripple ran down his body as he stretched out his front legs before strolling onto the road.

I sighed and stood as well. Typical Puss. There was no use speculating how he came by his knowledge. Questions only made him irritated.

Shouldering my pack, I strode after him. The road was well maintained, at least, the packed dirt solid and even. And already the spring air was dry enough to keep it from turning into a bog. From what I'd heard, it grew steamy and humid further south, but this part of Lanover held some of the dusty heat of the desert, although it was still lush enough to be green. It reminded me of home in lots of ways.

We walked in silence for an extended period, my eyes picking out unfamiliar plants and brightly colored birds I didn't recognize. But when our pace slowed enough to become noticeable, I stopped and held out both hands in a silent invitation.

Puss made no verbal response to my offer, but he leaped lightly onto my cupped palms, scrambling from there up my right arm. In a few deft moves, he slung himself around my shoulders.

"You're welcome," I said with a shake of my head.

He just purred in response, and I chuckled. Puss's purrs were as good as a thank you from the high and mighty cat.

I picked up the pace again, marveling as I always did at how light he was for such a large feline. I could have carried him all day without exhausting myself. But I had learned that he would be offended if I offered before he had need of the assistance.

"All that time in the desert was good for something, at least," I said into the silence as we continued on our way. "After endless days walking across the sand, walking on this road feels delightfully easy."

It is a great improvement on that unpleasant place, Puss acknowledged.

"Perhaps we should splurge and sleep in a real bed tonight," I suggested with growing enthusiasm. "It wouldn't do to spend our coin on such indulgences every night, but once would be all right. It would be nice to feel a proper mattress beneath me again."

Puss's purr deepened, so I continued. "What are you most looking forward to in Tarka?"

Human towns do not interest me. They are all the same.

"That's not true!" I twisted my head to try to get a view of his face. "I've been dreaming for years of visiting new places and experiencing other kingdoms for myself. How can you be so uninterested in our first experience of Lanover?"

Must I remind you that I come from the Palace of Light? Puss growled softly. *Human towns do not interest me.*

I cast up my eyes. "I really don't know what you're doing here with me, then! Why don't you go back to the Palace of Light if you dislike the kingdoms so much?"

When the time is right, I will.

"Well, I'm excited for Tarka, even if you're not," I said with determination. I couldn't wait for my first night sleeping on this side of the desert.

Puss's head snapped up, and for a brief second I thought his movement was in response to my words. But his nose quivered, sniffing the air, and one paw batted at me.

I smell prey. Let me down immediately.

I looked around but could see nothing. But I wasn't likely to spot the sort of small game Puss was interested in. Crouching down, I leaned to one side, allowing him to slide gracefully off.

His tail went up, and he slunk away into the undergrowth beside the road without looking back. I sighed and stretched, looking around.

The road remained the same, as did my surroundings. Undergrowth grew close against the verge, but the low greenery did nothing to block my view in both directions. Only the stretch of road directly ahead of us was obscured, a clump of trees surrounding the road on both sides. Attracted by the promise of shelter, as well as the possibility of a water source, I strolled slowly toward them. As long as I didn't go too far, Puss would have no trouble finding me.

Up close, the trees were a mix of familiar and unfamiliar species. Most had glossy, green leaves, but my eyes were drawn to one that also had branches laden with a large fruit wrapped in rough green skin.

"Ooh." I stepped closer and gently cupped one, testing if it was ready to be pulled from its anchor.

I had heard many of the familiar fruits of home grew in different varieties here, and this one looked both like and unlike the avocados I knew from Kuralan. If it was what I suspected, it would make a pleasant accompaniment to whatever meal Puss was about to provide.

It came off easily in my hand, and I brought it to my nose, smiling at the ripe smell emanating from the skin. If even the roads in Lanover produced such abundance, I would have no trouble living up to Puss's expectations that I forage for my meals.

"Thief!"

The loud, accusing voice made me start and spin around. A group of youths approached from further up the road, their faces angry and shoulders tense. I backed away instinctively, my hand tightening around the fruit.

"I'm sorry." I was proud of my voice for not shaking. "I didn't realize this tree belonged to anyone. Do your families own these lands?"

"Are you mocking us?" a boy asked, making a fist.

I gasped. "No, of course not! I meant no offense with my words or actions. I'm new in these parts, and unfamiliar with—"

"New?" scoffed a girl. "You're all the same. Hiding behind your robes and thinking you're above the law."

"Hiding…" I looked down at myself. I had forgotten I still wore the voluminous, covering robes of the desert traders, although I'd pulled off the head covering that would have left only my eyes visible. "Oh, no, I'm not—"

"Where's our money?" a second boy demanded, stepping forward threateningly. "Since it's obvious you're not here to deliver our goods."

"Your…goods?" I swallowed, looking around wildly, but there was no sign of Puss or anyone else. "I'm sorry, but I have no idea what you're talking about."

Several of them exclaimed angrily. I took two large steps backward, but the movement stirred the group into motion, and within seconds I was surrounded.

My legs trembled beneath my robes, but I forced myself to hold my place and straighten my spine, making myself as tall as possible. Some of my adversaries had the advantage on height, but their faces still bore the mark of youth, and they seemed to be led by a girl who looked at least a couple years younger than me.

"I'm afraid I really don't know what you're talking about," I said in a cold voice. "You've got the wrong person. I've never been in these parts before."

"Maybe you haven't," the leader said, not backing down. "But one of you is the same as another. Your people have been here, and if they're not going to return, then you can answer for them."

I swallowed. "If you mean the desert traders, I don't belong to a caravan."

"Do you take us for fools?" All of the youths stirred angrily. "We know how your lot dress."

"It's true I just left Caravan Golura," I said, "but I was merely traveling with them for a short time. If they have unfinished business with your families, you must direct your inquiries to—"

"Caravan Golura is well-known here," a boy said, latching on to the caravan name and ignoring the rest of my words. "But we don't recognize you. You must be with the new caravan. Cobolt. The cheats."

I frowned. The traders I traveled with had spoken frequently of the other caravans, but I had never heard of one called Cobolt.

"I don't—" I began, but the group was closing in around me, their faces shut off, clearly uninterested in any protestation I might make.

The girl at the center reached out, and I instinctively shrank away, only to back into one of the boys behind me. He grabbed me by my upper arms, holding me firmly in position while I tried to wrench myself free.

"Let go of me!" I kicked backward with one boot.

But hands were reaching for me from all directions, and there was no avenue of escape. One of them grabbed my robe, wrenching it with such force that it unraveled, one of the seams tearing completely.

He pulled the material away from me, flinging it roughly to the ground.

"What are you doing?" I shouted.

The boy holding me let go, and all of them drew back slightly, glancing at each other in discomfort. Unlike those who'd grown up in the desert, I had never fully adjusted to the heat and had taken to wearing only my undergarments beneath my robe.

Their leader snatched the garment from the ground, and for a relieved moment, I thought she meant to hand it back to me. But her eyes narrowed as she looked down at it, and she reached for her belt instead.

"Stop!" I cried as she pulled out a knife. But it was already too late.

Slashing downward with vicious focus, she made a long cut down the center of the robe. I lunged toward her, but two of the boys caught my arms, holding me back as their leader shredded the material into useless strips.

When she had finished, she let it fall to the ground once more, no longer recognizable as a robe at all. She turned to me slowly, the knife still clenched in her right hand.

I shivered and tried to wrench myself free of the restraining hold, but their grip was too tight.

"Puss!" I screamed, the sound fueled by a combination of fear and anger.

The youths actually paused at my outburst, one of the girls snickering at my unexpected cry. Before she could make any comment, however, a roar echoed from the nearby trees.

As one, the youths pulled back. Swiveling to stare in the direction of the noise, their superior expressions fell away. The bushes rustled, and a menacing growl floated out, the unseen creature coming closer.

"What's that?" the youngest of the boys asked, all the bravado gone from his voice.

"Let's go!" the leader said. "It's probably just some animal, but we should tell the village that one of the traders is back."

A couple of them looked at me uncertainly, their expressions revealing their original plan. They had intended to drag me back to the village with them, unkempt and humiliated. But the growl sounded again from the closest bush, and all the youths turned tail and ran.

Only one boy paused, glancing back at me. With a shake of his head, he was about to follow the others when his eyes fell on my pack, abandoned beside the road. Eyes narrowing, he stooped and grabbed one of the straps, hauling it with him as he fled.

I screamed angry defiance after him, but my legs were frozen, my arms clutched protectively over my middle, one hand clamped on the purse, thankfully still hidden in its place against my skin.

A large orange figure padded out of the undergrowth, and at sight of Puss, my whole frame sagged. Two big tears rolled down my cheeks. I stumbled several steps toward him and dropped to my knees.

The cat regarded the fleeing youth with a fierce expression, but stayed at my side. With a large hiccupping sob, I threw my arms around him and buried my face in his fur.

I expected him to immediately shake me off, but he went still, letting me cry into his fur for several shaking breaths. His calm, steady presence soon leached through to me, however, and the tears receded. Anger flooded back in their place.

Sitting upright, I glared toward the road.

"How dare they?" I spat out. "I've never even heard of a Caravan Cobolt. I'm going straight into Tarka and—"

Caravan Cobolt? Puss shook his fur, looking down the road with narrowed eyes, although the youths had disappeared from sight. *There is no such caravan.*

"Exactly." I sat in the dirt, my brow creasing. "None of it made any sense."

Puss turned to look at me. *You appear to be insufficiently dressed.*

I looked down at myself and groaned. I had almost forgotten I was shamelessly sitting in the road in my undergarments.

"Unfortunately they took my pack. And, as you can see, the robe is now useless. I couldn't even use it as a handkerchief." I sighed. "At least there's no one else to see me but you, Puss."

The sound of a throat clearing made me straighten, my eyes widening as I looked around for the source.

"While I hesitate to correct a beautiful lady," a smooth voice said, "I'm afraid there is one other person present."

I scrambled to my feet, my fists clutching my petticoats until my knuckles whitened. A startlingly handsome young man with golden skin and dark hair watched me, the expression in his eyes half admiring, half amused.

CHAPTER 2

I swallowed, reminding myself silently that while it was hardly respectable to stand around in my undergarments, my shift was at least sufficiently covering.

"How long have you been standing there?" I demanded, letting some of my anger at my attackers buoy my confidence.

"I'm afraid I've only just arrived," he said. "It seems an earlier arrival might have spared you some misfortune."

His words were courteous, but he had a distracted air, as if I had interrupted him in the middle of something, and he was eager to get back to it. He waited patiently, however, his raised eyebrow asking for an explanation of my disheveled state.

I cleared my throat. "Your earlier arrival would have been timely on this occasion, Lord…?" I trailed off with my own look of inquiry. Now that I'd had a moment to absorb the quality of his garments and his air of confidence, I felt sure this was no ordinary townsman.

His amusement grew, one side of his mouth curving upward. "Not a lord, I'm afraid. But I'm most sorry not to have been able to assist in your moment of distress—uncertain of its cause though I still am."

I sighed, pushing my now-messy braid over my shoulder.

"I was cornered by a group of youths who seem to have mistaken me for someone else. I can only imagine they come from Tarka." I nodded up the road.

"Mistook you for someone else? How unfortunate." The politeness of the tone gave a hint of disbelief to his words.

I crossed my arms. "I'm no trader. I've never even heard of a Caravan Cobolt."

A crease appeared between his brows. "Cobolt? Is there such a caravan?"

"Ten minutes ago I would have said no, but now…" I shifted my weight, glancing at my torn and abandoned robe. "Those youths certainly seemed to believe in its existence."

There is no such caravan, Puss said with certainty.

The young man started, his relaxed stance shattering as he tensed, staring at the cat.

"Did that animal just…speak?"

I grinned. I never tired of seeing people's first reactions to Puss.

Are you dense? Puss asked, apparently still on edge after the attack.

The young man stiffened. "I'm not usually accounted so. But I confess to being unfamiliar with talking animals." He paused. "Although, I have heard stories of a talking—"

I suppose you mean to say horse, Puss cut him off. *But now is not the time to be discussing Arvin. What exactly do you mean to do about those…children?* He looked as if he'd wanted to use a harsher word to describe my attackers.

The young man raised both eyebrows with an exaggerated expression of surprise. "Do about them? Do you take me for their parent, perhaps? I am a fellow traveler and do not even hail from Tarka."

"Certainly you can't be expected to do anything about a group of people who have already left," I interjected, taking back control of the conversation. "But unfortunately they also took my pack, so I would appreciate some minor assistance."

The man immediately swept into an elaborate bow. "Nothing could give me greater pleasure." He took the cloak from his shoulders and moved toward me as if he meant to place it around me himself.

I snatched it from his hands, wrapping myself in it with as much dignity as I could manage.

"Thank you," I said stiffly, irritated by his manner, but conscious I was at a disadvantage in the whole encounter.

He stepped back and surveyed me with a considering eye. "I'm sorry it's only a half cloak. It's so warm here that I haven't had need for more."

I looked down with a groan. The cloak was better than nothing, but I still presented a disreputable appearance.

"This is not how I wanted my first introduction to Lanoverian society to go," I said. "If I turn up in the town like this, what are they all going to think?"

The man cleared his throat, the twinkle back in his eye. "While I'm glad you seem unharmed, apparently my assistance is still needed. It's not much further to Tarka—shall I go ahead of you and procure some clothing? I may even be able to recover your pack."

"Oh, could you?" My eyes lit up. "I can easily wait here for another hour or two before it starts to get dark. I would much rather enter the town properly attired. Especially since those youths have likely already turned the townsfolk against me."

The man nodded gravely. "It would be my honor to assist." He hesitated and looked at the cat. "And what of you, Sir Feline? Is there anything you require?"

Me? Puss regarded him in astonishment. *Need aid from you?*

"Of course not," the man corrected hurriedly, the laugh back around his mouth. "But perhaps you can guard the young lady in my absence."

Puss's fur stood up, a slight growl sounding in his words. *Do you think I need your instruction to do so? I always guard my own.*

The man looked over at me. "I can see you will be fine here without me. You are fortunate to have such a loyal companion."

I nodded, remembering the way Puss had saved me earlier. "I am most conscious of it."

Puss's fur relaxed at my words, but he continued to glare at the man as he gave us both a deep bow and took off at a fast stride.

"It's Kali," I blurted out, calling the words after him. When he turned with a quizzical look, I flushed and gestured at myself. "My name is Kali."

His lips twitched, but he bowed deeply before turning to resume his journey. I watched him move out of sight among the trees and then sank down with a deep sigh.

Drawing the cloak around me, I put my head in my hands. "What a terrible beginning. This is not how it was supposed to go."

I thought ladies liked being rescued by handsome young men? Puss asked.

Despite myself, a slight flush rose up my cheeks at the memory of the stranger's good looks and confident air. But I shook my head resolutely.

"I would far rather be rescued by you, Puss."

A most natural desire, Puss conceded, beginning to wash one of his front paws with his tongue.

I sighed. "I wonder how long he'll take? I don't like relying on a complete stranger, but neither do I want to arrive in the town looking like this." I gestured at myself.

Is it such a great matter? Puss asked. *You seem to have coat enough still.* He eyed my undergarments.

I laughed. "It's not that I'm uncovered, it's a matter of looking like a disheveled waif versus a capable woman of means. One is a decided disadvantage over the other, I promise."

Puss switched to the other paw only to pause. *If humans only had enough good sense to grow fur, you wouldn't need to bother with such nonsense.*

I laughed again. "Unfortunately we don't have any say over the matter."

Puss didn't bother answering, and we both fell into silence. In spite of my intentions to remain cheerful and patient, I soon found myself reliving the unpleasant encounter with the town youths. But no matter how I thought through the events, I couldn't come up with any alternative course of action on my part that would have avoided the unpleasantness.

After an hour of waiting, I began to pace, stretching my legs and trying to drive back the rising anger. How dare they treat a stranger in such a way? And what lies were they spreading about me in the town?

When another hour had passed, I picked one of the avocados, my mood defiant, even though I had been mistaken in thinking the locals were claiming the tree. The delicious taste placated me somewhat, and I wished I still had my pack so I could take some with me for later. But when the sun neared the horizon, my patience ran out.

"Where is that dratted man?" I asked.

He appears to have abandoned you, Puss said without heat. *We should get moving now if we want to reach Tarka before dark.*

"Go like this?" I looked down at myself, making a frustrated sound in the back of my throat. I would have a difficult time convincing the townspeople to take me seriously after arriving in such a state. It was a sorry start to my adventure.

I sighed, slowly straightening. We could camp here for the night, but without my pack, we had no supplies. And I refused to behave in a cowardly manner. What else was this experience but the adventure I had claimed to crave? I would be ashamed of myself if I shrank back from it now.

"We should have gone hours ago and not waited at all," I said.

It would appear so. Puss nudged a small pile of rabbits in front of him with his nose. *At least it has given me time to collect these, however. I will offer them to the townsfolk as a peace offering, in case they are displeased with your lack of fur.*

"That's a good idea," I said, brightening. "You have had a successful hunt this afternoon."

The rabbits in this kingdom seem abnormally dull. I merely had to play dead, and they hopped straight up to me to investigate. He shook his head with disgust at the lack of challenge.

"Well I, for one, am grateful," I said. "To both you and the rabbits." I looked down at Puss's pile wondering how I was going to transport it the remaining distance to the town.

Eventually, with a sigh, I removed the cloak and used it to bundle the game into a workable load. When I neared the town, I would put it back on, and carry them awkwardly in my arms. But for now, this would be easier.

We set off at a brisk pace, racing the rapidly falling darkness. When we emerged from the trees to find buildings spread out in front of us, I growled. Tarka was even closer than I'd realized.

What could possibly have taken that wretched man so long? Had something happened to him? A tightness in my tummy made me squirm uncomfortably as concern blossomed. Had searching for my pack got him caught up in this strange business? Surely the residents of Tarka wouldn't have turned on him just for inquiring after it?

Just before I reached the first houses, I unwrapped the rabbits and donned the cloak. It was now marked and dirty as well as being too short, but I pulled it around me, covering as much of my body as I could manage.

Puss padded away from me down a side road. I was about to call after him when he popped back into view. A piece of rough burlap hung from his mouth, trailing through the dust. He dropped it at my feet with a satisfied expression.

"What is that, and where did you get it?" I asked warily.

It's a sack. And don't look at me like that. It was just abandoned on the ground. We can use it.

I hesitated, but Puss wasn't a thief. With a sigh of acquiescence, I loaded the rabbits into the sack and slung them over my shoulder.

Reminding myself to keep my head high, I resumed walking down the main street, heading for the town's central square. Despite the setting sun, people still moved through the streets, and all of them looked with curiosity at the new arrivals, whispers following our progress.

I took a steadying breath, my back straightening with every shocked look. This situation wasn't my fault, and I refused to show any shame in my bearing.

But the whispers must have spread ahead of us as well because we arrived in the square to a small crowd, all looking angrily in my direction.

Puss made a choking noise, as if hacking up a fur ball, and wound between my feet.

You had better let me present the game, I think.

Nodding silently, I let the sack slip to the ground, not taking my eyes from the milling people. Puss took a firm hold of the burlap in his mouth and dragged it forward, his strange behavior attracting the attention of everyone around us.

With the weight of their eyes lifted, my breath came more easily, and I surreptitiously examined our surroundings. We stood in a large square ringed by elegant stone buildings, so it must be a town of respectable size. A circular fountain tinkled in the middle of the empty space, although my view of it was almost entirely obscured by the gathered townsfolk.

As my gaze swept across the crowd, they caught on a familiar figure. I stiffened, my eyes narrowing as I took in the stranger from the road. I had made myself uncomfortable imagining all the terrible accidents that might have prevented him from returning, but he looked unharmed and relaxed, not a hair out of place.

I cast him another sideways glance. There could be no mistaking it—he was definitely the man who had promised to return to me. But his face remained calm and open under my scrutiny, the same amusement lingering around his mouth and eyes that I had glimpsed on the road. Not even the smallest shade of consciousness or guilt colored his bright eyes.

CHAPTER 3

Fury stirred in me. Had I been forgotten so easily? Or had it all been part of some twisted game? Perhaps the stranger had never had any intention of returning.

My hands clenched into fists just as Puss dropped the sack at the feet of the tall man standing at the front of the group.

Greetings, noble residents.

The entire crowd reacted, calls and shouts sounding as half of them drew back while the other half surged forward to stare at Puss. He gave them a satisfied smile.

Yes, it is I, Puss, speaking to you. I present you with this gift from my companion, Lady Kalila of Kuralan.

Most of the crowd were still staring at him with open mouths, but the man from the road looked swiftly up at me at the cat's words. I met his eyes squarely, defiance in my gaze as I waited for some sign of guilt.

There was none. His head tilted slightly, his eyes narrowing before an amused smile flickered across his face.

I barely held back an enraged snarl. Shameless. Utterly shameless.

The Lady Kalila apologizes for not bringing a greater gift, but she met with violence on the road and has been robbed of her possessions. We have come to throw ourselves on your legendary benevolence.

I spluttered slightly, giving Puss a glare. Did he have to overdo it?

But the townsfolk seemed awed by his words, frowning at each other and peering at me cautiously as they exchanged whispers. Apparently the words of a talking cat were taken seriously.

Their leader cleared his throat. "Apologies, Lady Kalila, but are you indeed from Kuralan? You're not a desert trader?"

From the corner of my eye, I saw a single eyebrow raise on the stranger from the road, the already familiar smile pulling up one side of his mouth. But for all his languid amusement, I couldn't shake the certainty that he was like a coiled spring, dangerous and ready for action, despite his outward manner.

I shook off the feeling and tried to focus on the townsman.

"No, I am not a trader, although I have ties to them. I have never even heard of a Caravan Cobolt. If you have some grief with them, I'm afraid I can't be of assistance."

The man looked dismayed at my words, his gaze shooting across the square to someone who lingered near one of the houses. A girl—the one who had destroyed my robe—immediately slunk backward down a side street.

The town leader seemed lost for a moment before remembering the sack at his feet. Stooping, he retrieved it and peered inside.

"An excellent catch," he said. "And a welcome gift. I am Greyson, and I have the honor of being mayor of Tarka. You must spend the night with my family so you may share in this bounty."

I bowed from the waist, keeping my face grave. While I welcomed the hospitality, I didn't mean to let them off quite so easily.

"There is the matter of my possessions..."

Greyson looked back at the crowd, and a young boy ran

forward, dragging the pack with him. From his features, I suspected he was Greyson's son and likely the younger brother of the girl who had led the attack on me.

I accepted the pack, my posture relaxing. As always, Puss had proven himself more than useful. Everyone who met him recognized how remarkable he was, and some of that favor spilled over to me.

At a few curt commands from Greyson, the crowd dispersed. They appeared reluctant to go, but from their pointed looks and wide eyes, it was the presence of Puss and not anger at me that motivated them.

As usual, the cat was entirely uninterested in the wonder he had generated, far too busy cleaning his ears to bother returning any of the looks he received.

I slung my pack over my shoulders and looked expectantly to Greyson. But he had turned to the one person in the crowd who hadn't moved. The stranger from the road.

My hands tightened into fists around my pack straps, but I kept my face as calm as I could. If my new acquaintance didn't mean to acknowledge me or our interaction on the road, I wasn't going to make a further scene—particularly not when I looked ridiculous in my petticoat and dirty cloak.

The cloak. I froze, guiltily remembering what I had used it for and its current state. But a moment later, I shook my head. He had given it to me with a promise to return, and he had been the one who had failed his end of the bargain. I could consider the cloak forfeit.

Seeing his clothing again, as well as the elegant, expensive sword at his waist, I didn't think he would have any issue replacing the garment.

Greyson turned, ushering me forward to join them. I went slowly, on reluctant legs.

"Lady Kalila," he said, "it is an unusual, but fortunate, chance that there is a fellow Kuralani here to greet you. We aren't usually so graced as to host two from the new lands across the desert."

My eyes flew to the stranger's. He was Kuralani? After all my dreams of new places and people, almost the first person I had run into in this strange land had been a countryman? Although he had deserted me in my hour of need, the humor of it still hit me. But as soon as I started to smile, the action reminded me of the man's earlier amusement, and my irritation returned. I glared at him.

Sparks must have been flying from my eyes because something in his own gaze flashed, and he stepped forward, taking my hand in his as if I really was a grand lady. Was I finally getting an apology?

"But perhaps introductions aren't necessary?" Greyson continued, turning to me. "You likely already know—"

"Xavier," the stranger said smoothly, cutting him off with a devastatingly charming smile, directed at me. "And, of course." He brought my hand to his lips, his eyes meeting mine with such warmth, I could feel the physical sensation of it. "Well met, Kali. Although I am sorry for the misfortune that overtook you."

I drew in an incensed breath at his subtle reference to our conversation on the road, but he gave me a sharp, quelling look that made me choke over my words. The nerve!

Greyson cleared his throat, his attention on the edge of the square again.

"Excellent, excellent," he said, apparently not noticing anything charged in our exchange. "Perhaps you could show Lady Kalila the way to my home, then, my lord? I should run ahead and inform my wife of our honored guest."

He didn't wait for a reply, speeding off across the cobblestones. Xavier, who had dropped my hand, offered his arm with a gallant bow.

I glared at him again as I reluctantly slipped my hand into the crook of his elbow and allowed him to lead me forward at a much slower pace.

"My lord?" I gave him an accusing look. "So you're apparently a lord now?"

"A mere honorific," he said breezily. "Not to be considered."

I looked away, irritated at his unwavering assurance. Didn't he feel the least bit guilty about abandoning me?

"I'm surprised you're so pleased to see me," I said coldly, the words slipping out despite my intention not to mention the matter while looking a total mess.

"How could I not be pleased to meet Kuralani nobility?" He smiled urbanely, looking down at me with that same amusement in his eyes.

I tore my gaze away, struck by the familiar accent—one which had not been in evidence before but which sounded entirely natural. This annoying man really was Kuralani. What did he know of the Kuralani nobility? Was he familiar with all the families?

I had been against the whole business of the false title from the beginning, but Puss never listened to me, insisting he knew more about my background than I did. And since the traders were uninterested in such things, it hadn't seemed to matter. Now I wished I could sink into the ground.

Kuralani on her father's side, Puss said, without missing a beat. *Although the noble line is from her mother who was of the desert nomads.*

"The desert nomads?" Xavier sounded even more amused, although he didn't outright deny the claim. "I didn't realize they recognized any titles."

Puss yawned. *Now they do not, perhaps, but once the Sea of Sand was a garden paradise, ruled over by emperors. And who could deny the daughter of emperors use of the most basic honorific?*

Xavier bowed, hiding his expression. "Who indeed?"

I glared at Puss. Even now, when we had been caught out, the wretched cat refused to own up to his error.

"Please forget the matter of my distant ancestors," I said. "Just Kali is more than sufficient."

Xavier bowed again, although I caught the amusement in his eyes before he lowered his head.

"Just Kali it is, then."

I ground my teeth together. At least we would arrive at the mayor's house soon, and I would never have to see Xavier again.

"I'm delighted to have such a charming fellow guest," Xavier said, as if aware of my thoughts and deliberately teasing me. When my horrified eyes flew to his, I could clearly see the laugh in their depths.

"You're also a guest of the mayor?" I managed to choke out, and Xavier nodded gravely.

"Although not so exalted as yourself, of course." For the first time his amusement fell away as his eyes flicked down to take in my dirty, torn state. "Nor as wronged," he said softly. "I hope you truly weren't harmed during the misunderstanding?"

I wanted to snap back, but I couldn't entirely dismiss the new note of sincerity in his voice.

"I'm unharmed," I said, wishing I sounded more natural.

He looked away, gazing across the town as if looking at something more than neat rows of houses.

"I think once you're cleaned up, a further conversation with the mayor is in order," he said. "There's something strange here."

I sighed softly, but he caught the sound, looking back down at me, and tightening his arm so that my hand was pressed against his side.

"Do not fear, Kali. I don't believe you'll be assigned any more blame."

"Fear?" I snapped, my earlier moment of softness swallowed by a surge of indignation. "Who said anything about being afraid?

Something strange is certainly going on, and I intend to get to the bottom of it."

A look almost like admiration crossed his face, and he gave a low laugh.

"Do you indeed? Most commendable." He stopped outside a large stone house surrounded by a small, riotous garden full of bright colors. Gesturing toward the door, he gave a small bow. "I hope I may be of assistance in the task."

I pushed open the door and stepped through, pausing to glance back at him.

"I already have someone to assist me, thank you. Someone *reliable*."

Even at those words, he didn't have the grace to look ashamed. His eyes held mine, curiosity and interest reflected back at me without a speck of guilt.

She means me. Puss pushed past my legs to enter the house first, nudging me to follow him. *Naturally you can't compare. Kali has no need of you.*

"Does she not?" Xavier's soft voice chased me into the house, but I didn't turn around to meet his gaze. I had no desire to see those eyes laughing at me again.

CHAPTER 4

The mayor's wife apologized over and over again, bustling me away to clean up and change into fresh clothes. Once I was respectable again and feeling more myself, she produced her daughter. The girl trotted out a dutiful apology of her own, her eyes fixed firmly on the ground the whole time.

At that point, my discomfort had eased enough that it was easy to offer a gracious response. Even so, the girl slipped away and made no further appearance, including at the evening meal. Her younger brother was present, though, so the conversation was light, carefully skirting the topic that was clearly on all the adults' minds.

I ate ravenously, trying to ignore the amused eyes that watched me from the other side of the table. Puss reclined on a cushion at my side where I fed him whichever of the dishes most caught his fancy. The mayor's son was fascinated by the cat, not taking his eyes off him the whole meal, and he clearly would have liked to stay after the food was cleared. His father sent him off, however, and the boy left with a disconsolate glance back at Puss.

"After the terrible behavior of our children, you're owed an explanation," the mayor said to me without preamble. "I hope you can forgive the delay. We try to avoid talking of the matter around the children."

I inclined my head. "Of course. I understand."

The mayor looked at his wife, his eyes heavy, and she sighed.

"It's that caravan," she said. "Caravan Cobolt."

I frowned, exchanging a look with Xavier in spite of my resolution not to glance across the table. On the road he had seemed as confused by the name of the caravan as I was. The same concern was reflected in his eyes now.

I cleared my throat. "I'm afraid I've never heard of that caravan." I hesitated. "Are you sure you have the name correct?"

"Of course," the mayor said sharply, before rubbing his hand across his forehead and sighing. "Forgive me. It's a matter of grave concern here. We would not mistake the name."

"You had best tell the story from the beginning," his wife said, and he nodded.

"Tarka survives because we're a way point for both the desert trader caravans and the regular traveling merchant caravans. They meet here to exchange goods, bringing custom and goods to our town despite our remote location."

I nodded. This much I knew.

"Recently, we hosted a desert caravan we hadn't encountered before, calling themselves Cobolt."

Xavier leaned forward. "It didn't strike you as suspicious that they were newcomers?"

The mayor's lips twisted. "In retrospect, it should have. But they claimed that their usual routes kept them in the south of the kingdom, around Largo, and there was nothing especially unbelievable about that. The caravans all have different primary routes, depending on the location of their hidden oases."

"That's true," I said thoughtfully. "So this caravan claimed to be a southern one."

I glanced at Puss with raised brows. Could it be true? Was that why we hadn't heard of Cobolt?

There is no such caravan, he said with calm certainty.

The mayor paled. "Can you be sure of that, Sir Cat?"

Puss is fine. He looked up briefly before returning to his after-dinner wash. *And of course I'm sure.*

The mayor cursed, and his wife looked as if she was about to cry. Neither of them questioned Puss's knowledge further.

"I'm sorry," I said softly. "I take it you had some sort of dealings with this false caravan?"

The mayor nodded as his wife drew out a small package wrapped in leather. Unwrapping it carefully, she held up a short length of material.

I gasped, staring in wonder at the soft silk. When she held it out to me, I took it, marveling at its fine texture and the way it slipped through my fingers.

"I've never seen anything like this," I breathed, my eyes captured by the colors which shifted in the light as the material moved. I seemed to be holding a piece of living sunset.

Xavier bent across the table, reaching a hand out to run a finger over the fabric.

"I have," he said.

I looked up, meeting his eyes again in surprise. His brows were knit.

"Some of the Lanoverian court have garments made in material like this. But from what I understand, the supply is extremely limited. It comes from silkworms in one of the kingdoms across the sea. They only produce such wonders in their home environment, and the kingdom of Arcadia has the exclusive trade contract here in the Four Kingdoms."

The mayor nodded, a hint of eagerness edging into his voice. "Precisely. Gowns made in this material are extremely expensive. And Arcadia won't sell the material to other kingdoms—only the finished products. But Caravan Cobolt has arranged their own supply. It's an incredible opportunity."

"Or so they claimed," his wife said bitterly, and his face fell.

"They weren't eager to do business with us," the mayor said with a defensive note. "They were on their way to Lanare, intending to take their caravan all the way to the capital to arrange deals with the seamstresses there—an unprecedented undertaking. Even our initial offer of a favorable deal was rebuffed until we showed them the skill of our local workers. Once they saw the quality of our work, they finally agreed that it would be easier to do business near the desert."

Xavier sat back and sighed. "Experienced swindlers, then. I'm sorry for it. I wish you'd mentioned the matter sooner."

"We were still hoping..." The mayor exchanged a look with his wife. "Only a small delegation from the caravan came into the town, and we gave them enough gold for a large shipment. In fact, we purchased the entirety of their current stock which they claimed to have with their main caravan on the border of the desert. They should have returned by now, but we thought maybe..."

"You already gave them all the gold?" Xavier raised an eyebrow, and I couldn't help leaping to the defense of the townsfolk.

"The desert caravans have earned implicit trust! They might drive a hard bargain, but their entire existence is based on having built a rock-solid reputation. No desert caravan would go back on a trade deal, let alone abscond with gold without delivering the goods."

"That's right," the mayor said. "We were so pleased to have secured the deal, it never occurred to us that..."

Xavier's frown deepened. "The caravans won't be happy to hear about these swindlers using their name, then."

"Not happy is an understatement," I said. "They'll be beyond furious. These cheats threaten everything they've built over generations."

"Can they do anything about it, though?" he asked. "What authority do the caravans have over each other?" He seemed to consider me the expert on the topic, and since neither the mayor nor his wife attempted to interject, I answered.

"The desert caravans come under the merchant council and consider themselves bound by its rules and treaties. But the council is largely run by the traveling merchant caravans, and when a council of caravans is called, the desert traders usually send only a couple of representatives north. The meetings are almost always too far away from the desert. I don't think they've ever called a council meeting themselves. But while the desert traders usually handle any issues among themselves, this matter is serious enough to warrant the attention of the traveling merchants as well, I think."

I glanced at the mayor for confirmation, and he nodded, although he looked less certain.

"We have to inform the desert traders, then." Xavier looked to me. "You just left Caravan Golura, didn't you? We should seek them out at once."

I shook my head. "That would be a dangerous endeavor. They dropped me at the edge of the desert and continued south immediately. Unless you have an intimate knowledge of the desert and a camel stashed somewhere, it would be beyond foolhardy to attempt to catch them."

He grimaced, looking like he found it hard to accept the warning.

"Unlike the traveling merchant caravans, the desert traders have separate agreements with the Lanoverian crown, though," I said to the mayor, "since they're geographically tied to Lanover in a way the traveling merchants aren't. You should send a report to Lanare. The king will surely wish to hear of this. And he'll have means to get in contact with the desert traders."

Xavier nodded in agreement. "Given his second son is married to a desert trader, he certainly does."

"Ah yes, Princess Tillara." I grinned. "Although she came from

Caravan Adira, I get the impression all the caravans are extremely proud of her."

"With reason." Xavier gave a reminiscent smile. "She is beautiful, charming, and gracious. True nobility."

I glared at him with narrowed eyes while he smirked across the table. Was I being overly sensitive in imagining there was an implied comparison in his words?

The mayor's wife gripped her husband's arm. "Yes, I'm sure Princess Tillara will be concerned about this matter." She turned to me. "Thank you for your expertise. We will send a messenger in the morning."

"I only wish I could do more." I sighed. "I can understand why your youngsters were so worked up. It must be a great blow to lose so much."

She swallowed. "The opportunity seemed so good that we gathered every coin we could possibly find. If it can't be recovered, the whole town will feel the effects for years."

I gave her an impulsive hug, my eyes catching on Xavier across her shoulder. He looked sympathetic, but I could also read an underlying frustration. The opportunity had been too good to be true, but the townsfolk had let greed stop them from asking enough questions.

I glared at him. From his clothing and manner, he was clearly a wealthy oldest son, traveling for his own amusement. What would he understand about the struggles of those who worked every day for their bread? Could they be blamed for hoping for better times?

When the mayor's wife drew back, I patted her hand as comfortingly as I could.

"Thank you for your hospitality," I said. "I will gratefully stay here tonight, but I must be off myself in the morning."

"So soon?" she asked, but I could hear the relief in her voice. These people didn't have an excess to share at the moment.

I nodded firmly. "Puss and I are bound for the capital and prefer not to linger in our travels."

"How did you find such a companion?" she asked me in a lowered voice, her eyes flicking sideways to the cat who now appeared to be napping on the cushion.

She didn't find me, he meowed without opening his eyes. *I found her. Naturally.*

I stifled a laugh. "It's true enough. I think I could be more accurately considered Puss's companion than the other way around. Although he won't tell me what his urgent mission is—just that he has come from the Palace of Light."

The woman's eyes widened at this mention of the dwelling place of the High King.

"Well, in that case, we must find a nicer bed for such an exalted guest." She sounded breathless, as if she doubted her ability to produce the promised luxury.

"Do not disturb yourself," I said quickly. "Puss likes to sleep in my bed. There is no need to provide him separate accommodation."

"In your bed?" Xavier raised his eyebrows, meeting my gaze with a silent laugh.

My eyes narrowed, and I surged to my feet, reaching for Puss. He came willingly, allowing me to sling him around my shoulders, apparently unconcerned by Xavier's comments or manner.

I decided I also wouldn't deign to reply. Instead I stuck my nose in the air and strode from the dining room, the mayor's wife hurrying after me.

Once free of Xavier's gaze, I slowed, calming my breathing.

"My apologies," I said. "I'm merely weary after the day's events."

"Oh! Of course!" She instantly looked guilty, making me feel bad.

I put a hand on her arm. "I'm fine, truly. Just tired."

She gave me a grateful smile and led the way to the guest

room I had used earlier. "We'll have a morning meal ready for you whenever you awaken, however early that may be. I know travelers like to get on the road promptly."

I regretfully considered the appeal of a real bed and a lazy morning before nodding my head forcefully. It was worth the sacrifice to escape the house early and avoid another meeting with Xavier.

"Yes," I said. "I'll be on the road early."

CHAPTER 5

*D*espite my resolution, I would have overslept if not for Puss's unwelcome wake up. His claws dug into my arm, stopping just short of puncturing the skin. I shot up into a sitting position, sending him sprawling in the process.

I glared at him unrepentantly. "Was that really necessary?"

He stretched. *You claimed to want an early start.*

I grumbled to myself but didn't make any more serious protest since it was true. As promised, the mayor's wife was already up, and her cook had prepared a simple breakfast. It didn't take me long to eat and send a farewell message to the mayor.

As Puss and I strode out of town, my pack across my back once more, I was doubly glad to be leaving so early. Not only had I seen no sign of the mayor's other guest, but few of the towns-folk were up either. Although I understood them better now, I had no desire to run into any of the youths who had harassed me the day before.

The road beyond Tarka was more established than the one that led to the desert. Lanoverian travelers and merchant cara-vans traversed it on this side, and it was both wider and smoother. We made swift progress, gaining as much ground as we could before the day began to warm. Even this early in the season, it got hot in the middle of the day.

I spotted several more avocado trees, pleased at the indication that foraging would be easy in this abundant kingdom. Puss seemed pleased with the signs of game around us as well, although he stayed by my side during the morning.

I'll hunt when we get closer to the next town, he said in his usual perspicacious way after our second brief stop. *You won't want to carry them far.*

"That's a good thought," I said. "Arriving with a gift did seem an effective strategy at Tarka."

As I walked, I tried to focus on the beautiful day and the soft breeze that kept the air fresh. But my mind constantly circled back to the unfortunate situation of the townsfolk I had just left. I wished I could have helped them, but I couldn't think of a single thing I had to offer.

Although at least I had been able to offer understanding, I thought sourly. Xavier had been both useless and callous—despite his interfering and officious manner—so at least I was a small improvement on their other guest.

What was a nobleman's indolent son doing in a position of honor in the mayor's house, included in his counsel? Had he paid his way there? My mouth pursed. A rich good-for-nothing was the last thing Tarka needed in a crisis—and the last thing I needed as well, I assured myself, a little too fervently.

Biting my lip, I stared down at the road in front of me without really seeing it. Was it my father's voice in my head dismissing an adventurer in such a way?

He had always talked like that—his voice pointed, although he stopped short of naming me. Others in the community hadn't been so circumspect. And yet, despite all the discouragement, I had always dreamed of adventure and had sought it out at the first opportunity. Did that make me as useless and self-centered as Xavier?

Even my mother—the one to plant the seed in my heart with stories of her nomadic childhood—had told me innumerable times about all the advantages of a settled life. I knew she had wished for me to have the same stability she enjoyed—the willing and happy wife of a miller.

I didn't even blame her. After the massacre of her people—a massacre she only escaped because she had chosen a life with a tradesman—a little fear was understandable. How could she not worry about the future of her only daughter?

I had never allowed myself to be swayed by her gentle comments, though, any more than by my father's forceful ones or the spiteful words of those in the markets. But now, on only my second day in Lanover, every critical statement came back to circle in my head. In the face of true pain and need, I couldn't help but wonder if they were right. Was it nothing but selfishness and indulgence that led me to seek adventures and freedom instead of being satisfied to work with my hands and serve the community that raised me?

If you're going to be such poor company, I'll be off, Puss said sourly, startling me out of my reverie.

I looked at him guiltily. How long had I been silent? But he was already stalking away.

After a few more steps, I shook my head and rolled my eyes. We often walked without talking. Puss was just in a mood. He would be back soon enough, as he always was.

I picked up my pace, though, hoping the increased physical exertion would drive away the uncomfortable thoughts and the churning in my belly. According to the mayor's wife, the next closest town, Dilwen, was a two-day journey on foot. I would have to look for a place to camp for the night, but it was still morning, and I had much more ground to cover before that.

There was still no sign of Puss when I stopped for the midday meal, but he would easily be able to provide himself with a meal of mice or some other cat delicacy. Fields lined the road now, but regular stands of trees broke up the bare monotony, and greenery ran down both sides of the road. The thin strip of untouched undergrowth provided a pleasant green fringe between the road and the bare fields waiting for plowing. Puss would easily be keeping pace without being seen.

As the afternoon wore on, I began to feel anxious. Surely I hadn't done anything to make Puss truly angry. Had I missed something that upset him? I watched the undergrowth closely, listening for any sign of his presence.

When I reached the next clump of trees, I paused, staring between the trunks and trying to catch a glimpse of him. His shorter legs should be tired by now.

"Don't you want a ride?" I called out, hoping he was within hearing range. "We should try to make it a bit further before stopping for the night. We don't want too long a journey tomorrow."

Silence greeted the attempt, and I strained to hear the pad of cat footsteps among the leaves.

There! I frowned, angling my ear toward the trees on the right side of the road. Had that been the cat?

My eyes fixed on a large bush that seemed to be rustling slightly. Was he hidden among its leaves?

I stepped off the road, my eyes on the questionable foliage. The ground underneath my foot was spongy, but no roots tripped me up, so I increased my pace. I had nearly reached the bush when the dirt beneath me crumpled.

I gasped, my hands flying out, but there was nothing to grab hold of. I collapsed forward, plummeting downward.

I managed to twist as I fell, taking the brunt of the impact on my left shoulder and hip. For a moment, I lay still, soft dirt tumbling over me as I fought to regain my breath.

It was dark inside the hole, the dirt walls absorbing the light.

But from my back, I could clearly see the round top, giving a hint of the daylight that still existed up at ground level.

"Help!" I screamed when I regained my breath. "Puss!"

Only silence sounded in response. I drew a deep breath to repeat the call but stopped. If Puss was within hearing distance, he would have heard me the first time. The cat never missed anything.

But what was a pit like this doing just beside the road? What purpose did it serve?

Fury gripped me. There was only one possible explanation. Some reckless fool had built a trap pit to catch larger game and then abandoned it without filling it in. Inexcusable!

I made myself pause and think more logically. Perhaps they hadn't abandoned it. Perhaps they would be past soon to check for any catch.

I worried at my lip. But how soon? What if they only circled past every few days? It was a cruel thing to do, but some hunters didn't care about such things.

"When they do come, I'll be giving them an earful," I muttered, but the bravado of my words barely covered my fear.

Sitting up slowly, I checked for injury. Thanks to the soft dirt beneath me and my landing position, I didn't seem to have broken or strained anything. I would be bruised, but that was a minor consideration.

Far more worrying was the discovery that I had landed on my water skin. The force of the impact had burst it open, and the water had already drained away into the ground beneath me.

"It doesn't matter," I told myself, striving for calm. "Puss will come looking for me long before water becomes an issue. Or the hunter who dug the pit will return. All I have to do is wait."

But as the minutes stretched to hours, my certainty faltered. Every so often, I shouted again, calling for Puss as loudly as I could. I didn't dare keep it up, though. I didn't want to dry my mouth or exhaust myself when I had no water to sustain me.

The same thinking applied to my attempts to climb out of the pit. The soft dirt of the sides of the hole kept crumbling under my hands and feet, and when a whole chunk came loose, nearly burying me, I finally gave up. Puss couldn't rescue me if I was completely covered.

When it began to grow dark, my hold on my panic grew thin. What if I had misunderstood Puss's earlier words? What if he had deserted me completely?

But even in such desperate straits, I couldn't believe it of him. The more likely possibility was that he had continued on at my usual pace and was now far ahead of me, not realizing I wasn't keeping up. Eventually he would look for me, but would he think to circle back? Or would he push on, thinking he was the one to fall behind? At what point would he realize and retrace my steps? How long before he found me?

And once he did, how long before he could go for help? A talking cat was a great deal of help in many situations, but he couldn't possibly pull me from this hole unaided.

It took all my control to steady my breathing as I imagined the hours turning into days. Despite my repeated mental reminders that this could only be classed as an adventure, it took all my willpower not to start mindlessly screaming.

But as the light continued to dim, I questioned my restraint. An adventurer needed to use every tool at her disposal, and right now, all I had left was my voice. I stopped fighting it and screamed as loudly as I could.

Unlike my controlled calls earlier, I didn't pause to listen for a response. My instincts taking over, I shouted for help again and again, screaming my throat ragged.

Somehow, though, I retained just enough awareness to catch a sound out of place over my cries. I froze, going silent mid-scream. Had that been Puss? Was someone there?

I stared hopefully up at the opening of the hole, straining to hear.

"Where are you?" a human voice called into the silence.

"Over here!" I shouted back, my voice hoarse.

"Keep calling," the man said sharply. "I'll follow your voice."

"This way!" I called back, a little quieter this time, feeling the strain in my throat. "Over here. I'm in a hole. I think it's a trapping pit. Just to the side of the road."

"A pit? No wonder I can't see you."

"Careful!" I called. "The edges are fragile. They'll give way if you get too—"

My words dried up as a face appeared over the edge of the pit. An all-too-familiar face. I groaned.

"Are you hurt?" he asked quickly, his face creased with concern.

I cleared my throat. "Not in any significant way," I said stiffly.

"Oh, it's you." Amusement rippled over his face. "I was wondering where you'd got to."

"What are you doing here?" I asked sourly.

He raised an eyebrow. "I can leave if you like?"

"No!" I swallowed my irritation. "I'm sorry. I would appreciate your assistance, of course."

"Where's your cat?" he asked, not moving.

"Who knows? He went off for a walk." I struggled to keep my expression calm and unbothered by his interrogation. "I've been here for some hours and would prefer to chat once I'm above ground again."

A smile flashed across his face, as if he was suppressing a laugh, but he nodded. "Just give me a moment. I have a rope in my pack. I'll move back and throw it down to you. Wrap it around your waist, and then take hold of it as tightly as you can. If you brace your feet against the edge of the pit, I should be able to pull you out without much difficulty."

"Yes, I can do that." I scrambled to my feet and secured my pack across my shoulders as I waited.

When the rope appeared, tumbling down from the sky, I hurried to do as he'd instructed.

"Let me know when you're ready!" he called.

I gave a small tug at the rope to check it was properly wound around me and then called for him to begin. The rope immediately strained upward, and I scrambled to keep pace with it. Now that I had assistance, walking up the walls of the hole was easy compared to my previous attempts.

When I reached the top, he kept tugging me forward until I was well clear of the edge. As soon as I collapsed onto the ground, the rope went slack and his footsteps sounded.

I just lay there, too embarrassed to look up at him. For the second time in as many days he had found me on the road in a state of dishevelment and distress. Why did it have to be him of all people?

He knelt beside me, patting down my back and arms with surprisingly gentle hands. "Are you sure you're unharmed?"

I sprang up, scrambling back out of his reach.

"Yes, I'm fine. Just tired. And a bit bruised," I added truthfully.

He sat back on his heels. "It's a good thing I came by. I was thinking I might meet you on the road."

I glared at his laughing eyes, but justice made me force myself to speak.

"Thank you. I deeply appreciate your help."

"Don't speak of it." He gave a gallant half bow. "I'm sure someone else would have passed by soon, or Sir Puss would have returned."

"Perhaps." I held up my burst water skin, looking at it dispiritedly. "But since I managed to land on this, I might have ended up in trouble."

His brow creased. "You must be thirsty."

He didn't hesitate to hold out his own. I accepted it reluctantly, too thirsty to spurn his generosity. I was careful to drink sparingly, however, taking just enough to quench my desperate thirst and leaving plenty behind.

What's this? asked a familiar voice, more yowl than meow.

"Puss! Where have you been?" I glared at the cat, glad to have one legitimate object for my annoyance.

That is no business of yours. Were you really unable to manage without me for one small stretch of road?

"I…" I closed my mouth, opened it again, and then snapped it shut. What was there to say?

"I'm afraid Kali ran afoul of a trapping pit," Xavier said, unexpectedly grave. "She was stuck alone in there for some time and is justifiably shaken."

I looked away, my irritation irrationally growing at his understanding.

"I'm fine," I snapped, regretting the words immediately when both of them gave me doubt-filled looks. "Or I will be soon enough," I amended. "I'm just shaken and thirsty."

Puss frowned at my burst water skin. *The closest stream is some distance, and it is already getting dark.*

"We will have to camp together," Xavier said cheerfully. "Thankfully I filled mine at the last stop and can provide enough for us all until we reach the next stream tomorrow."

"Camp together?" I spluttered.

"You needn't fear for your safety," he said quickly. "I'm sure Puss would attack anyone who offered you harm, including me." He looked to the cat for confirmation.

Puss glared back at him. *Certainly I would do so. Not that you are any threat.*

"No, no," I said quickly, unable to think of an excuse in the awkwardness of the moment. Xavier had rescued me and had the water Puss and I both needed. I couldn't run away for no better reason than injured pride.

I swallowed my feelings and murmured my thanks.

Xavier smiled in a knowing way that set my teeth on edge but refrained from actually saying anything obnoxious.

"Not right here, though," I said. "I want to get away from that pit."

"There appeared to be a decent clearing among the trees on the other side of the road," Xavier suggested. "I saw it when I was trying to work out where all the screaming was coming from."

Screaming? Puss looked at me, but I refused to meet his eyes. If I had been screaming it was his fault as much as mine.

"Let's go, then," I said with as much dignity as I could muster, leading the way across the road.

With the sun now below the horizon, it was growing darker every minute, so we had plenty to focus on. Once we'd established the best position—a location with plenty of room for us all to stretch out comfortably but with enough surrounding trees to provide cover—we hurried to gather sufficient fallen branches for a small fire. I was more than usually eager for a cheerful blaze to keep away the shadows of the night.

Xavier worked swiftly, showing no sign of discomfort at the basic camping situation. He happily handed the cooking over to me, though, claiming I wouldn't want to taste what he could produce.

I took up the task eagerly, glad to have a way to repay his earlier favor. I even felt a small spark of warmth toward him when he smacked his lips after polishing off the bowl of rabbit stew, sitting back with a satisfied sigh.

"You make a good team." He smiled from me to Puss, acknowledging Puss's efforts in catching and preparing the rabbit—a task he did as well as any human, although never within my sight, so I had no idea how he managed it.

Would I travel with her if we didn't? Puss yawned and stretched himself out beside the fire.

Xavier stifled a laugh, regarding the cat with something close to fascination. I could tell he was full of questions but unsure how Puss would respond if he tried to ask them.

"You're right to restrain yourself," I said softly. "He doesn't like questions."

Xavier looked up at me in surprise but didn't deny my correct reading of his thoughts.

"He's a true marvel," he murmured back. "How did you come to meet him?"

I shrugged. "He was with my brother first. But Puss won't tell me how or why he ended up with Bernard."

"Your brother must have great faith in him if your family allowed you to travel so far with just a cat for company."

I stiffened, the brief moment of understanding between us broken. "I have no one left who can claim the right to question my movements."

Xavier's face fell, his eyes examining my face.

"I'm sorry for your loss," he said softly after a moment.

I turned away, not wanting him to see the grief that still lived too near the surface, even after so many months and so much distance.

"It's not your doing," I said after the silence grew too great.

"Nevertheless…" He hesitated. "I fear we have perhaps started off—"

"Greetings!" called a loud cheerful voice, making us both start and turn away from the fire to peer into the darkness. "What a cheerful blaze you have going. Can two travelers beg hospitality on this lovely evening?"

Xavier leaped to his feet and swept an elaborate bow. "By all means. We are but three travelers met by chance ourselves."

"Three?" A round faced man of middle age appeared in the circle of firelight, looking from me to Xavier before his eyes found Puss, still stretched out by the flames, apparently asleep. "Ah yes, indeed, indeed."

He gave us a slightly askance look, however, as he ushered a middle-aged woman forward to join him.

Puss opened one eye and examined them both. *You will do.*

The woman screamed, the sound reverberating through the trees.

"Did…did that animal just speak?" she whispered.

Xavier offered his arm to assist her to a seat across the fire from Puss.

"He's a most unusual cat." He lowered his voice dramatically. "From the Palace of Light, you understand."

"Oh." Her eyes widened even further. "Of course." She looked utterly bemused despite the platitude.

"What an interesting group," the man said, taking a seat beside the woman. "I'm Peter, and this is my wife, Loris."

"I'm Xavier," my companion said, and I jumped in quickly before Puss could give me a false title, or Xavier could introduce me and give the impression we belonged together.

"I'm Kali, and this is Puss."

"Most pleasant to make your acquaintance." Peter grinned broadly. "We're on our way to Tarka from Dilwen, and pushed on a bit long."

"And whose fault is that?" Loris asked in long-suffering tones. "I told you and told you it was time to be stopping and finding a place to camp, but you were always sure there was somewhere better just ahead." She threw me a knowing glance. "It's always the same way."

I tried not to grin too broadly. "Well, you're most welcome to join us. As Xavier said, we only met by chance ourselves just as dark was falling."

Loris looked me up and down, furrows appearing in her brow. "You look as if you've met some accident, my dear. Are you well?" She cast a suspicious look at Xavier.

"Yes, I'm afraid I did." I winced. "There is a trapping pit on the other side of the road, and I managed to foolishly stumble into it.

I was stuck for some time before Puss returned and Xavier passed by."

"A trapping pit?" Loris exclaimed, horrified, as her husband let out an explosive bellow.

"Another one!? Confound those wretched traders!"

CHAPTER 6

"Traders?" I stared at him, and even Puss raised his head with interest at the unexpected response from the couple.

"That dratted Caravan Cobolt, or whatever they call themselves," Peter said. "What they're doing out of their precious desert, I don't know, but we don't want them around here—as we told them! Leaving pits everywhere and taking all our game! Dilwen sent them on their way, and we thought we'd found all those holes. I'll have to report this one before someone else gets hurt."

He continued muttering furiously under his breath while Xavier and I exchanged a surprised look.

"So Caravan Cobolt passed through your town as well?" Xavier asked in a carefully neutral voice.

"That they did." Loris gave her husband a reproving look, taking over the narrative. "But our mayor is the suspicious sort and wanted to know what a desert trader caravan was doing so far from the desert. We thought we'd sent them on their way immediately, but it turned out they had continued lurking in the area, stripping it dry. They even tried to harvest some of the spring crops in the outlying fields, the cheek! After that we made sure they were really gone."

I wondered if I should mention the trouble Tarka had experienced with the supposed caravan but decided against it. It wasn't my information to share, and they might not want their misfortune spread widely.

"I'm glad you were able to be rid of them in the end," Xavier said. "I'm actually on my way to the capital to report them to the king. We suspect they are criminals masquerading as a desert trader caravan."

"I knew it!" Peter exclaimed. "You'll stop in Dilwen, I hope, and hear the full report from our mayor?"

Xavier agreed, and we were soon each finding a comfortable place close enough—but not too close—to the flames. It was hard to settle to sleep, though. Every time I closed my eyes, I remembered the dark sides of the pit. And when I opened them, my mind raced with thoughts of the false traders. What sort of trouble were they sowing along this road?

Eventually I managed to sleep, but I was up with the first stirrings of dawn. To my surprise, I wasn't the first awake.

Xavier had already risen and prepared a simple breakfast. I accepted the offered food, not feeling bad since I'd provided the meal the night before. I felt a little more guilty accepting his water skin, but my mouth was so dry I couldn't bring myself to refuse it.

Puss showed no such compunction, happily lapping up the water Xavier carefully poured into a cupped leaf for him.

"Do we just leave them?" I asked, looking down at the sleeping Peter and Loris.

Xavier nodded. "We're going opposite directions anyway. And they seem well provisioned." He nodded toward their full packs.

I joined the road at Xavier's side, unable to use the excuse of going a different direction to him. At least Puss showed no inclination to stray on this occasion, staying unusually close to my feet. He hadn't offered any apology for disappearing the day before, but I chose to consider his current behavior as regret for abandoning me.

"Are you really Tarka's messenger to the king?" I asked when the silence grew too awkward.

Xavier smiled. "Is it so hard to believe? I'm generally considered quite reliable, you know."

I stiffened as he threw my previous words back at me. Unbelievable! I'd nearly forgotten his behavior on the road to Tarka, but the reminder was timely. For all his assistance the day before, it wouldn't do to forget the capricious nature of my temporary companion.

"I thought you were heading toward the desert," I said, not looking at him.

"Did you?" From the corner of my eye, I saw him tilt his head and look at me curiously. "I suppose I was, originally. But as you aptly pointed out, I couldn't go further than its border on my own. And I found I wasn't in the mood for waiting around for the next caravan to visit."

I quirked an eyebrow but kept my eyes ahead. Of course he was picking up and putting down plans based on his whims. I just hoped he wouldn't tire of this task as well and leave the people of Tarka in the lurch.

His eyes remained on my face, something in their bright depths making me more determined than ever not to look sideways and meet their gaze.

"For some reason, I found myself eager to be on the road back to the capital," he said. "So it was only natural to offer to take the message. None of the inhabitants of Tarka can easily bear the expense and time of the journey at present."

He spoke so seriously that I hoped he understood the importance of his message. I silently resolved that when I reached the capital I would do my best to check that Xavier had indeed arrived and sought an audience with the king. No doubt he would arrive there first as he could travel more quickly than Puss and I could.

"I suppose you'll procure a horse at Dilwen," I said.

His eyes drew together as if disappointed, but the look passed quickly, his own eyes returning to the road.

"Yes, I must do so. It's not a message that can wait. Especially now we know the caravan has been causing further trouble." He frowned into the distance. "How far ahead of us do you think they are? I don't suppose it's possible we'll encounter them before we reach Lanare."

The idea shocked me enough that I didn't comment on his reference to *we*, as if we were truly traveling together.

"Do you think so?" Without thinking, I wrapped my arms around myself, an unconscious shield.

Xavier turned toward me, concern in his eyes, but Puss spoke first.

You need not be alarmed. Naturally I will not let anyone do you harm.

"Oh really?" I asked, unable to keep the acid from my voice. "Perhaps you should tell that to the trapping pit?"

Puss cleared his throat, looking uncomfortable for the first time since I had known him. *A pit is not the same as a person.*

"No, but it can be deadly just the same," Xavier said softly, finally surprising me into looking at him fully.

Had he just reprimanded Puss? I waited for Puss's dismissal of his words, and when it didn't come, my head swiveled around to look at the cat. Had he just taken criticism from a stranger?

I shook my head. Apparently this leg of the trip was going to continue shocking me.

No one spoke again, and we walked on in surprisingly comfortable silence. After everything that had happened, I couldn't bring myself to question Xavier on his background and situation, and he seemed distracted by his thoughts, more concern in his expression than amusement since the encounter with Peter and Loris.

At every stream we passed, he filled his water skin, so we experienced no lack of water. Without the opportunity to replace my own skin, however, I couldn't part ways with Xavier.

We pushed on with few stops, my accident the day before having cut short our progress before night fell. Thankfully we saw the first buildings in the distance just as the sun was approaching the horizon.

"Thank goodness," I muttered, turning to Xavier and offering him my hand. "Thank you for your assistance, and I wish you all the best with your errand. I hope the crown acts swiftly and decisively."

Xavier stopped and frowned at my hand, glancing at the town in the distance. I didn't let my arm drop, though, and after a moment, he took it as he had in the central square of Tarka.

Bowing over it, he pressed his lips to my knuckles, sending an unwelcome frisson through me. He looked up at me with the old laugh back in his eyes.

"Thank you for your well wishes, my lady," he said with false gravity.

I whisked my hand away and glared at him, but he didn't appear in the least daunted.

I waited for him to hurry off toward the town, intending to follow at a slower pace, but he didn't move. When I gave him a pointed look, he just smiled at me mischievously.

Why have we stopped? Puss meowed irritably. *There is hot food and a soft bed over there. I, for one, see no reason to linger out here on the road.*

I growled softly, put my chin up, and strode toward the town as quickly as I could manage. If Xavier had any consideration, he would be the one to take a slower pace.

Apparently he had none. He immediately started moving as well, easily keeping pace with me with his longer legs.

When I glared at him, he merely grinned back, taunting me silently. I considered reprimanding him, but what could I say?

Fuming silently, I entered Dilwen at his side. I knew we must look as if we were a purposeful pair, like Peter and Loris, but I couldn't do anything about the assumptions of others.

"Dilwen is a larger town than Tarka," Xavier said conversationally as we neared the central section. "But still only large enough to have a single inn."

I ground my teeth together, carefully not looking sideways to see his laughing face. There was no use suggesting to Puss that we push on and find a spot to camp just out of town. His earlier words had made it clear he wanted the greater comforts offered by an inn.

With a sigh, I trailed behind Xavier as he led the way into the courtyard of Dilwen's lone inn. It was a prosperous looking place, the main building crafted of gray stone with a large, free-standing stable beside it.

"They look as if they should have horses to spare," I said pointedly, but Xavier just chuckled.

Inside, we were greeted immediately by a delighted, matronly woman who clearly recognized Xavier.

"We didn't expect you back so soon, my lord! I hope it's not due to any misfortune." She sounded pleased, despite her words.

I took the opportunity to regard him with narrowed eyes. Here was someone else addressing him as my lord. Had he lied to me about his rank?

"I'm afraid it's bad tidings that are sending me back to the capital," Xavier said. "But your worthy establishment is a bright spot in a melancholy business."

She beamed at him, clearly long since won over by his charm.

"I'll need to speak to the mayor before I leave," he added.

"And he'll need to hire a horse," I put in.

He cast me an amused glance while the innkeeper turned a suspicious eye on me.

"And who might you be?" she asked.

"This is Kali," Xavier said. "A fellow traveler. She also needs a room here tonight for herself and her fine companion." He gestured at Puss.

The innkeeper let out a shriek at sight of the cat.

"Out!" she cried, trying to shoo him toward the door. "Whatever are you thinking, Miss? You can't bring your pets in here!"

Pet? Puss meowed in icy tones. *I am no one's pet.*

The poor woman shrieked again, and I felt a swell of sympathy.

"He's not an ordinary cat," I said hurriedly. "And I promise he'll cause no trouble. He sleeps in my bed, but you'll find he sheds very little, despite his size."

Puss turned an offended look on me, but I gave him a glare. If he wanted a night in an inn, we needed to placate its keeper.

"I can vouch for him," Xavier said. "A most magnificent creature all the way from the Palace of Light. You should consider your establishment honored by his patronage."

Although the innkeeper had looked unimpressed at my words, she visibly softened at Xavier's contribution.

"The Palace of Light did you say? Naturally it's different if he's an enchanted animal." She regarded Puss with wonder. "Wait until word spreads around town! My dining room will be full tonight!"

I murmured my thanks, hurrying for the room we were assigned as quickly as possible, Puss stalking at my side.

Am I a performing animal? he meowed indignantly.

"We should be grateful she let us in," I said, the words turning into a sigh of satisfaction as I swung the door open and saw a large room with a soft, clean bed, two chairs, a neat fireplace, and a scrubbed floor. "She runs a lovely inn."

Puss looked around before taking a place by the low fire. *I suppose it is well enough for a human den.*

"Well enough?" I raised an eyebrow. "Who was talking about soft beds and hot food not so long ago?"

Oh that. Puss began to clean himself fastidiously. *I was merely assisting you with the human man.*

"Assisting me?" I sputtered. "I don't need assistance with… him!"

Do you not? Puss looked at me consideringly. *Perhaps it is so. But I doubt it.*

He returned to his cleaning, unmoved by my glare.

After a long moment of glaring at him, I erupted in a laugh. "Perhaps you're right, Sir Puss."

Don't you start with that nonsense as well, he said without looking up.

I chuckled again and left in search of a warm bathtub.

Once I was scrubbed clean and dressed in fresh clothes, I felt a great deal better. And my good mood only improved after I smelled the scents wafting from the inn's kitchen. I stuck my head in and requested two meals from the serving girl inside, directing for them to be brought to my room.

Puss had fallen asleep by the fire, but he roused at my return with a hopeful expression.

"Yes, yes, dinner is coming soon," I promised. "And it smells amazing. I ordered a whole meal for you, so you may pick out whatever you like best."

Puss yawned. *Perhaps I will eat it all. It has been a tiring business.*

Curiosity filled me as to his activities during his absence the day before. In all the chaos, it hadn't come up, and I knew he wouldn't respond to questions now. The only chance of getting information out of him was to surprise him in the moment.

When a knock sounded on the door, I sprang to answer it, my stomach rumbling. But when it swung open, it wasn't the serving girl on the other side.

"What are you doing here?" I demanded, trying to peer

around Xavier in the hope my dinner might be lurking behind him.

"I heard you ordered dinner to your room," he said cheerfully. "So I've come to fetch you."

"Excuse me?" I stared at him.

"You can't eat here," he said. "You heard what the innkeeper said. She's relying on you to be present downstairs so that all the people already flooding in from the town can admire Sir Puss. They won't stay to eat and drink if he's not there."

"He is not a performing ani—" I started to say icily, but was interrupted by Puss himself.

Really, Kali, aren't you always saying we should be considerate of people who are just trying to earn their living? I assure you I won't melt because of a few stares.

"Why, you..." I glared at him as he strolled from the room, accompanied by Xavier's chuckles.

Drawing a deep breath, I shut the door firmly behind us. "I have no issue with eating downstairs for myself."

Sweeping ahead of them both, I hurried down the steps in the lead, trying to block out the polite words Xavier was directing toward Puss, that infuriating laugh hiding behind every one.

CHAPTER 7

s promised by Xavier, the dining room of the inn was already packed beyond capacity. At our arrival, murmurs swept the group, everyone surging forward in an effort to see us. For a moment I drew back, instinctively unnerved by the pressing, rowdy crowd.

But Xavier managed them with ease, a few words and gestures clearing a path to the central table for all three of us. Relief filled me as he pulled out a chair and held it for me.

I even smiled at him, earning a return smile so charming that my traitorous heart actually fluttered. As he turned away, however, I caught sight of a cluster of town girls over his shoulder. They were clinging to each other and giggling, their eyes fixed on Xavier's handsome face. And there was no mistaking the envious glances they kept shooting at me.

Instantly, my irritation returned. Did they think we were together? Just as I had feared, the manner of our arrival had created a false impression—one only confirmed by Xavier's subsequent maneuverings. What was he playing at? Did it amuse him to toy with me?

I crossed my arms and glared at him as the innkeeper bustled up, her face creased with a large grin.

"Welcome, welcome," she said, her attention focused on the cat and not the good-looking young man. "What can I get for you? My kitchen stands ready to prepare any dish that might meet the fancy of such an exalted personage."

Puss had been regarding the crowd around us with a tolerant eye, but at these words he brightened considerably.

I will accompany you to the kitchens myself, madam, to give my instructions to your staff. He paused and looked at Xavier. *You may place my cushion on the table. I'll be back shortly.*

He strolled away, a path opening through the crowd and closing behind him, mouths agape all across the room. Xavier chuckled as he moved the cushion the inn had provided for Puss from its usual place on the floor onto the table.

"I'm glad he's gotten into the spirit of the evening," he said.

"The innkeeper won him over with talk of a special meal." I shook my head. "He's not usually so easily swayed."

"I think he feels bad," Xavier said softly, taking the seat across from me.

"Bad?" I stared at him. "Whatever for?"

"For abandoning you on the road yesterday. He might not show it like a human, but he must be genuinely fond of you. He wouldn't travel with you otherwise."

"Wouldn't he?" I muttered doubtfully, thinking of Puss's efforts to persuade my brother to cross the desert. I didn't have the impression the requirement to have a miller's child as companion had come from Puss himself.

"I'm sure of it." Xavier smiled knowingly, making me want to get up and leave him to eat alone. "I'm still learning how to read feline expressions, but I'm sure he's been looking guilty ever since I pulled you out of that pit."

I shivered. "Please don't remind me. I have no desire to remember that particular incident."

"My apologies," Xavier said with a half bow. "You'll have to forgive me for wishing to keep it in my own memory."

I stared at him, my brow creasing as I tried to make sense of his words. Was he taking pleasure in my misfortune?

He met my eyes without shame, a laugh lurking in his expression. Apparently he had no consideration for the suffering of others.

A stir on the far side of the room told me Puss was returning, but I was too focused on Xavier to pay attention. He was determined to amuse himself by grouping us together, so at least I could use that to my advantage.

Back in Tarka, when I had told him I intended to help uncover the wrongdoings of the false caravan, I had merely been speaking in anger. But the determination hadn't faded. I had come to Lanover in the belief that an adventure would find me—preferably one where I could be of use to someone. And now the remnants of my mother's people were in danger again.

The desert nomads of the east were no more, but their survivors had joined their brethren in the western desert trader caravans, and I saw them all as kin, however distant. I might not have been raised as one of them, but that gave me greater freedom. Unlike the traders themselves, I wasn't tied to a caravan and the desert. And I wasn't going to stand by and do nothing while their whole way of life was at risk.

If Xavier was the official Tarkan messenger, taking news of Caravan Cobolt to the capital, then the mayor of Dilwen would give him an open account of the false caravan's doings in this town. He might even appoint Xavier as their official spokesperson on the matter as well. Given the warm welcome from the innkeeper, they seemed to know and like Xavier here.

"Taken in by a charming face," I muttered.

"Excuse me, what was that?" Xavier leaned forward, his brow quirking.

"Nothing," I said hurriedly, looking away.

Xavier would meet with the mayor, and since he had paired us together, I would tag along. The more information I had, the more use I could be if he disappeared before delivering his message to the crown.

Puss appeared, leaping onto the table and settling himself on the cushion with a satisfied look.

This inn has a most satisfactory kitchen. We will dine well.

I shook my head. How could we enjoy a meal when surrounded by staring faces, as if we were the newest exhibits in a menagerie? Puss seemed unaffected by the attention, however, neither preening for the crowd, nor put off by their presence.

The innkeeper followed in Puss's wake, leading two servers who came weighed down with dishes.

Xavier leaped to his feet at their arrival, helping clear enough space for them to unburden themselves onto the table. Before sitting again, he pulled the innkeeper to one side.

"Have you heard from the mayor? I need to speak to him at his earliest convenience."

She gave him an indulgent look. "Never you worry, my lord. He stands ready to speak to you. As soon as you've finished eating, you can go—"

"Food can wait," Xavier said. "I'll go now."

I jumped up, stepping over to join them. "Of course, this matter is too important to wait on niceties."

Xavier looked at me, surprise in his eyes.

"You needn't hold your own meal, Kali. You must be hungry."

I shook my head. "Naturally we must speak to the mayor first." I gave him a determined look, daring him to deny that we were on the same mission.

He glanced behind me at the table where Puss had already begun to eat.

"No, no," he said, "you must leave this burden to me." He raised his voice slightly, enough to carry to the crowd around us.

"I know everyone is looking forward to hearing your account of how you came to be traveling with such a magnificent creature as Sir Puss."

"Yes, yes, you must tell us!" cried multiple voices around us, the crowd pressing forward.

They had been hanging back, their fascination with Puss balanced with caution, but they felt no such uncertainty about me. Within seconds, I was trapped inside a throng of people.

As I was swept back and deposited in my chair, I glared across at Xavier. His lips twitched, his eyes laughing at me as he used the distraction to make his escape. At the door he turned back and saluted me, the fire in my gaze only making him chuckle—a sound that was lost in the eager voices asking me to tell them more about Puss.

"I am going to kill him," I muttered.

Why? Puss looked up from his meal. *We've never received such treatment elsewhere. He seems to be taking excellent care of us.*

I stared at him. Was he really so lacking in perception all of a sudden? He had always seemed so canny in the past.

With a sigh, I turned my attention to the people around us and the meal on the table. Even if I could somehow escape at this point—an eventuality that seemed unlikely—Xavier was gone. I'd missed my opportunity. So I might as well enjoy the enticing spread and the eager company.

Xavier hadn't returned by the time we retired for the evening, although I'd kept an eagle eye out for him, intending to waylay him and force him to tell me what the mayor had said.

The next day I was up early, despite Puss's complaints. I didn't want to miss Xavier again. Surely after the late night, he wouldn't have left before dawn?

The innkeeper was dismayed at our intention to depart after only one night, but I was determined to push on. I had originally intended to proceed to Lanare at a leisurely pace. But the news about the false caravan had given me a pressing sense of urgency to arrive in the capital. We would be moving much more slowly than Xavier, since we were traveling on foot, but I still wanted to reach our destination as soon as possible.

We only stopped for a simple breakfast—all I could fit in after the feast the previous night—before stepping out into the courtyard of the inn. My efforts were rewarded by the sight of Xavier, deep in conversation with an older man who looked like the stable master.

Xavier held the reins of a saddled horse, so I could only assume he had already arranged transportation for himself for the next leg of the journey. He finished the conversation with the man with a smile, turning in my direction.

When he caught sight of me, his smile grew, and I had to remind the fluttering feeling around my heart that a handsome face had little worth without substance to back it up.

Xavier led the horse over to join me and Puss, bidding us both good morning.

"I was hoping to see you before I left," he said, as if he hadn't been the one to run away from us the previous night. "I'm afraid I can't linger, much as I would like to."

I immediately forgot my own grievances and stepped forward. "It was bad news from the mayor, then?"

His lips tightened. "I'm afraid so. Worse even than I feared. He not only confirmed everything Peter said—and more misbehavior he didn't mention—but he's also had reports from Berk, the next town along. They were fooled in the same manner as Tarka and have been swindled out of a large amount of gold."

He sighed, his grip on the reins tightening. "The caravan visited Berk more recently than it did Tarka, though, so they're still celebrating their good fortune in making the deal."

"How recently?" I asked. "Will you catch the caravan before reaching the capital?"

An unexpected pang of concern hit me. If Xavier ran into the large group of criminals on his own, he could find himself in significant danger.

He shook his head. "No, their visit wasn't that recent. And I don't think they would dare go near Lanare. I'm guessing they will have left this road and continued northeast, making for the coast below the capital." His face set into grim lines. "There are plenty of towns along that route for them to swindle."

"But..." I stared at him in dismay. It really was worse than we'd realized. "How many do they mean to cheat? Surely they realize they'll be caught at some point!"

"Their brazenness only worries me more," he said. "They must have a plan of escape to give them such confidence. If they aren't stopped before they reach the coast, they may sail away and never be seen again."

"Then you must ride at once!" I cried.

He nodded. "I'll need to stop in the next town to hear their report firsthand—I'll need accurate information to present to the king—but even so, I should be able to reach the capital in plenty of time for them to send troops to the coast. At least the effrontery of these criminals is working in our favor as far as time is concerned. They clearly don't think anyone will have realized what's going on so quickly."

We'll hope to hear good news when we reach the capital, Puss said gravely, making me start. I had almost forgotten his presence.

Xavier nodded respectfully at him. "It is a matter of great gravity if even an inhabitant of the Palace of Light is concerned."

Puss nodded solemnly back, and Xavier pulled himself into the saddle, riding off with a single wave in our direction.

"What was that about?" I asked Puss. "Since when have you been so concerned about human matters?"

Of course I'm concerned, he meowed calmly. *This is not a foolish matter such as the amount and type of fur you're wearing at any given time. People might be hurt.*

"People might be hurt?" I shook my head. "I suppose falling into a pit didn't put me in danger of being hurt?"

Puss turned away without deigning to reply, but for a moment I thought I saw a hint of guilt on his face.

CHAPTER 8

*A*s we traipsed out of town, I realized I had one reason to rejoice at least. On horseback, Xavier was already long gone. Given his faster pace, we wouldn't cross paths again.

An uncomfortable feeling filled me. Relief—it was relief, I told myself firmly. Maybe without the irritating man around, I could enjoy a calmer journey.

Sure enough, the day proceeded without incident—almost as if Xavier had been the cause rather than the witness of my various embarrassing misadventures. I had replaced my water skin before we left Dilwen, even procuring a spare in case of emergencies, although I didn't fill it up, not wanting the extra weight.

There was no need to carry excess water since we passed plenty of water sources, giving me lots of opportunities to replenish our supplies. Puss stayed close as well, only leaving to catch a rabbit for our evening meal. By the end of the day, I couldn't look at him without a swell of affection.

Xavier really had been right, and the infuriating cat felt bad for abandoning me in the hole. It meant all the more because of Puss's general attitude toward humans.

Will we reach the next town tomorrow? he asked, making me hide a smile.

Puss was usually the one with all the answers, and I suspected he was making an effort to let me feel useful.

I nodded. "We'll reach it before nightfall. The towns seem to be fairly evenly spread in this region—you could sleep in an inn every night if you traveled on horseback or by fast enough coach. But…" I hesitated.

Puss looked at me inquiringly.

"Shall we skip this one?" I asked in a rush. "We need to conserve our coin, and…" My words trailed off at Puss's knowing look.

I turned away, feeling a flush rising up my cheeks. The innkeeper had refused any payment at our last stop, given the custom Puss had brought to her establishment, so it was a weak excuse even in my own ears. But I refused to acknowledge the real reason I wanted to avoid the town.

Xavier was on horseback and would be sleeping there tonight. If there was only one inn, as there had been in Dilwen, stopping in Berk would likely mean running into him again.

Certainly we may do so, if you wish it. Puss sounded bored, giving me the courage to turn back to face him. *It is of no great moment to me.*

"That's settled, then," I said firmly, and turned the conversation to the meal.

The next morning we hadn't been walking long when we heard wheels behind us, coming in the same direction. Ambling over to the side of the road, we made room for the vehicle to pass us.

A wagon drawn by two horses appeared, and I raised a friendly hand of greeting, meaning to wave as they passed. But the driver grinned broadly and pulled his horses to a stop at sight of us.

"Well met!" he called. "I've been keeping an eye out for you."

"You have?" I stared at him in confusion, sure I'd never seen him before.

He removed his hat and scratched his head before replacing it. "The whole town's been full of talk about the cat that can speak as well as a human."

A great deal better, in fact, Puss meowed with a trace of acid.

"Aye, aye!" the man said in unabashed excitement. "I didn't hear the news in time to make it to the inn to see you which was a great disappointment. But I thought to myself that if you were walking, I'd like as not see you on the way through. And here you are." He was evidently greatly pleased with his efforts of deduction.

"Here we are," I said blankly, not sure what else to say.

"You'll hop up and ride with me, of course," he said, gesturing at the broad wooden seat beside him. "I'm bypassing Berk, and Erva beyond it, and going near as far as the capital. I'm visiting my daughter who married a fine young man with a farm near Lanare."

"Congratulations," I said, responding to his evident pride.

"Thank you muchly," he said. "Done very well for herself, she has."

A timely arrival. Puss leaped up without discussion, perching upright beside the driver.

I rolled my eyes but followed him without complaint. I couldn't argue with a break from walking, even if I would have liked to be consulted.

The driver—a voluble man by the name of Erwin—kept up an almost constant stream of conversation as we traveled. He was clearly delighted at the company, despite Puss's lack of return interest, showing great astonishment and pleasure every time Puss spoke.

"That cat will be insufferably conceited by the time we part ways," I muttered to myself as we made camp. But I had to admit admiration had very little impact on Puss. He treated it as a given, not worth enough to have any effect on how he viewed himself.

There had been no question of stopping in Berk in the end, since thanks to the ride, we passed it long before nightfall. I didn't even feel the lack of a proper bed, since I slept with Puss, nestled in the hay that filled the back of the wagon. Erwin had been most insistent that we sleep there, while he took the ground. It was a kindness I only accepted because I knew it was directed more to Puss than to me.

A day of talking had done nothing to slow Erwin, who talked all the next day as well. We bypassed the fourth and last town between the desert and the capital around midday, and I felt a thrill to think we were so close to our destination already.

The only shadow on the unexpected good fortune was that the traffic had increased as we neared the center of the kingdom. All too often, hoofbeats sounded behind us, and every time they did, I flinched, afraid we were at last going to run into Xavier again. But when more and more time passed without any sign of a familiar face, I finally relaxed. He must have outpaced us at some point, perhaps when we were camped off the road.

Sunset was nearing when Erwin finally exclaimed that it was time for him to turn off the main road to reach his daughter's farmhouse. I tried to bid him farewell, but his insistence that we join him for a night was so effusive that Puss and I eventually capitulated.

He had been sure his daughter would be delighted to host us, and his predictions proved accurate. The daughter was nearly as talkative as the father, and her constant stream of conversation made it clear she was truly pleased to host guests.

"The neighbors won't believe me, that they won't," she assured me as she showed me the trundle bed she had made up for me. "A talking cat! Whoever heard of such a thing? You must stay as long as you like!"

I thanked her for the kind offer but insisted we would be on our way in the morning. The home was a comfortable one, and after listening to him talk non-stop for two days, I felt as if Erwin was an old, familiar acquaintance. But knowing the capital was so close made my feet itch. I wanted to keep moving.

Would they have already sent troops after the false caravan? I wondered as I lay in bed, staring at the ceiling. Would I find the capital abuzz with talk of the happenings in the surrounding towns?

I had less than a day's walk before me, but we still left early the next morning, taking more than enough provisions with us, thanks to the generosity of Erwin's daughter and her husband, a man who smiled far more than he talked.

"A well-matched pair," I said to Puss with a laugh once we were back on the main road.

Indeed. It counts to your credit that you don't feel the need to talk incessantly.

I laughed. "Is that a compliment? I'm shocked!"

Puss regarded me with a surprised look. *I can't imagine why. I often compliment you.*

"What?" I stared at him for a moment before bursting into laughter. "Do you? I can't say I'd noticed."

I continue to travel with you, don't I?

I laughed again. "I suppose that is a compliment of sorts."

My quick pace continued as the day wore on, my body refreshed by the break on the wagon. The weather had been dry since we left the desert, though, and the dust had grown bothersome. By the time it reached afternoon, I felt coated in it.

"It's a pity to arrive in Lanare after all this time looking like this." I surveyed myself with a sigh.

We will reach the city soon. You should wash yourself in that river and change.

I stared at Puss. "Since when do you care about how I look?"

He gave me a reproving look. *You seemed greatly concerned about it when we were arriving in Tarka.*

"Yes, but…" I trailed off and chuckled. It was difficult to refute such a point. I looked around instead. "I can hear flowing water, although I hadn't noticed it until you mentioned a river. Do you see it?"

It's there. Puss indicated the right side of the road with his head. *I will keep watch for you.*

"That's very kind of you," I said, impressed. "In that case, I think I will quickly wash." I couldn't resist the chance to be clean, especially for our much-anticipated arrival in Lanare.

Hurrying off the road, I found a slow-moving river, only just big enough to earn a title grander than stream. At a spot just down from us, the water spilled out into a small pond-like section to one side of the central current.

"That's perfect!" I exclaimed enthusiastically. "The water is even still enough that it might have picked up some warmth from the sun." I pulled off my first layers before hesitating and looking at Puss. "Are you sure there's no one around?"

Quite sure. Puss sat upright, his manner relaxed. But something about the way he held his tail gave the impression of alertness.

I relaxed. Puss always knew everything happening in his surroundings. If he said we were alone, then we were. Giving in to the impulse for a full wash, I stripped off all my clothes and plunged into the water.

I squealed as it closed over me up to my neck.

Is it not warm, then, after all? Puss asked without turning from where he surveyed the screen of trees that hid us from the road.

"No, no, it's quite lovely," I assured him. "It was just a shock at first. It always is."

A most displeasing way to wash.

I chuckled. "For a cat, perhaps. But I promise it's delightful for a human. I feel better already."

Pushing off the bottom, I stroked across the pond, keeping my head above water. Despite the temptation, I didn't intend to wash my hair. It would take too long to dry, and wet hair would only attract more dust.

"Are you sure you don't want to give it a try?" I called over my shoulder. "It's beautiful in here."

I got no answer which made me laugh, knowing his aversion to water. But when I turned, the smile dropped from my lips. There was no sign of Puss on the bank where I'd left him.

"Puss? Puss!" I stroked back in his direction. "Where are you?"

What harm could possibly have befallen the cat in the few moments I had been turned? I'd heard no sound. Surely no large animal could have taken him so silently.

I shook off the thought. I couldn't even comprehend Puss being taken off guard in such a manner.

"Puss!" I shouted again louder. "Where are you?"

Was there someone nearby? Fear gripped me at the idea he might have gone to investigate some new arrival. I had to get out of the water!

I scrambled awkwardly up the bank, only to freeze when I looked toward where I had left my pack. It was gone, along with the clothes inside that I had intended to wear.

A new sound, frighteningly like hoofbeats, made me launch back into motion. Never mind my pack, I would have to wear my old outfit.

I turned toward the rock where I had thrown my old clothes in my hurry to enter the water. It was empty.

"What? Impossible! Where are—"

I leaned forward, trying to see if they had fallen to the other side. There was no material in sight, however.

A fresh sound, this time like words, although too muffled for me to make out their meaning, reached my ears.

Squealing, I leaped back into the water, stroking over to where a patch of rushes made it impossible to see beneath the water's surface. How could this have happened? Where was Puss?

I was trapped in the water, unclothed, without so much as a towel to allow me to climb out.

The words came closer, the voice the familiar one of Puss. A second's relief washed over me before I registered the words.

Help! Help! he yowled. *We've been robbed! Help!*

"Robbed?" I stared in the direction of the sound, torn. How could we have been robbed in those few moments?

But I had never heard the cat call for help in all the months I had known him. Had he been injured in some way? Even if I was unclothed, I couldn't leave him to bleed out to spare my embarrassment.

Groaning, I pushed out from the reeds, only to hear the sound of another voice and a horse coming closer. Instinctively I shrank back into cover again, just as a single rider appeared.

His eyes swept the surface of the water, concern lining his features as he searched for someone.

"You!" I cried in horror, losing my chance to remain hidden.

Xavier's eyes flew to mine, the concern slowly dropping from his face as he took in my situation.

"Well," he said, the ever-present laugh in his voice. "We meet again."

CHAPTER 9

"What are you doing here?" I asked, my brain struggling to comprehend the awful situation in its entirety. How had I ended up in this position *again*?

"Riding gallantly to the rescue, I thought." He looped the reins over the front of the saddle and sat back, regarding me from his vastly superior height. "Having never seen Sir Puss in such a state, I feared some terrible fate had befallen you."

"Do you mean to tell me that awful animal flagged you down?" I cried, my horror merging with a new wave of anger. "Where is he now? I'm going to..." My words died off as I remembered that I was stuck in the water.

Xavier seemed to have been struck by the same thought because a smile slowly grew over his face. "What will you do exactly? You find me full of curiosity."

"Never you mind," I said icily. "If you have a single compassionate bone in your body, you'll see if you can find my clothes. They seem to have gone missing."

"Stolen, if your companion's cries can be believed," Xavier said with a total lack of sympathy. He even had the gall to chuckle. "I haven't seen any sign of these disreputable persons, however."

"The cat has run mad," I said through my teeth. "I only had my head turned for a moment. How could they have been stolen?"

"I must admit, seeing you unharmed, I'm inclined to suspect the cat of some plot too deep for us to fathom." Xavier swung down from the saddle, stepping toward the water.

"Don't!" I shrieked, making him freeze. "You can't come over here!"

His lips twitched. "What exactly are you wanting me to do, then?"

"Just…just…turn around!" I snapped.

Stifling a chuckle, he obediently turned away. "Would you like me to obscure the horse's eyes as well?"

"Wretched man! Do you have no compassion?"

"I offer my humblest apologies for my lack of feeling," he said in suspiciously grave tones. I could no longer see his eyes, but I suspected they were dancing with hidden laughter. "Consider it an overwhelming reaction to seeing you unharmed."

I groaned. Right now I would rather be fully clothed and bleeding on the river bank than stuck here in the water with no way to get out.

Before I could think of anything to say, Xavier straightened, his attention snapping to something beyond the trees.

"Did you hear that?" he asked.

"Hear what?" I shrank back. What fresh disaster was about to occur?

"It sounds like a large group of riders." He spun back around, stopping himself just before I came into view and giving a sound of frustration. "Do you really not have anything to wear?"

"I did have several outfits, but they've all disappeared along with that dratted cat," I said stiffly.

"Well, it can't be helped, then."

He rummaged for a moment in his saddlebags before

producing several folded items of clothing. "You'll have to wear something of mine for now."

In the distance I heard something that sounded suspiciously like Puss calling for help from the approaching group.

"What is that cat up to?" Xavier ground out. "Quickly! You can't be in there when a whole group arrives."

For once I agreed with him wholeheartedly, but I still hesitated.

"Come on," he said, dropping the clothes on the same rock where I had left my own outfit. "I'll be over here, keeping watch. I swear I won't turn around. Hurry!"

As promised, he led his horse some distance away, although he kept where I could see his broad back, obediently turned away. Drawing a deep breath, I gathered my courage and shot from the water, scrambling inelegantly up the bank.

With the sound of the approaching riders in my ears, and my eyes firmly fixed on Xavier's back, ready to cover myself if he so much as twitched, I shook out the garments he'd left.

With frantic, trembling fingers, I pulled on the dark shirt. Fumbling, I got one leg and then the other into the trousers, tucking the much too large shirt into the oversized waist. Thankfully Xavier had also left a belt, and I pulled it to the tightest notch, securing the whole lot in place.

"I'm done," I announced.

Xavier turned, freezing for a moment at sight of me. I grimaced, aware I must look ridiculous in the oversized male clothes. Swallowing, Xavier shook off the momentary hesitation just as the first riders appeared through the trees. His hand flew to his sword as he spun to face them, but at sight of their faces, his arm dropped.

"Xavier!" the man in the lead exclaimed. "What are you doing here? Don't tell me you're the thief?" He laughed as if such a thought was ridiculous.

I stared at the man, my eyes flicking to the woman at his side.

Both their horses had perfect proportions, and the outfits of both man and woman were in luxurious materials, perfectly fitted to their figures. My heart sank into my stomach, dropping all the way to my feet when the next rider to appear wore the uniform of a guard. Who were these people?

Xavier laughed, but the sound was a little forced for once. "No, I haven't taken to thievery in my brief absence."

The man's eyes moved along the bank. When they reached me, his expression froze, his eyebrows slowly rising as he took in my appearance, before his eyes flew back to Xavier.

"What exactly is this?"

Xavier cleared his throat, a momentary flicker of discomfort passing over his face, before his usual assured manner returned.

"This is the victim of the theft. She was swimming when all her possessions, even her clothing, were stolen. I arrived moments before you did and was able to provide some covering at least." He looked at the woman hopefully. "I don't suppose you have something more suitable with you, Evie?"

"Of course!" she said, warm sympathy in her voice. Her eyes turned to me. "How unpleasant for you!"

"Naturally Evie doesn't leave even for a day trip without bringing spare clothing in case of an unexpected accident," the man said with fond amusement in his voice. "She has saved me on more than one occasion."

The woman, who appeared to have a similar stature to me, although she must have been at least ten years older, laughed. "I may be a princess now, but I can't entirely leave the seamstress in me behind."

"Princess?" I immediately dropped into an awkward curtsy, realized I was in trousers, and swapped to a bow, nearly toppling over in the process. "In that case, I couldn't presume to..."

"Do you only accept the clothing of princes?" the man asked in a wry voice.

"Princes?" I gasped, looking at him with wide eyes.

Had I strayed into a dream? The whole conversation made less and less sense.

"Of course she could not refuse the only help she had on hand," Evie said reprovingly. "Even if wearing Prince Xavier's clothing was hardly to her liking. You mustn't tease her, Frederic."

The man smiled at her with the same affection as earlier, although I suspected it hadn't been teasing that had led him to view me with suspicion. They continued to speak to each other, but my brain had latched on to two ominous words. Prince Xavier.

My eyes flew to his to find him watching me with open laughter on his face. Prince Xavier? My Xavier was Kuralan's *Prince Xavier*. Not mine, I corrected my thoughts. I appeared to have lost the ability to even think straight from the shock.

Of course I had known Kuralan had a prince named Xavier. I had even seen him from afar at royal parades. But what was he doing here in Lanover, wandering around *alone*? Princes didn't do that.

Surely it couldn't be him.

But more guards had appeared now, along with two more people in equally noble dress. Was it more likely this group were impersonating the local royalty? Hardly. And they seemed sure of Xavier's identity.

"Oh, Tillie, there you are!" the woman named Evie called to the second woman.

Tillie? I swallowed. As in, Princess Tillara, the desert trader girl who had married the second Lanoverian prince? My eyes traveled to the other man. Did that make him Prince Cassian?

"This poor girl is in need of our assistance." She turned imperious eyes on the men and the guards. "You all clear out. We'll come out to the road when we're ready."

Crown Prince Frederic grinned, as if knowing there was no use arguing. "We'll go in search of that remarkable cat. I wouldn't have believed it if I hadn't heard it with my own ears." He looked across at Xavier. "Come on, the girls have the matter in hand now."

Xavier hesitated, glancing at me before nodding and swinging himself back into the saddle. Once astride, he bowed formally in my direction.

"Have no fear, Lady Kalila. You're in good hands with Evie and Tillie."

"Lady Kalila?" Prince Frederic looked between us.

"Of Kuralan," Xavier said with a completely straight face, making me gasp, although it was soft enough the others didn't seem to notice.

"Oh, you know each other?" Evie beamed at me. "That makes it a little less awkward. I didn't realize any other Kuralani nobility was in Lanover."

"I've just newly arrived, Your Highness," I said with another bow.

I wanted to deny the title, but how could I do so when Xavier —a Kuralani prince—had just assigned it to me? And Puss would no doubt back him up, the rotten traitor. If I didn't want to look even more ridiculous than I already did, I had better keep my mouth shut.

"We met on the road earlier," Xavier said lightly. "But had parted ways since I needed to make for the capital with speed. I'm glad I came by at the right moment to be of assistance, however. I would never wish to leave a fellow Kuralani in distress."

"No, no, of course not," Frederic said, his earlier suspicions seeming to be laid to rest. "But what brought you back with such haste? I thought you were making for the desert."

Xavier's eyes drew together. "As to that, it's not good news, I'm afraid. Come, I'll tell you while we search for Sir Puss."

The three princes directed their horses back into the trees, the guards trailing behind them. The last two guards hesitated, but Princess Evie waved them away.

"We'll be right here, well within earshot," she said. "Lady Kalila will be uncomfortable if anyone else remains in view."

"Just Kali, please," I managed to choke out.

The princess smiled at me. "And you must call me Evie. And this is Tillie. We're delighted to meet a friend of Xavier's. We were sad to see him go when he got sick of Lanare and decided to resume his adventuring."

"Kuralan must be an interesting kingdom to allow their princes such freedom," Tillie said, her curious gaze friendly.

I rubbed the back of my neck, giving a nervous laugh. "The twins have never been ones to follow royal protocol. Everyone says they're the despair of the sultan."

Both princesses laughed at that.

"I can well believe it," Evie said. "But he seems to have at least been of some assistance to you in your hour of need."

I looked down at my outfit and grimaced, but I couldn't deny it.

"Don't worry," Tillie said sympathetically. "We'll have you in something more appropriate soon enough."

Evie slid down from her horse and dug through her saddle-bags. "Tillie's too tall, but we're a similar size, luckily. Here, this should fit."

She drew out a tumble of soft silk in brilliant blue. Elegant golden embroidery flashed as it unfolded.

I gasped. "Oh no, I couldn't possibly—"

"Nonsense," Evie said briskly. "They're just clothes. It's an old outfit, I promise. I wouldn't have stuffed it in a saddlebag otherwise."

"Evie used to be a seamstress," Tillie explained with a grin. "She can never resist making herself new outfits."

"It's a weakness," Evie agreed with a sigh. "I already have more clothes than anyone could possibly need, but when the inspiration comes…"

"Not a weakness at all," Tillie said. "You're just maintaining Lanover's reputation as the richest and most stylish of the kingdoms. An important task for its crown princess."

I looked between them, struck by Tillie's words. She was so certain in her support of her sister-in-law's passion, not seeming to consider for even a moment that it was a distraction from her true duties.

Evie laughed lightly at Tillie and held out the dress to me. When I reluctantly took it from her, she turned back to her saddlebag. "I even have some undergarments here. Just give me a moment."

"Of course you do," Tillie laughed. "What don't you carry around in that bag?"

"Old habits," Evie murmured into the depths of the satchel. "It used to be my job to make sure the royals were never without the clothes they needed, remember. Even on the road."

"Are there really thieves in the area, though?" Tillie asked. "That's concerning. They must be brazen to snatch your things in broad daylight like that."

I shifted uncomfortably. "I didn't see anything. I just turned around for a moment, and when I turned back, everything was gone. Puss was supposed to be keeping watch…"

"That talking cat?" Evie and Tillie both fixed me with bright, excited eyes. "Wherever did he come from?"

"The Palace of Light according to him. But I met him in Kuralan. We've been traveling together."

"How thrilling." Tillie sighed. "But Kuralan really must be more relaxed than the Four Kingdoms if a cat was considered enough of an escort for a lady—even an enchanted cat from the Palace of Light."

"Oh, well…" I wanted to say I was no lady, but I still couldn't manage the words. "My father passed away recently, and my mother a few years ago. There was no one to tell me I couldn't go."

I managed a tremulous smile, but the older girls exclaimed in sympathy. Both of them surged forward to hug me in unison, and for the first time since my father's death, I found myself enveloped in the warmth of a caring embrace. Despite myself, tears welled in my eyes and overflowed.

They murmured soothing words until I managed to get myself under control. Pulling back, I mopped at my cheeks.

"I'm so sorry! I can't believe I'm crying all over you."

"Nonsense," Evie said firmly. "But I'm sure you'll feel at least a little more yourself once you've changed. Let me help you. You don't need to feel the least bit embarrassed—just pretend I'm your seamstress."

With efficient, business-like movements, she helped me strip off Xavier's ill-fitting clothes and don her own outfit instead. Within an astonishingly short time, I was standing before them, clean and dressed fittingly for the fictional Lady Kalila of Kuralan.

I surveyed Xavier's clothes with dismay. "They're very wet. I ended up using them as a towel, I'm afraid."

"That doesn't matter." Evie folded them and tucked them away in her saddlebags. "They'll dry well enough when we get back to the palace."

"The palace?" I stared at her.

"Of course! You can't think we'd cast you out on the streets when all your possessions have been stolen."

All my possessions. Fresh horror washed over me. Last time my pack had been taken, I'd had my purse of gold on my person. But I'd taken everything off for the swim. Which meant I really did have nothing.

"Especially not one of Xavier's friends." Tillie smiled at me kindly. "We're in the middle of negotiating various trade treaties with Kuralan, you know."

"Oh. I...I didn't realize..."

"Despite this unfortunate beginning, I hope you'll soon find Lanover to be a welcoming and hospitable kingdom." Evie took her horse's reins, gesturing for me to walk beside her. "We're usually considered so."

I joined her, looking about us as we walked through the trees. Where was that cat? What role had he played in the inexplicable disaster that had just befallen me?

"Puss!" I called when we cleared the trees, and a moment later, I caught sight of him, draped calmly across Prince Frederic's saddle.

He turned and surveyed me with a look of utter satisfaction.

"Why, you..." I stalked forward, but Xavier stepped in front of me.

"Are you all right?" he asked in a disarmingly soft voice, his eyes warm as he took in my new attire.

I crossed my arms defensively, trying to peer around him.

"I'm fine! But that cat!"

"Carefully," he said softly, too low for the others to hear.

I looked up swiftly, reading a caution in his eyes I didn't entirely understand. But it was enough to make me subside. I would have it out with that audacious feline, but maybe not in front of the gaggle of royals.

Frederic had crossed over to Evie and Tillie and was talking in a low, rapid voice. Both girls looked shocked, Evie's hands flying to her mouth.

"We need to get back immediately," Frederic said. "Our visit to Erva will have to be deferred. I need to consult with Father at once."

"Of course!" Evie stepped close to him, ready to be tossed up into the saddle. But as soon as she'd gripped her reins in competent hands, she started, turning toward me. "Oh! Kali! What about you? You don't have a horse. I suppose your mount was stolen as well."

"She can ride with me," Xavier said quickly. "You'll all want to hurry, but we can follow more slowly if we fall behind from the extra weight."

Evie nodded agreement, turning to say something to her husband.

I turned my glare from Puss to Xavier. Did he really expect me to ride in front of him on his horse? I'd never ridden a horse in my life.

"Don't worry," he said with an infuriating grin. "I'll hold on to you. You'll be fine."

My eyes narrowed, my determination immediately rising. No matter what it took, I wasn't going to fall off that horse.

Xavier swung himself up onto his mount, gesturing for a groom to toss me up in front of him. My courage almost failed as I was grabbed by the waist and thrown upward, but Xavier's waiting arms caught me firmly, positioning me sideways within the circle of his arms.

I gasped at the feeling of his embrace, and he chuckled.

"Don't worry, you're safe here. I'm considered expert on a horse."

I remembered who he was and stiffened even further. How many girls had the notoriously flirtatious prince carried in front of him on his horse?

"At least you must have had plenty of practice," I said icily. "You'd better not drop me."

"What's that supposed to mean?" he asked in a voice of pretended offense. "I don't let just anyone ride in front of me, Lady Kalila."

I straightened again, twisting to glare at him. "About that!"

"Shhh," he murmured, glancing significantly sideways at the guards who milled around us, the royals just beyond.

I narrowed my eyes but obediently fell silent. Here was yet another conversation that would have to wait for a more private moment.

The whole company had mounted, and we set off at a brisk pace that made me forget everything except clinging to the saddle and pressing myself back against Xavier's chest.

As I cowered against him, he made a low noise of satisfaction that filled me with irritation. But I was too focused on not falling off to accuse him of enjoying my discomfort.

I barely managed a look at our surroundings as we reached the famous city of red sandstone, cantering up the main road to the sprawling, single-story palace, built in the same stone as the rest of the city. Despite its lack of height, it still stood out, located at the top of a hill and surrounded by vast, lush gardens in every imaginable color.

Further hills spread out behind it, a suitable backdrop to the attractive and inviting building. Evie had claimed Lanover was warm and hospitable, and its palace, at least, seemed to proclaim that fact. But I had never imagined I would ride into the capital surrounded by royalty, carried on horseback in the arms of a prince.

PART II

THE PALACE AND THE SEA

CHAPTER 10

Xavier and I had fallen slightly behind, just as he predicted. So by the time we arrived at the double doors of the palace, they were already flung wide, people streaming in every direction. It appeared the unexpected return of the royal group had caused half the palace's occupants to come pouring out.

A groom spotted our arrival and ran forward to take the horse's reins, a footman close behind to help me down. Xavier dismounted after me, seeming unfazed by the chaos around us.

He flagged down a passing guard whose insignia suggested he was an officer of some kind.

"The king's been informed?" Xavier asked, appearing to know the man.

"Yes, sir." The guard nodded to one side of the doors where the younger royals I'd met earlier were huddled around an older man with gray hair.

"Excellent." Xavier strode off toward them.

I hesitated, unsure what to do. He halted mid-stride and looked back, giving me a questioning look. I made an uncertain face, and he gestured for me to join him. Reluctantly I did so.

As we neared the group, I caught sight of a large feline body, obscured among the legs. Puss.

I was still angry with him, but it was also a relief to see a familiar face in a very unfamiliar place—even if it was the face of a cat. My pace increased, and I circled the group to where Puss stood. But when I crouched down to his level, he gave me such a haughty look that I immediately stood again.

My movement attracted the attention of the older man.

"Who's this?" he asked sharply, clearly on edge.

I took an instinctive step closer to Puss, and the man's face lightened.

"Ah, you're the girl traveling with the cat. Lady...Kal...something." He inclined his head toward me. "Apologies, you've found us in a state of upheaval."

"Lady Kalila of Kuralan, Father," Frederic said in a reproving voice. He turned to me. "This is my father, King Leonardo of Lanover."

"Your Majesty." I immediately sank into a deep curtsy, my skirts swishing softly around me.

The king's face shifted. "Kuralan, did you say? You're most welcome, my lady. Urgent matters are underway currently, but my wife and I will look forward to welcoming you properly later."

"No, indeed, Your Majesty," I said, alarmed. "You need not consider me."

Her mother was of the desert nomads, Puss meowed, making the king start.

"Remarkable," he muttered. "Does one ever get used to it?" He looked from the cat to me. "The desert nomads, is it? If you're kin to our traders, you'll understand the importance of the current situation."

"Yes, of course," I said. "It's only been days since I parted company with Caravan Golura, and I'm greatly alarmed about this false caravan. If there's any way I can possibly help..."

My words trailed off as I realized how foolish they were. How could I help the king of Lanover? He could command countless people better trained and equipped than me.

"Very gracious." The king nodded at me. "You must bring your cat to talk with me once everything has settled down."

I opened my mouth to say that he wasn't my cat, but the king's eyes had already moved on to Xavier.

"So you really are back!" he said. "Does my son have the situation correct?"

He rattled off a list of the details we'd heard from Tarka and Dilwen, adding a few I hadn't yet heard about Berk and Erva.

"That's the sum of it, Your Majesty." Xavier's expression was unusually serious, his eyes alert and muscles taut, ready for action. "My fear is that they'll take ship somewhere along the coast and disappear before they can be brought to account for their actions."

"We can't allow that to happen," the king said. "While the crown can replace lost gold, that wouldn't be enough in this situation. We must prove they're not desert traders if we're to restore the people's confidence in the caravans."

I nodded, pleased to see the king was already considering the full scope of the issue and that he had the appropriate level of concern for the desert traders. My impression of Lanover went up several notches.

"We're turning out the guard," Frederic said to Xavier. "Squads are about to depart for every port—both official and unofficial. And a larger force will track them through the towns between here and there. I'm hopeful we'll catch them swiftly and put the whole matter to rest."

No wonder there were so many people scrambling in all directions. I could barely see the surrounding gardens for the constant moving bodies.

"I'll send delegates to the eastern towns," the king said. "We'll need an exact accounting of the deals made and property stolen.

But I'd rather wait a couple of days in the hope they can take positive news with them."

"And the caravans?" I blurted out, flushing as soon as I felt the weight of six pairs of royal eyes.

The king took my interruption in stride, however. "Contacting the caravans can't wait. I'll send express messengers to every caravan immediately, but it isn't an easy task to track them down. We'll have to wait for them to make appearances in one of the towns or cities along the desert edge."

I nodded. Royal messengers would have the same problem that had faced us from the beginning in Tarka. Following the caravans into the desert was a foolhardy endeavor.

An officer approached to speak to the king, and both he and Prince Frederic turned aside. Tillie took the opportunity to pull me slightly back from the others, Evie coming with her.

"I didn't realize you were a desert nomad!" Tillie exclaimed. "I know the connection between the eastern desert nomads and western desert traders is very ancient, but I wonder if we have any ancestors in common?" She looked so pleased at the idea that I couldn't help smiling back.

"My mother left her tribe to marry my father, and I never had the chance to meet my grandparents before the massacre. So I don't know if I have any living relatives."

Tillie squeezed my arm, her eyes full of sympathy. "Of course you do! All the traders are your family, which makes us cousins." She twined her arm through mine and beamed down at me.

"There's nothing we can do out here," Evie said. "King Leonardo has it well in hand. We should find you a room, Kali."

"Is it really all right for me to stay here?" I looked around at the frantic activity with discomfort. The Lanoverian palace already had enough on its hands.

"Of course it is!" Tillie tugged me toward the open doors. "The maids can easily make up an unused guest room. The palace is emptying of people, not filling up."

I glanced back, checking Puss was keeping pace with us. He was, maintaining an unusual silence given the conversation so far. I narrowed my eyes at him, and he gave me such a look of innocence that I snorted.

Tillie twisted, following my gaze.

"Oh, yes, you must come as well, Sir Puss. Would you like a room of your own, or will you be comfortable with Kali?"

"Don't pander to him," I muttered, as Puss replied for himself.

I will be perfectly comfortable with my companion, thank you.

"He likes to steal the blankets and all the warmth of the bed," I said. "So I'm sure it wouldn't suit him to lodge alone."

No, certainly it would not, Puss meowed without shame.

The princesses led me through various corridors, collecting a bevy of servants as they traveled. By the time we reached the chosen guest suite, work was already underway to prepare it for inhabitants.

"Oh!" I cried when I saw the size of the room and elegance of the furnishings. "This is much too grand for me."

It is not, however, too grand for me. Puss strolled inside, looking around approvingly. *And I am willing to allow you to stay with me.*

Evie and Tillie both laughed, as if he had been joking, but I rolled my eyes. Clearly Puss wasn't going to let me turn down the room.

"I'll raid my wardrobe and find you some outfits to use for now," Evie promised. "We'll have some things made up for you, of course, but it will take a little time to have them ready."

"Please don't go to any such trouble! Any old thing will be sufficient for me."

"Nonsense!" Evie smiled. "Remember I have my pride as a seamstress."

In the face of her insistence, there was nothing I could do but thank her profusely. Within a surprisingly short time, I was standing in the middle of the grand room, alone but for Puss.

"Did that really just happen?" I asked dazedly.

Of course it did. Puss leaped up onto one of the plush chairs. *My plans never go awry.*

"Plans?" I jumped on the word, glaring at him. "I knew it! What did you do?"

What needed to be done. He began to clean one paw. *I don't know what you're complaining about.*

"Puss! Did you somehow know those royals were coming?"

He smiled slyly, his tongue working into the grooves of his paw.

How else were you supposed to enter the capital in the proper manner and raiment of a lady?

Wrath filled me. "What did you do with my purse? Where's all my gold?"

Puss merely continued to clean his paw, and I sank into the other chair, covering my face with my hands. Puss would never admit to fault.

"How can you be so happy with this situation?" I asked, anyway. "We're here under false pretenses."

I don't know what you mean. Your blood is as noble as any of theirs, and their hospitality has been freely offered.

I looked up, glaring at him rebelliously. "It's really thanks to Xavier, not you, that they believed the story. When he introduced me as nobility from Kuralan, obviously they believed him. Your whole plan might have failed if he hadn't happened along."

Well, naturally. Puss didn't look up from his cleaning.

"Wait." My mouth fell open. "Was Xavier part of your plan as well?"

Puss merely smiled.

"You deliberately left me stranded like that and sent *him* there to find me?" I screeched, leaping up and flinging a pillow at the cat.

Puss leaped down just in time to avoid the missile, looking up at me with hurt eyes.

Everything I'm doing is for you. The least you could do is show a little gratitude.

"Gratitude! Gratitude!" I grabbed the next closest pillow and chased him across the room with it.

He scrambled up the wardrobe, perching on the top and hissing at me.

What are you doing? This is very undignified. I'm not used to such treatment.

"I'll show you what treatment you can get used to," I muttered, wondering if a thrown cushion would make it high enough to hit him.

A knock on the door made me hesitate, looking over my shoulder.

Do you mean to make a scene? Puss asked. *Or can I come down now?*

I sighed and dropped the pillow on the nearest surface. "Oh, come down, if you must."

Puss leaped down, looking far too pleased with himself as two maids entered the room, their arms laden with several gowns. And despite my discomfort with the situation, I would hardly have been human if I hadn't managed a little pleasure at the sight of so many beautiful items intended for me to wear.

There was no use trying to get Puss to acknowledge he was in the wrong. Which left me with a decision. Did I confess to the royals about my true background as a mere miller's daughter? I could feel the reluctance as I looked at the gowns, but the feeling only made me wary of my ability to make the right decision.

When the maids had carefully hung the gowns in the wardrobe and left, I turned to Puss.

"You didn't make this situation alone," I said, although he hadn't asked my intentions. "There's someone else I need to talk to before I do anything drastic."

Puss stretched out on the bed with a yawn, pointedly ignoring me. I considered hitting him with a cushion while he was unprepared, but decided he would likely sense my intentions and somehow leap out of the way.

"At this point, I'd almost believe you left me on purpose to fall into a hole," I muttered under my breath.

Puss caught the words, opening one eye to give me a cautious look.

My own eyes widened, my breath coming fast. "Puss! If you really...I'll..." I choked on the words, too flustered to finish a sentence.

There's no need to get so worked up, he purred in a superior voice. *I don't know what nonsense notion you've got in your head.*

I relaxed slightly, although I continued to watch him suspiciously. It hadn't exactly been a denial, but then I wasn't sure I wanted to know the truth. I exhaled slowly, deciding to let it go.

Eventually my gurgling stomach reminded me of how long it had been since I last ate. Surely even with so much going on, the palace inhabitants would still eat an evening meal? I seemed to have been forgotten, however.

Sighing, I opened the door and poked my head out into the corridor beyond. Although Puss had appeared to be asleep on the bed, he moved instantly in response to the door opening, joining me by the time I stepped out of the room completely.

It's this way, he meowed, starting down the corridor to the left.

I shook my head and followed. "How do you do that?"

Do what?

"Never mind. It's a handy ability, I must admit."

It's a wonder to me you humans ever manage, given you don't seem to know where you are half the time.

"It's certainly a trial," I agreed lightly. "But we do the best we can."

He didn't hesitate as we took several turns, finally arriving at a spacious room, not quite large enough to be considered a hall. A long, oak table took up much of the open space in the center of the room, and a number of people milled around it.

"Puss," I hissed as soon as I got a good look at them. "We were supposed to be going to the kitchen."

He looked back at me with a raised brow. *Were we?*

I groaned, but we'd already been seen. Xavier, who had been in conversation with Evie near the door, hurried to my side.

"You're here!" His charming smile focused only on me, and I forced myself to remember all the unpleasant situations we had shared before I forgot who I was dealing with.

"I was about to come fetch you," he added, making my eyes narrow.

An easy thing to say after the fact.

"Puss brought me," I said, and Xavier laughed.

"Is there anything that cat doesn't do?"

Despite myself, I couldn't help a smile. "Swim. But I think that's a dislike rather than an inability."

"It's good to know he shares some characteristics with a regular cat," Xavier said, shaking his head.

A quiet bell sounded, and everyone moved toward the table. I hesitated, but Xavier swept me along with him, depositing me in a chair beside Tillie before taking a seat himself directly across the table.

To my relief, the king wasn't present—presumably still busy making arrangements to track down the false caravan—but an older lady I hadn't yet seen took the seat at the foot of the table. When I caught her eye, I quickly stood again and dropped into a curtsy.

"Goodness, child," she said comfortably. "You mustn't worry about such things at the meal table. I suppose you're the girl from Kuralan. The one with the cat."

I cleared my throat, looking apprehensively at Puss. He padded along the length of the table, stopping beside the queen's chair. Lowering his head respectfully, he purred loudly.

"What a large, handsome fellow," she said in surprise. "But do you really speak, Sir Cat? It seems a strange rumor."

I do indeed speak, Your Majesty, he meowed with astonishing compliance.

"Goodness!" She stared at him. "What a remarkable thing. So you really come from the Palace of Light, then?"

Certainly, Queen Viktoria.

"Well, you're most welcome in Lanover, I'm sure. My youngest daughter has told me much about a talking horse, but I never thought to see such a wonder for myself."

Puss made a hacking sound in the back of his throat. *Arvin has also spoken of the Princess Celine.*

A loud laugh made me look at Prince Cassian who was seated between his wife and mother.

"Wait until I see Celine next," he said with a chortle. "She's even infamous at the Palace of Light."

Frederic, who sat across from his brother, grinned. "Are you surprised? If Eldon hadn't taken her off our hands, she would have driven Mother into an early grave."

"Nonsense," the queen said calmly. "What things you both say." She gestured with one hand, and servers stepped forward with large trays of food. "You'll give our guests a very strange idea of us all."

"By no means, Your Majesty." I eyed the array of dishes. "I can already tell that no one could fault Lanover's hospitality."

She gave me a satisfied smile. "We do our best."

The taste of the food lived up to the appearance, and I relaxed as the meal progressed, in large part thanks to Tillie's comfortable conversation. She was full of questions about the current state of Caravan Golura, showing herself to be knowledgeable about its people, despite having come from Caravan Adira herself.

Only the weight of Xavier's gaze, all too often fixed on me, ensured an uncomfortable note remained as the meal progressed. Several times I tried glaring back at him, but my ire only seemed to amuse him. After a while I decided not to look at him at all, a determination that took a surprising amount of effort to maintain.

When the meal finally finished, I bid a hasty farewell to the queen, exhausted and eager to be back in the privacy of my room. But Puss, who I had expected to join me, didn't leave his position at the queen's side. Even when I glared at him, he merely purred with satisfaction. I didn't know if he'd truly taken a liking to the imperturbable queen or if this was part of some plot to weasel into her good graces, but apparently he intended to abandon me to the endless corridors.

"I'll show you the way back," an unwelcome voice said from my other side.

I turned slowly, catching a slight movement from Tillie, as if she meant to join us, as well as the look Xavier sent, warning her off. When he looked back at me and saw I'd noticed, he merely smiled.

"Don't you think we have something to discuss?" he murmured quietly.

I ground my teeth together, but he was right. Insufferable man. I drew a steadying breath before inclining my head in acquiescence and leaving the room at his side.

CHAPTER 11

*W*e strolled down the corridor in silence at first. I shot a sideways glance at the man beside me. Now that I had adjusted to the truth of his identity, I wondered why I hadn't seen it before. Everything about his air of confidence proclaimed someone used to authority.

His situation might have been out of character for a prince, but everyone knew the Kuralani royal twins had no interest in formality and royal protocol.

But where was his brother, Xander? I had never known them to be apart in Kuralan—another reason his true identity hadn't occurred to me. I considered asking but didn't want to risk his taking it as an impertinence. I didn't want to put myself at a disadvantage for the coming conversation.

"Well?" he asked after the silence stretched on. "Don't you want to thank me?"

"Thank you?" I turned my head to stare at him, forgetting all about his royal status. "I suppose you mean for the loan of your clothes. But I only wore them for a matter of minutes, and they haven't come to any harm. And look at the mess you've landed me in as a result! I wish you'd ridden straight past and ignored Puss's cries!"

He frowned, examining my face. "Are you serious? Of course I couldn't have done so. But whatever do you mean? What have I done now?"

I gestured around us as we walked past an elegant statuette positioned beside an elaborate tapestry.

"Why did you tell them I was a noble?"

He raised both eyebrows. "I thought I was doing you a favor. I thought you wanted to be known as one."

"Of course I don't! What do you take me for? Don't you know enough to recognize Puss's nonsense? I've asked him to stop often enough, but the wretched creature never listens to me."

I narrowed my eyes at him. "But at least he only attributes me with some vague, imaginary bloodline. Thanks to your lies, the Lanoverians have the entirely wrong impression."

"Did I lie?" Xavier asked with a mischievous twinkle. "According to the cat, you have the right to the honorific, and you do come from Kuralan, don't you?"

I growled at him in frustration. "You know perfectly well that's not the impression your words gave. They think I have an actual Kuralani title."

"I'm sure I didn't say so." His lips twitched, as he fixed me with a grave look. "Surely you don't intend to go to my friends and accuse me of being a liar?"

I stopped, drawing in a slow breath as I swelled with rage. "Surely you don't expect me to stay here, taking advantage of their hospitality?"

He halted as well, looking back at me.

"But of course," he said mildly. "Although I would call it *accepting* their hospitality rather than taking advantage. Surely you've noticed that being hospitable is a matter of pride for them. And didn't you hear what the princesses said? Evie used to be a seamstress and Tillie a desert trader. I promise you're the only one here worried about titles or backgrounds. These people would help anyone they encountered in need." He gave me a roguish smile. "Especially a friend of mine."

"Friend?" I cried, stalking swiftly past him. "Is that what we are?"

He caught my arm, swinging me around to face him.

"Only if you want to be," he murmured, his quiet words meant just for my ears.

My breath caught in my throat at his sudden proximity, my heart beating riotously against my chest. No one so undeserving should have such a face. It scrambled my thoughts in an unforgivable way.

"I…" I swallowed, trying to pull my eyes from his and failing.

A slow smile spread across his face at my silence, and I tried not to fixate on his lips. It didn't matter how close they were to mine right now. This man could not be trusted.

I managed to get my limbs moving again, wrenching myself free.

"Use whatever word you like," I snapped, wishing I could make a dramatic exit but unsure which way to go without his direction.

His mouth twitched, his eyes too knowing. "I will, then."

When I didn't respond, he grinned and gestured down a side corridor. I followed, sending silent insults back in Puss's direction for leaving me in this situation.

When we reached the door of my room, I gave the prince a stiff goodnight. He responded in the same relaxed manner as always, the infuriating amusement lurking in his eyes. I slammed the door, letting my emotions get the best of me, but regretted it as soon as I heard his low chuckle receding down the hall.

A good night's sleep managed to soothe some of my turbulent emotions. Even Puss's heavy purrs contributed, and I couldn't maintain my anger at him. He insisted on doing outrageous things, but he truly seemed to believe he was doing them all for my good. How could I expect a talking cat from the Palace of Light to behave and think in the same way as a human?

Although he was being difficult for now, I had to believe that he had merely stashed my gold somewhere safe and intended to retrieve it at the right moment. He clearly wanted this visit at the palace and thought I might rush off if I had the means to do so.

He even stuck close to my side the next day until Evie arrived to sweep me away for fittings, full of plans for my new wardrobe. When the fittings were completed, I awkwardly mentioned the matter of payment, but the princess brushed my words aside.

"Don't be ridiculous! It's the least we can do after your own coin was stolen so close to our capital."

"I…" I hesitated, unsure how much to say.

Despite my fury at Xavier, his words from the night before had wormed into my brain. Could I call him a liar to his friends when he had merely failed to correct a possible misconception?

"I don't have any connections in Kuralan to help with forging favorable treaties," I said at last. "There really isn't any need to treat me so well."

Evie looked upset at my words, immediately making me feel guilty.

"Did you think that was why we were doing all this? Of course we don't have any such expectations." She gave me a coaxing smile. "A girl and a cat are not exactly a normal foreign delegation, you know."

I chuckled reluctantly. "No, I suppose not."

"Consider yourself as doing me a favor," she said. "It's good to have something to take my mind off the waiting."

When I gave her a questioning look, she grimaced. "Frederic

rode out late last night with the guards pursuing the caravan. I know he's not riding into battle, but I still worry…"

"I'm sorry." I gripped her hand, squeezing it. "I didn't know. Of course you'd be anxious. But I didn't hear any accounts on the journey here of the caravan being violent. I'm sure he'll be back safe before we know it."

"Yes." She brightened. "The time will pass quickly with your wardrobe to consider. "In fact…I have an idea."

Grabbing my hand, she pulled me from the seamstress's room, only pausing to direct someone to find Reya, whoever that was. Leading me through a dizzying number of turns, she barged unceremoniously into a suite even larger and grander than my guest one.

"Don't worry," she said, "Cassian went with Frederic."

My eyes widened as I realized whose room we had just charged into, but my concern was soon forgotten at the cry of welcome from Tillie. Turning from the window, she hurried over to us.

"Have you come to rescue me from myself?" she asked her sister-in-law with a smile.

"Of course!" Evie grinned back. "Kali has given me an idea. Remember that dress I talked about making for you for the soiree? You didn't want to wear it on your own, but now you won't have to be alone." She gestured at me triumphantly while I looked back and forth between the women uncertainly.

Tillie's eyes slowly widened. "Would you, Kali?"

"I…Of course I'm happy to do anything I can to help, but I'm not sure what we're talking about."

Tillie laughed. "Did Evie drag you here without an explanation? She gets overly excited about new dress designs."

"Didn't I explain?" Evie gave me an apologetic look. "You'll have to forgive us both. Our brains have been scrambled by our children. They do that to you, you know."

"Children?" I frowned, wondering why I hadn't seen any sign of them.

"It's not usually half so calm around here," Tillie said with a laugh. "When we planned the trip to Erva, we sent our children for a pleasure trip to one of the northern beaches. They left with a veritable army of nannies, guards, and companions, but I'm still glad they're nowhere near the route of this caravan."

"Do you have a lot of children?" I asked.

"Enough." Evie exchanged an amused glance with Tillie. "My oldest, Leo, is best friends with Tillie's oldest, Luca, and the pair of them get up to so much mischief they feel more like ten children."

"How nice to have a close cousin like that," I said softly, thinking of how many times I had wished for a sibling or cousin of a similar age.

"The girls are close, too," Tillie said. "My twins, Iris and Violet, are only a few months younger than Evie's Beatrice."

"I can't believe my baby is already seven," Evie said wistfully. "I miss them, but I'm determined to put their absence to good use. I'm going to make these dresses."

"What dresses?" I asked nervously, unsure what I was being dragged into.

"It's all because of this book I found." Tillie picked up an ancient looking tome from a small table beside the window. "For the past eighteen months, I've been researching my people's history in the royal library. The caravans keep few written histories since we have to carry everything with us, so it's been a slow process. There aren't many books dedicated to the desert traders, so it's mostly just a chapter here or there in more general Lanoverian histories."

"Have you found anything about the eastern desert nomads?" I asked eagerly. "I've never seen a book about them."

"There aren't any direct references," she said, her face becoming animated in response to my interest. "There aren't any mentions of Ardasira or Kuralan at all, so we always believed there was nothing but wasteland beyond the desert. We didn't know half of our ancestors had gone east."

I frowned. "I know the Four Kingdoms thought so, but didn't the desert traders always know?"

She made a wry face. "The elders knew it, but it's not information they give the youngsters. They like to wait until the rasher phases of youth are past before sharing the information. And even then, it was only senior caravan members who knew. The stories told by the nomads who trickled across from the east to join us were too concerning to make the crossing worth the risk, but I think trader parents have always been afraid their more adventurous youths would decide to attempt the crossing anyway."

I bit my lip, feeling the familiar weight of judgment, although Tillie wasn't directing her comments at me.

"When Cassie—you'll know her as Princess Cassandra of Ardasira—showed up in Lanover eighteen months ago, it was an enormous shock," Evie said. "We were all in an uproar, and I'm sure many wouldn't have believed her tale if she hadn't come with such an extensive delegation."

"I was especially fascinated by the idea of our people splitting," Tillie said, "with some establishing themselves in desert trader caravans to the west, while others became the desert nomad tribes to the east. And I finally found a book that claims to recount some of our people's history before the split."

"Back before the Sea of Sand became a desert?" I asked with wide eyes, leaning forward to peer again at the book.

She nodded. "Since you're from Kuralan, I believe you'll be familiar with the legend of the three brothers—the treachery of the youngest brother, the creation of the treasure caves, and the subsequent transformation of their garden empire into a vast desert—but the story didn't survive on this side of the desert. I first heard it from Cassie eighteen months ago, but I found it repeated in this book! According to this historian, he lived only a couple of generations after the upheaval. It must be one of the oldest books in the library."

I gulped. I wouldn't even dare touch the pages.

"Don't worry," Tillie said in response to my expression. "The book itself isn't that old. It's been copied out several times since then, although it's still old enough. The library is actually making several new copies at the moment at my request."

"The important thing," Evie said, cutting into the conversation, "is that it has pictures."

"Pictures?" I frowned at her, trying to imagine what sort of pictures it might contain. "Of the wonders of the old empire?"

Tillie chuckled. "There's only one wonder Evie is interested in." She picked up the book and flicked through it, clearly looking for something in particular. Stopping at a page, she held it out to me. "Clothing design."

I leaned forward to look. An ink sketch showed a young woman wearing a dress unlike any I'd seen before. The fitted top was short, showing a flash of skin near the waist, but her middle was largely obscured by a sweeping drape of material across one of her shoulders.

"It's hard to tell from the picture," Evie said, "but I'm almost sure it's a single stretch of material wrapped around the waist to form the skirt and then swept over the shoulder. Isn't it elegant? I've been begging Tillie to let me make her one. It only seemed right that one of the descendants of these people should be the one to wear it. And now there are two of you, so she has to let me!"

I considered the idea of attending an event in such a gown and couldn't help smiling. "It would make a sensation, don't you think?"

"Exactly!" Evie's eyes were shining the same way Tillie's had when she spoke of our people's history. "It's the perfect way to introduce you to the people of Lanover."

A soft knock at the door preceded the appearance of a head, peering around it.

"Your Highnesses? They said you wanted me?"

"Reya!" Evie pounced on the young woman and dragged her into the room. "There you are! This is Kali. She's one of the desert nomads from across the desert, and she's helped me convince Tillie to wear the dress."

"Really?" Reya's excitement told me she must be one of the seamstresses.

"We've got our work cut out for us," Evie said, although she looked delighted at the prospect. "We need two dresses in time for the soiree."

"Two?" Reya looked me up and down in a business-like way. "She'll look good in it at least."

"Thank you?" I said uncertainly.

Tillie laughed, and pulled me over to one of the chairs by the window. "Ignore them. They'll be too distracted for reasonable conversation now. But look at what else I discovered in here."

She opened the book and gestured at another picture, clearly settling in for a protracted conversation. I smiled, leaning forward. For the first time I didn't feel out of place in the palace. I understood Tillie's interest completely since I had always been fascinated by my mother's people. I was more than happy to talk to her on the topic for as long as she wanted.

CHAPTER 12

The next day both princesses were occupied with royal duties of some sort. After a brief fitting with Reya, who kept muttering to herself and apologizing for pricking me, I found myself at a loose end.

Reya was only a couple years older than me, but she had clearly been a seamstress for a long time and had Evie's full trust. Something about her determined focus made me feel out of place again. Reya was the kind of girl my parents had wished me to be —someone dedicated to her trade and settled into her place in the world. She probably never felt the itch to be off to places unknown, seeking new experiences and adventures.

Puss had also disappeared off somewhere.

"Probably weaseling his way into the good graces of the queen," I muttered, remembering the way the ungrateful cat had eaten beside her again at the meal the night before.

Eventually, I couldn't take the confinement of walls and rooms anymore and headed out into the palace gardens. They were so extensive that I could spend hours wandering through them without retreading any ground.

The fresh air swept away some of my poor mood. It was hard

to maintain a downcast attitude amid such beauty. Even the air was laden with the scent of the blooms, each breath bringing a new and intoxicating smell.

I had heard the palace in Kuralan had a similar garden, but the Kuralani version was enclosed in high walls, and I had never seen it for myself.

"They're generous here," I murmured to myself. "Leaving this wonder open for anyone to enjoy."

As the calm seeped through me, I shook my head at my earlier discontent. The Lanoverian royals had offered not only physical hospitality, but friendship as well, and it was easy to imagine a protracted stay in this beautiful place.

"Help!" A piercing cry broke through the peace of the afternoon.

I spun, trying to ascertain which direction the call had come from.

"Help!" It came again, the voice nearer now.

Had that been a child?

"Here!" I called back.

Steps sounded as a small body burst through a nearby cluster of bushes.

"Help, please help!" the young girl panted.

I hurried to her side. "Are you hurt?" I surveyed her but could see no sign of injury.

"No, no." She shook her head frantically. "Not me. Back there!" She pointed back the way she'd come.

I seized her hand, a rush of fear filling me for whoever she'd left behind.

"Where? Show me!"

Was it another child hurt? A younger one under her care, perhaps?

The girl grabbed my hand and pulled me after her, returning through the bushes she had pushed through before. I was significantly larger than her, however, and the branches pulled at me, scratching my skin and catching on my clothes. I ignored them, though. She must be scared if she wasn't even bothering with the neat paths that crisscrossed the gardens.

I had already made it some way from the palace building in my wanderings, but she led me further away still. Beyond the bushes, we passed through a small rose garden, coming after that to an area near the edge of the gardens.

We were behind the palace, in the northern section of the gardens which seemed wilder and less frequented than the section between the front of the palace and the rest of the city which spread out to the south. And this area seemed even less landscaped than what I had seen so far, as much wilderness as garden.

The girl stopped, and I looked around in all directions but could see no sign of anyone else.

"Over there." She pointed north, toward the hills that stretched behind the palace.

I stepped forward and peered down at a small section of sheer cliff. A part of the hillside must have broken off in some ancient landslide, leaving behind the unnaturally steep spot, jagged rocks visible far below. I managed to absorb as much before I registered the identity of the person hanging by their fingertips from a small ledge part way down.

"Seriously?" I groaned. "You?"

Xavier looked up, surprise flitting across his features. But his face was tight, the strain of holding on showing in his expression. The sight of it sobered me.

"What happened?" I asked, even while I examined the situation, trying to work out the best course of action.

"It's my fault." The girl started to cry. "All the others can jump down to the ledge, and climb back up easily. They kept laughing at me for being a baby because I was too scared to try. So I decided to practice on my own, so I could show them next time."

I winced. "You got stuck?"

She nodded, her face streaked from where the tears had mingled with the dirt. "I got down all right, but then I couldn't climb back up." She lifted her chin, a trace of defiance on her face. "I'm shorter than the rest of them." She looked woefully down at Xavier. "I was stuck there for *hours* before he came past and heard me calling for help."

I peered over the edge again, measuring distances with my eyes. "But how did you end up like that?" I asked him.

The girl answered. "He jumped down to join me, but I panicked and stepped back and nearly went over the edge. I would have fallen if he hadn't grabbed me and tossed me up. Only he lost his balance in the process and slipped off." She sounded like she was going to cry again.

"That's all right, Suzanna," Xavier said in a strained voice. "You brought back help."

"Just give me a moment," I said. "I'm trying to work out what to do." I worried at my lip, glancing back toward the palace. "I don't suppose you can hold on long enough for me to go for help?"

"I don't...think so." He grunted out the words, clearly struggling to talk.

I sighed. It had seemed unlikely.

"I'm going to have to jump down to you. I don't see any other way." I gave him a stern look. "Don't you panic like Suzanna did and fall!"

He gave me a look that attempted some of his usual amusement.

I hesitated, more nervous than I was showing, but delaying only heightened the risk. He must be losing strength.

Taking a deep breath, I sat on the edge of the cliff, focusing on the small ledge and trying to block out the longer drop beyond it. I pushed myself forward, half sliding, half falling down, landing on the ledge with a thud and collapsing into a crouch.

Holding the position for a second, I sucked in rapid breaths, waiting for the stone beneath me to give way. It held firm, however.

Fighting the instinct to press myself back against the sturdy stone of the hill, I edged forward and peered down at Xavier. There was just room on the ledge for me to crouch, taking a firm grip on a tree root that protruded from the sheer hillside behind me. With the other hand, I reached down toward him.

"I'm ready," I said, trying to sound more confident than I felt.

He didn't hesitate, letting go with his right hand and using it to grab tightly onto my wrist. My hand reacted instinctively, clamping onto his wrist and locking us together.

The sudden weight jerked me forward, but the tree root kept me anchored as I adjusted to the increased strain. Leaning as far back as the hill would allow, I heaved him upward by his arm. I wouldn't have been able to pull him up with my strength alone, but he pushed up off his other hand, his legs finding purchase on the slope below.

With a grunt of effort, I strained upright, pulling him with me. At the same moment, he swung his right leg onto the ledge.

As soon as he had purchase, he heaved the rest of his body over, colliding with me and pinning me back against the hill. For a moment we remained frozen in that position, both of us breathing raggedly.

"Don't move," he said as soon as he'd caught his breath.

I nodded, my eyes squeezed shut as I tried to control the surge of relief mixed with the existing fear. He straightened, reaching over our heads to the top of the broken section.

I opened my eyes again as he gripped something out of my sight and hauled himself up and away. I had no idea how his exhausted arms had any strength left, but within seconds he had disappeared completely.

With a deep breath, I pulled away from the hill slightly to peer upward. His head appeared, looking back down at me. He'd managed the climb easily, and Suzanna had said even the kids could do it. But it looked insurmountable to me.

I squeaked, the sound slipping out before I could stop it.

"Don't worry," he said in deep, reassuring tones, his eyes not leaving mine. "I'll help you. Just take my hand."

He reached down for me, and I forced my feet under me. Standing, I grasped his wrist, feeling the reassuring strength in his fingers as they wrapped around my wrist in return.

But I couldn't seem to make my other hand let go of the root. My fingers had clamped around it and weren't responding to my mental commands. I looked down at my hand in panic.

"Look at me!" Xavier's command broke through my fear, and I swung my eyes upward again.

He captured them, his own gaze steady. "Let go. You can do it. I've got you."

I swallowed and nodded, forcing my fingers to flex open one by one. As soon as I'd let go, he pulled.

My body flew upward. Xavier pulled me up and over the edge, making it look easy. The momentum carried me away from the cliff as I collided with him, both of us falling backward.

His arms gripped me, pulling me down on top of him, protecting me even as we fell. The force of the impact still knocked the breath out of me for a moment, and he groaned, clearly worse off.

For a breathless moment, I lay there, flat against him, with his arms wrapped around me. Then I came to my senses and scrambled inelegantly away.

"Are you alive?" Suzanna cried in a panic.

Xavier groaned again and pushed himself up by his elbows, still on his back.

"Yes, we're both alive."

"I'll go find help," Suzanna said on a sob of either guilt or relief.

Before either of us could protest, she took off running toward the palace.

"Wait," I called after her, but she was already gone.

I slowly stood, shaking out my skirt. Looking down at it in dismay, I realized I had damaged one of Evie's loaned gowns—probably beyond repair. I groaned and glared at Xavier, still lying on the ground.

"How have we ended up in another mess together?" I looked away. "At least it was me rescuing you this time," I muttered.

"I'm very grateful," Xavier said humbly, making me whip around to look at him suspiciously.

He was smiling at me, having sat upright at least, but there was a shadow at the back of his eyes. Exhaustion, perhaps? His muscles must be jelly at this point.

"Come on." I held out a hand to help him up. "We should start back to the palace. We could both do with a proper rest."

He took my hand, but instead of leveraging himself up, he gripped it firmly and pulled me down to sit beside him.

"Hey!" I tried to stand, but he hadn't let go of my hand. "What are you doing? We can't just sit here."

He dipped his head apologetically. "I've twisted my ankle, I'm afraid. I'm not sure I can walk all the way back to the palace."

"What?" I stared at his feet but couldn't distinguish the injured one. "In that case, I'll go and fetch—"

He shook his head, once more pulling me down as I tried to stand. "You're going to leave me here all alone and injured?" He gave me a pathetic, woebegone face. "Suzanna's already gone for help."

I snorted but stopped trying to stand. For all I was trying to put on a brave face, my own legs were still a bit wobbly.

"Fine, I'll stay with you."

"Will you, Kali?" His soft voice took me by surprise, and I looked up swiftly, catching my breath when I realized how close we were sitting.

Clearing my throat, I shuffled to one side, looking pointedly down at our joined hands. "At least until some more qualified rescuers arrive."

He laughed and let me go.

"Thank you, by the way," he said. "I think I would have gone over if you hadn't arrived and acted so swiftly."

My insides spasmed, clenching at the thought of the drop below the ledge.

"Nonsense," I said in a strangled voice. "Suzanna was running through the gardens like a mad thing. She would have found someone if I hadn't been there."

He didn't reply, and after a moment, I spoke again in an awkward voice. "Thank you for helping me up. I don't know why I froze like that." It was embarrassing for someone who claimed to want adventures.

"Fear can do strange things," he said in a conversational tone that eased some of my tension. "It isn't logical either."

"I'm not usually afraid of heights," I said in a more normal tone. "I don't know why it hit me so badly."

"It wasn't exactly the same sort of situation as standing on a high balcony," he said with a chuckle. "It would have been unnatural not to feel fear. We need that reaction to keep us alive—it makes us sharper in the moment."

"Yes," I said thoughtfully. "I wouldn't have thought myself capable of doing all that normally. I'm not particularly strong."

He grinned sideways at me. "It's exhilarating, isn't it?"

"Yes," I said slowly, realizing to my surprise that now that the feeling was draining away, I missed it.

"I knew it," he said with satisfaction. "You're just like me. Not everyone understands the appeal, you know. But I thought someone who set off across the desert with only a cat for companion must surely be an adventurer at heart."

My lips twisted. "Much to the dismay of my parents."

One side of Xavier's lips quirked up, but sympathy lurked in his eyes. "I understand that feeling too. My parents have often bemoaned that I'm not more like Rek."

I started at the name of his older brother—the crown prince of Kuralan. I had almost forgotten that when Xavier spoke of his parents, he was speaking of a ruling sultan.

I looked away. "I didn't have to deal with that, at least. My older brother clashed so badly with my father that they shipped him away to a distant apprenticeship at fifteen. And since I was only five at the time, I basically grew up as an only child."

"I'm sorry," he said. "For all my parents' complaints, I wouldn't trade my siblings for anything."

His forehead creased, and I had to look away again, shaken by the concern on his face. He didn't just have siblings but a twin—no wonder he couldn't imagine being without them. I tried to imagine their childhood in the Kuralani palace and faltered. Searching for another topic of conversation, I blurted out the first thing that came to mind.

"Even if you are a thrill-seeker, you shouldn't have done something so reckless!"

"Sorry?" He stared at me in confusion.

"We both could have died," I told him sternly, warming to the topic. "Suzanna said she'd waited on that ledge for hours. She wasn't dangling by her fingertips, so she could have waited a little longer. You could have gone for proper help—or at the very least a rope."

Xavier rubbed his jaw ruefully. "I suppose that's true." He gave me an unrepentant grin. "But, then, I've always been the reckless one."

When I gave him an unimpressed look, he adopted a penitent air.

"How could I walk away and leave her? She was exhausted and terrified, even if she was secure enough. She'd been there so long and thought no one was ever going to come."

I softened, remembering the aftereffects of fear still showing on her face. I didn't think I could have left her in his place.

"No, I don't suppose you could have just walked away," I said with a sigh. "Still, I wish you had managed the business without dragging me into it! Now I've ruined Evie's dress!"

"I'm sorry," he said meekly. "I'll buy her a replacement, if you like."

I looked at him and burst out laughing. "As if she would accept it! She would probably insist she prefers to sew her own."

"Probably." He grinned at me. "I am sorry, though."

"Don't be." I shook my head. "I should be grateful to have a chance to repay the favor after you rescued me."

"Twice, don't forget," he said with a laugh.

I narrowed my eyes. "The first one doesn't count," I muttered. "That was just restitution for earlier."

"Restitution?" He frowned at me, apparently still unwilling to acknowledge our first encounter.

"Never mind," I said stiffly.

He looked as if he intended to press the issue, but a shout interrupted us.

"Oh, good, rescue is here." I jumped to my feet and hurried toward the clump of worried-looking guards.

"It's all right," I called. "He's just hurt his ankle."

They rushed forward, and I made way for them, glad to hand the prince over to someone more capable.

CHAPTER 13

I pretended not to hear when Xavier called my name, escaping the group that swarmed around him and returning to my room alone. By the evening meal, the story had spread through the palace, and Xavier was being hailed a hero. The girl was the daughter of two of the servants, and her mother had apparently already come to thank Xavier in person, crying all over him if the stories were to be believed.

When I went to find Evie to apologize about the dress, she was with Tillie. Both women listened to my account of the incident with wide eyes. Several times they exchanged knowing looks that made me squirm, but when I finished, they both insisted I was also a hero. Evie told me so many times not to give the dress a second thought that I eventually put it from my mind and even accepted their praises with only the slightest awkwardness.

You did well, Puss told me, surprising me with his praise. *It's a good thing I wasn't there.*

"What's that supposed to mean?" I asked.

Merely that you must be allowed to stretch your wings.

"What am I? A baby bird?" I muttered.

He flicked one ear. *Thankfully not, or I would have already eaten you.*

"You would have..." I stared at him for a moment before bursting into laughter. Somehow Puss always managed to win me over, no matter how outrageous he was.

The next day, the two Lanoverian princes finally returned. Word of their arrival spread through the palace like wildfire. Evie, Tillie, and I hurried to the front doors with what seemed like half the staff.

We emerged into a scene of chaos, the number of people, carriages, horses, and guards far more than the ones who had left in company with the princes. For a hopeful moment, I thought they had brought back the false caravan to face justice, but a piercing scream split the crowd, and three short figures in expensive dresses launched from the middle of the mass of people to attach themselves to Evie and Tillie.

"Beatrice!" Evie cried in delight, embracing her daughter's head. "You're home!"

Tillie was greeting the two girls hugging her in a similar manner, so I could only assume they were Iris and Violet.

"But where's your brother?" Tillie asked. "And what are you doing home already?"

"Father fetched us," one of the twins said, at the same moment that the other said, "The boys are probably already up to trouble. Did you know we were stuck in a carriage with them the whole way here?"

"They smelled bad," Beatrice said with a frown. "Why do they have to be so obnoxious?"

I stifled a laugh as the two mothers tried to prize information from their daughters, all of whom seemed ready to launch off into any tangent that crossed their minds.

"We didn't find them," a tired voice said from behind the girls, and all three of us looked at Frederic in dismay.

"What do you mean?" Evie asked. "Had they already made it onto a boat?"

"We're still waiting for confirmation from the teams we sent down the coast," Cassian said, coming forward to hug his wife. "But there's no sign of that. They just...disappeared." He sounded frustrated. "Almost like they realized we were coming and went to ground. But where could a group that size conceal themselves?"

"Since we're not sure where in the kingdom they are," Frederic said, meeting his wife's eyes, "we thought it was best to collect the children ourselves on our way back. Sorry for making you wait."

"No, no, you're quite right." Evie gripped her daughter more tightly.

"So that's it?" I asked, dismayed. "They've just gotten away?"

"Don't worry." Frederic sounded both grim and exhausted. "We'll find them yet. We've already got teams on all the coastal roads, but we'll send more. We'll search the whole kingdom inch by inch if we have to."

It was a noble sentiment, but I didn't need the look of dismay being directed his way by Evie to know it was more easily said than done. Lanover was a large kingdom with numerous different regions, many of them with inhospitable terrain, such as the large jungle that covered the middle of the kingdom.

"Surely we can rule out the jungle, at least," Evie said, apparently thinking along a similar vein to me. "What would desert dwellers know of surviving the jungle's many dangers? They wouldn't risk it."

"That's assuming they actually are from the desert," Tillie said. "Something I highly doubt. Just because they've found themselves some camels doesn't mean they grew up in the sand."

Evie winced. "Of course. I'm not thinking straight." She sighed. "You had better all come in and clean up and rest. There's nothing to be done about it this second."

She gave a significant look at the children, and the other adults all nodded their agreement.

"I would also like to track down our son if we can manage it," she added.

Frederic chuckled. "He'll appear at some point. I think he missed you, even if he won't admit it."

The whole group moved toward the palace, and I trailed behind, out of place, but not sure where else to go. I couldn't stop thinking about the missing caravan. Where could it have gone? I wanted to ride out and start searching myself, but it was a ridiculous notion. I knew nothing about Lanover and wouldn't have any idea where to start. But I hated the idea of sitting around in the palace, doing nothing.

The distance between the royals and me slowly lengthened until I lost sight of them disappearing into one of their suites. I halted, but before I could decide on a course of action, I heard my name being called from a side corridor.

"Kali!"

I turned to see Xavier hurrying toward me, Puss keeping pace at his feet.

"What news?" he called. "Is it true they're back?"

I nodded and filled him in on what Frederic had said. He exclaimed, slapping his fist into the other palm.

"How did they manage that? At least one of the towns saw the full caravan. It was a small one, but still a large enough group to make it hard to hide—and with camels as well!"

Are you surprised? Puss asked. *They've already proved themselves both cunning and brazen. We must assume they have untold tricks up their sleeves.*

Xavier sighed. "Perhaps more disappointed than surprised. Seeing the havoc they already wrought east of the capital, I was hoping to see the matter resolved quickly."

I nodded, thinking of Greyson's desperation. "Have the

Lanoverians heard anything back from the real desert traders, do you know?"

Xavier sighed. "It's too soon for that. The message likely hasn't even reached them yet. But I imagine once it does, we'll have angry traders on our doorstep."

I winced. "And how will they be treated on their journey to the capital?" I could still clearly recall the sensation of being surrounded by the Tarka youths.

Xavier stepped closer with a look of ready sympathy. "The king is sending messengers to every affected town. He'll make them understand it isn't the fault of all traders but of this one rogue group."

"I hope they succeed." I sighed. "And of course the real traders won't be traveling alone, so they won't be such an easy target."

Neither are you traveling alone, Puss meowed. *What am I? Chopped herbs for the pot?*

"Of course not," I said quickly. "And you were a great assistance on that occasion."

Xavier smiled at the cat, and I had to suppress a sudden urge to wallop him. For once I hadn't been thinking of Xavier's own role in that particular drama, but he could at least look a little self-conscious at the topic.

"I'm going back to my room," I snapped.

Turning on my heel, I marched off, sending only one look over my shoulder, directed at Puss. He hesitated before giving the feline equivalent of a shrug and following me.

Xavier remained in place, watching me leave with an expression I couldn't read. At least he wasn't laughing anymore.

With their children back and more plans to be made for finding Caravan Cobolt, the royals were all busy over the following days. I continued to meet with Reya for various fittings and consultations, but once again I was reminded that I didn't belong here. Even surrounded with luxury, I was quickly becoming bored. I wanted to be out with one of the teams on the road, doing something active.

I filled in my time exploring the palace—a large, rambling place that fascinated me. It was nothing like the tall, regal palace of Kuralan, but it had a charm of its own.

I met many of the servants and some of the courtiers in my wanderings, all of them, regardless of rank, full of talk about the false caravan and the upheaval they had brought to the usually peaceful kingdom.

"We haven't had trouble since the princes were married," was a refrain I heard often repeated. "Everyone knows how the High King smiles on kingdoms ruled by love."

"So where are his godmothers now?" was the usual reply, but no one had an answer to the question.

I quickly got used to hearing wise women referred to as godmothers. As a miller's daughter, I had no tie to them, so I couldn't call one to assist us, but it was a different story with the Lanoverian royals.

Unfortunately, according to Evie, they weren't responding to anyone's calls.

"It's always like that," she said with a sigh. "They don't just come on command." A moment later, she brightened though. "But it must mean they believe we can sort the matter out ourselves."

For a ridiculous moment, I almost suggested that they might have sent Puss in their place. Then I remembered what the cat was like and laughed at myself. Now that we'd reached the palace, he didn't even seem particularly perturbed by the situation.

Only one encounter proved unpleasant. On my third day of exploration, I had only just set out from my rooms when I nearly walked into a short man with tight features and carefully combed hair.

"Watch where you're going," he snapped, pulling away from me with exaggerated movements.

"I'm sorry," I said automatically, although the near collision had been as much his fault as mine. "I didn't see you there."

"You should try opening your eyes if you're going to insist on charging around a palace!" he said.

I frowned. The corridors in this section were busy, and I often saw near collisions—events that were usually brushed off by both sides.

The man's displeased expression only deepened as he surveyed me from head to toe, sending a tendril of unease creeping down my spine.

"You're the trader girl, aren't you?" His nose wrinkled, as if he could smell the scent of camel lingering around me. "Your kind have caused enough trouble. You should have the decency not to go putting yourself in the way of respectable people."

"Excuse me!" I gasped. "Cobolt isn't a true caravan, and they're likely not even from the desert. The traders have nothing to do with this."

He scoffed. "So they're claiming. Very convenient if you ask me." He looked down his nose at me, although he was only a couple of inches taller. "Not everyone is so easily fooled, you know."

I drew myself up to my full height, sucking in an angry breath. "Are you insulting the king now? I think he knows the situation in his own kingdom better than you do!"

The man laughed. "Perhaps. And perhaps not."

My brows snapped together. "What's that supposed to mean?"

"Don't question me, girl," he spat. "Don't you know who I am?"

"No, I have no idea," I said rudely. "I can't imagine you're anyone too important."

He swelled at my words, the anger on his face growing. I held my place although I could have bitten my tongue. What was I thinking purposely provoking him? He might be someone important enough to cause me trouble.

"Why, you little..." He stepped forward, his manner threatening.

I swayed, torn between holding my ground and fleeing. It went against the grain to run before a bully, but it might be the wiser course of action.

He moved even closer, his eyes narrowing, but hurried footsteps behind us made him draw back slightly.

"Kali, there you are."

I breathed a sigh of relief, all the tension disappearing. For once, I was relieved to hear Xavier's now-familiar voice.

Xavier strode up to stand at my side, so close our shoulders almost touched. He looked the man up and down with a raised eyebrow.

"Is this man giving you trouble?"

The man drew himself up, but he couldn't match Xavier's height.

"It's this girl who's causing trouble." He sniffed. "But I suppose it's only to be expected that you foreigners would stick together. So it doesn't matter what lies she tells."

"Excuse me?" Icy air seemed to emanate from Xavier, and I was almost surprised not to see frost spring up on the obnoxious man's skin.

He pasted a false smile on his face, bowing slightly.

"No offense meant, Your Highness."

Xavier stepped forward, looming over the man as he lowered his voice, somehow making it more threatening in the process.

"Offense has been taken. I suggest you get out of our sight immediately and stay out of our way in the future. *Both* of us."

The man raised an eyebrow, looking for a moment as if he meant to argue, but after a look at Xavier's broad, muscled shoulders, he gave another hasty bow, muttered something inaudible and hurried away down the corridor.

Xavier watched him go, only relaxing his tense stance when the man turned a corner and disappeared from sight. He turned to me.

"Are you all right?"

I shook myself. "I'm fine. They're just words." I hesitated. "But thank you for defending me."

"Of course." His eyes laughed at me. "We foreigners have to stick together after all."

I laughed weakly. "I suppose we do."

"If he bothers you again, let me know." Xavier looked back toward where the man had disappeared, his eyes narrowing.

"I'm sure he won't," I said, recovering myself. "This place is so large, there's no reason to think I'll run into him again. I've been exploring for days, and this is the first time I've seen him." I frowned. "I don't suppose you know who he is?"

Xavier shook his head. "But I intend to find out," he said softly before looking at me and smiling. "Are you off for further exploration now? Shall I join you?"

I hesitated, unable to believe I could be considering voluntarily spending time with the infuriating prince. But I couldn't deny he had just saved me—again.

"I suppose you might as well," I said.

Xavier laughed. "How could I turn down such a gracious welcome?"

I reluctantly smiled back. "You're forgetting I come from Kuralan, Your Highness. I'm well aware that neither of the royal princes need further flattery to build up their already overbearing egos."

He winced. "Has our reputation truly spread so far?"

"I'm surprised they haven't heard it here in Lanover," I said gravely. "I suppose I'll have to consider it my duty to inform as many as I can."

"Don't you dare," Xavier said, but his lips were twitching.

"And there's no need for all this *Your Highness* business. It was much more comfortable when you were calling me Xavier."

I frowned at him. "That's another complaint against you. Why didn't you tell me who you were from the beginning? I don't appreciate being set up to make a fool of myself."

I expected him to turn off my complaint with another laugh, but he frowned back at me.

"You didn't recognize me? I was sure you did from the beginning."

"Recognize you?" I rolled my eyes. "Not every Kuralani in the kingdom has your features memorized, *Your Highness.*"

"Of course not. But…" He examined my face. "You truly didn't recognize me?"

"No! What do you take me for? I would have said something if I did!"

"Very well, then," he said, but the confused frown still lingered around his mouth.

CHAPTER 14

Various teams had been sent from the palace, joining the ones already searching for the missing thieves, but none of the royals accompanied them. Instead they held seemingly endless meetings, strategizing, reading reports, and issuing fresh orders.

When not present at the meetings, Evie and Tillie threw themselves into planning the soiree.

"It's the first one of the season," Evie explained to me. "It's especially important now since we need to demonstrate to the court that the kingdom is functioning as usual, despite the furor over the false caravan. We're even hoping some of the representatives from the caravans might arrive in time to attend. We want to show everyone that we remain on good terms with the true desert traders."

"The king has already received at least one report of a true caravan being turned away from a town that was swindled by the false one," Tillie added in dejected tones. "My people will be in trouble if more follow their lead."

"Don't worry." Evie gripped her hand. "That won't happen. We won't let it."

I helped as well as I could with preparations for the soiree, given I couldn't help with anything else. It was an evening event, and despite her worry, Evie couldn't help being excited about the gowns she had helped Reya craft for Tillie and me.

And she was right to be proud. They looked incredible. I had originally felt some doubts, but as I returned to my room after my final fitting the day before the soiree, I admitted I was looking forward to wearing the finished outfit. Evie had chosen a pale aqua for mine, somehow finding satin for the bodice and silk for the skirt and wrap that exactly matched in color.

Reya had spent hours embroidering flowers across it in metallic thread that reflected the light and spoke of wealth I didn't actually have. But I would wear it proudly for the sake of my new friends.

Absorbed in thoughts of my new outfit, I rounded a corner and had to leap sideways to avoid colliding with someone coming the other direction.

"Oh! I'm sorry," I said, the words dying away as I recognized the antagonistic man from the other day.

"Still parading around as if you own the place, I see," he said with poison in his voice. "If you haven't learned your place by now, it looks like I need to be the one to teach you."

"Surely you can't still think the traders are at fault for any of this," I said, unable to help myself engaging.

"What does it matter if they are or not?" he asked. "They're a blight on our kingdom and should have been driven out years ago. Maybe they would have been, too, if our prince hadn't been a fool and fallen for a pretty face."

I stared at him. "Are you talking about Prince Cassian and Princess Tillara? Are you a fool? What can you be thinking to talk so in the palace of all places?" I shook my head. "And from everything I hear, the crown was on good terms with the traders even before the wedding. I don't know where you got the idea the traders would have been spurned if not for the wedding, but I'm sure it's false. Which makes you doubly a fool."

"Are you so sure I'm the fool?" he asked in a tight voice. "You'll all see the truth soon enough."

"I've heard enough nonsense." I stalked past him, trying not to make it obvious I was tense, waiting for him to grab me or hit me from behind.

He let me go, however, although I could feel his eyes burning into my back all the way down the corridor. But I refused to give him the satisfaction of looking around.

When I reached my room, I slumped into a chair, my breathing coming unevenly. What a poisonous man! Had Xavier discovered his identity? I should report him for his treasonous talk. Did he think it was safe to speak to me like that because I was a foreigner? Didn't he know I was friends with the princesses?

As I sat there, my anger faded, but it was replaced with a growing concern. What exactly had he meant by his comments? We all feared the misbehavior of the false traders might damage the kingdom's relationship with the real traders, but he sounded like he wanted that to happen. Was it possible he had some tie to Cobolt?

I jumped up and paced over to the window before pacing straight back again. It was a worrying idea, but I didn't have any actual evidence to back it up. I didn't even know the man's name. How could I go to any of the Lanoverian royals and accuse one of their people on only vague suspicions?

I bit my lip. But how could I stay silent? What if his words were significant? I might be the only one he was showing his true face to. He certainly seemed to be enraged past good sense over my presence in the palace. Maybe I provoked him into speaking more of the truth than he intended.

"I'll talk to Xavier," I said aloud after further thought.

He would be better placed than me to know if it was worth

mentioning the matter to the Lanoverians. And perhaps he would even know the man's name. I hated to admit it, but I needed Xavier for this.

Talk to the prince? What about? Puss uncurled from the center of the bed, startling me into shrieking.

"Have you been there the whole time?"

Of course. He stretched. *I was having a lovely nap until you started babbling to yourself. What's amiss now?*

I felt a little foolish saying it aloud, but I told him all about my two encounters with the man.

It's a pity I wasn't with you, he meowed matter-of-factly. *I would soon have straightened him out.*

He leaped lightly down from the bed and padded over to the door. When I didn't move, he looked over his shoulder at me.

Well, aren't you coming?

"Coming?"

To see the Kuralani prince. Wasn't that your plan?

"Right now?" I stared at him blankly. "But I have no idea where he is."

Puss gave me an impatient look. *You may not know where his room is, but I am not so ill-informed.*

"His room?" The words came out as a squeak. "You want me to go to his room?"

We are going to his room. I thought you were concerned? Or isn't this a matter of importance, after all?

I groaned. If there was any chance my suspicions were right, then I should act sooner rather than later. But still…

"Fine." I joined Puss with reluctance.

The cat led me only a short way down my own corridor before stopping outside a similar door to my own. I blinked at it in surprise. Had Xavier been so close this whole time?

I flushed, reminding myself that it didn't matter where the prince slept.

Puss yowled and scratched at the door before I'd managed to

bring my misbehaving emotions under control. It swung open far too promptly, and I had to stop myself from pressing my hands to my cheeks.

"Kali!" Xavier leaned against the frame and grinned lazily down at me as if he had been expecting me to turn up at his door.

My ire rose, driving a different sort of heat into my face.

"Puss insisted we come," I said shortly.

Xavier gave a half-bow. "My thanks, Sir Puss."

The lady has something to tell you. Puss slid past Xavier. *Best not discussed in the corridor.*

Xavier raised both eyebrows but stepped back, gesturing courteously for me to follow him into a small but nicely appointed sitting room. I took a deep breath and followed.

The prince closed the door behind me, turning to give us both a welcoming smile.

"You find me filled with curiosity."

"Have you discovered the name of that man we met in the corridor the other day?" I blurted out. "The rude one?"

Xavier immediately straightened, the smile falling from his face and his eyes becoming sharp.

"His name is Taylan, and he's the oldest son of a prominent family in the city. Has he been bothering you again?"

"I can handle it," I said. "It's just that—" I hesitated, wondering how to explain my fears without sounding like I was jumping at fancies.

Xavier stepped forward, one hand curling into a fist.

"Tell me! What has he done to you?"

"No, no." I held up my hands placatingly. "It's not me I'm worried about. He just said some strange things that made me wonder..."

I sighed. "I might be imagining things, but I didn't want to risk staying quiet if there was any chance I was right. That's why I came to you. I'm hoping you can tell me I'm being foolish."

His brows knit, his eyes fastened on mine. "Not likely. But tell me exactly what he said."

I repeated it, as best I could remember, adding the suspicions that had grown up since the conversation.

"But I still don't even know who he is," I finished. "So I couldn't exactly go to Evie or Tillie."

Xavier rubbed the back of his neck, looking thoughtfully into the distance.

"It's a difficult matter. Nothing he said is exactly a confession, but I understand your suspicions. And I don't think we can afford to ignore anything right now. They've still found no sign of the missing caravan, and it's starting to make the locals nervous. If this goes on much longer, they may start to doubt the crown's ability to keep order in the kingdom."

I gasped. "Is it that bad?"

"Not yet. But it could get there."

"That's why they're so determined to go forward with the soiree tomorrow," I said.

Xavier nodded, but his thoughts were obviously still on the man.

"Taylan's family are wealthy and influential merchants which is probably why he thinks he can get away with behaving so obnoxiously."

"That might explain why he dislikes the desert traders," I said. "I've heard it's expensive to get goods south by ship given the complex reefs down the coast. And of course the jungle is even harder to traverse. He probably dislikes that the caravans have an easier route through the desert."

Xavier nodded. "It's possible. Without the traders offering an alternative, his family could set up a more expensive trading route of their own, I imagine."

"He certainly seemed to hate me enough just for having trader heritage. What if this merchant family is somehow colluding with Caravan Cobolt? It could all be a plot to turn the kingdom against the desert traders."

Xavier sighed and ran a hand through his hair. "Again, it's possible, but we'll have to tread gently. We can't accuse such a powerful family without any evidence. That would just sow more chaos. Especially if he turns out to be a single individual with unsavory opinions, not a representative of his whole family."

"So what should I do?" I asked. "Should I talk to the Lanoverians?"

Xavier looked toward Puss who had been silently watching the conversation. "What do you think?"

Puss grinned in a satisfied way, as if Xavier had just proven himself by showing the good sense to seek Puss's opinion.

I think we can safely leave the matter in your hands.

Xavier raised an eyebrow, then chuckled and bowed. "High praise indeed from someone such as yourself."

Puss stood and strolled toward the door. *Come, Kali, we're done here.*

"What?" I stared at him. "Just like that?" I looked at Xavier doubtfully. "We're just going to dump it on him?"

Is there some way you think you can help? Puss fixed me with a knowing stare.

"You could at least pretend I'm helpful," I muttered.

Xavier caught my hand, taking me by surprise. I stared up at him.

"You've already been a big help. You're the one who came up with the theory, remember."

I looked away, trying not to seem too pleased at the praise. "The unproven theory. It might turn out to be totally wrong, and then I'll have bothered you for nothing."

He continued to smile. "Consider it you doing me a favor. I was about to lose it, stuck here in the palace with nothing to do."

I tried to tear my gaze from his, but I was trapped in place, his warm fingers wrapped around mine acting like an anchor, although he wasn't gripping them tightly.

A hacking sound from behind us made me finally jerk around, turning quickly to meet Puss's amused gaze. I hurried over to him, Xavier keeping pace, showing none of my discomposure.

At the door, I stared at the ground, afraid to meet his eyes again, but as I fixated on his boots, my eyes narrowed, remembering the last few times I'd seen him.

"Your ankle healed quickly," I said accusingly. "In fact, you were walking just fine the very next time I saw you."

"Yes, thankfully it was only a twist in the end, and was soon fine with a bit of strapping," he said cheerfully.

My eyes finally rose again to meet his, this time with suspicion.

"How convenient. Are you sure you didn't imagine it in the first place?"

"Whatever can you mean?" he asked, all too innocently. "Why ever would I do that?"

I remembered him holding my hand and begging me not to leave his side, claiming his injury made it impossible for him to walk. But when I opened my mouth, I found I couldn't voice the words.

The amusement in his face grew as he opened the door, holding it wide and gesturing politely for us to pass through.

I snapped my mouth shut and swept past him, his chuckle chasing me down the corridor.

CHAPTER 15

The next day dawned with perfect weather for the evening's entertainment—the bright sun and clear skies promising a warm evening. Evie and Tillie had made me promise to join them to prepare for the evening which was unsurprising given Evie's anticipation of her new outfits' debut.

In the late afternoon, I hurried through the corridors between my room and Evie's suite. I was so distracted by the upcoming event that it took me a moment to register who was approaching from the other direction.

As soon as I realized it was the rude man—Xavier had called him Taylan—my steps slowed. I didn't relish another altercation.

Sure enough, when he saw me, his eyes flashed. But instead of saying something insulting, he veered away, bypassing me on the far side of the corridor.

I watched him pass, relieved but also bemused. Something had happened to make him wary of me.

The memory of Xavier's clenched fist flashed through my mind, and I shot Taylan another look. He had no visible injuries, though, so I shook the thought aside. Of course the prince wouldn't have attacked him.

I reached Evie's suite in a subdued mood, but the brighter spirits of the two women waiting for me soon lifted my own. Evie and Tillie might both be more than a decade my senior, but they never made me feel young or foolish around them.

"They came out perfectly," Evie announced in satisfaction, as Reya arrived, carefully carrying the two new gowns.

"It does look beautiful," Tillie murmured, fingering the filmy purple silk of her own wrap. "I'm glad I let you talk me into it after all."

"Of course you are." Evie gave her creations a satisfied smile. "No one ever regrets wearing one of my dresses."

Tillie laughed. "You're right. I should have known it from the beginning." She grinned at me. "Or maybe it's just Kali lending me some of her youthful courage."

I coughed, thinking of the ledge on the cliff. "I'm not that courageous."

"Nonsense! You left behind everyone you know and came across the desert on your own, didn't you?"

I considered her words. "I did, yes, but I'm not sure it counts as courage. For me it was more like a necessity. I've always longed to travel the desert—it was more like I couldn't help myself."

"Well, whatever the cause, I still count it as courage," Tillie said. "But I do know what you mean about longing for travel." She sighed softly. "I love my life here with Cassian and the children, of course. But sometimes I miss the desert and the vast open skies."

"It's appealing to always be on the road, always visiting new places," I agreed, and she nodded, her eyes picking up the spark they always held when she spoke of her research.

"Isn't it strange to think that our shared ancestors weren't nomads at all? Our nomadic life is one shared aspect between the western traders and the eastern tribes, despite our separation— and yet the empire we came from wasn't nomadic at all. I wonder what it was about the destruction that made both branches into nomads?"

"Maybe it was just the terrain?" I said thoughtfully. "There's no other way to live in the desert. All the stories say the land used to be a garden paradise before the wickedness of the emperor brought destruction to his whole empire."

"Where do you think the capital was located?" Tillie asked. "It must have been near the eastern part of the desert, I think—given the treasure caves are in Ardasira and Kuralan, and that's where the majority of the population fled. Both of the eastern kingdoms are descended from the old residents of the empire as well. Only our people became nomads, but there were far more refugees than just us. Whereas the Four Kingdoms seem to have always existed alongside the empire."

"I guess we'll never know." I'd never considered the matter before. "Do you think there are ruins in the desert somewhere? They might lie there forever undiscovered since travelers always stick to the known routes between oases."

"I bet there are!" Tillie said. "There must have been plenty of cities in the empire. Imagine finding ruins like that!"

"How can you talk about ruins when you have a new outfit to try on?" Evie cried. "I refuse to listen to any more such talk. We have a party to attend, remember."

Tillie shot her a rueful look. "Sorry, Evie. You know how I get."

Evie laughed. "I know you're too beautiful to have ever had to worry much about your appearance. But the rest of us mere mortals need time to prepare for fancy events, you know."

Tillie protested, but I was distracted from their affectionate bickering by Reya approaching with the bodice of my outfit. With expert care, she helped me discard my regular gown and don the new one, arranging the unfamiliar length of material so that it draped elegantly across my shoulder.

"You look perfect!" Evie breathed, signaling for me to spin

while she looked me up and down with critical eyes. When I'd finished, her face split into a broad grin. "Absolutely perfect."

Reya helped Tillie next, while Evie slipped into her own, more traditional, gown. It was an elegant creation, but I could tell she'd purposefully gone for something simple, not wanting to attract any attention away from us.

Maids appeared not long after that, bringing with them brushes and various other implements for arranging our hair. They arranged a string of pearls across my head like a tiara, piling some of my hair up behind it, while the rest trailed down my back in a single braid. The whole arrangement was modeled after the picture in the book, and Tillie's sleek black hair was done the same way.

As a finishing touch, they had even managed to procure flowers that matched the colors of our outfits, pinning them into place in our hair.

"It's like you stepped out of history. But even more beautiful," Evie said when we were finally ready. "I can't wait for everyone to see."

"The first trader delegates arrived this afternoon," Tillie said triumphantly. "They must be tired, but they're going to attend, of course. It's fortunate they arrived in time."

"Come on," Evie said. "It's time for your grand entrance."

She led the short parade out of her suite, having already told me that the children were tucked away in the old nursery for the evening under the supervision of their nannies, and Frederic had been banished to Cassian's rooms.

We arrived together, just the three of us, at the large ballroom hosting the soiree. Our arrival had been perfectly timed so the night was still young, but the majority of the guests had arrived before us.

Unlike a formal audience there was no one announcing new arrivals, but a ripple spread through the crowd when we stepped inside the doors and paused at the top of the shallow steps that led down into the room.

For the first time I was conscious of the narrow band of skin showing between the bottom of the bodice and the top of the skirt. But I reminded myself that most of it was covered with the sweep of material over my shoulder. And the bodice itself had small sleeves. The design was merely unfamiliar, not immodest.

Evie led us triumphantly down the steps into the crowd, making directly for the small knot of people I recognized as desert traders, although none of them were familiar faces from Caravan Golura.

"What do you think?" she asked them in a carrying voice. "Tillara and Kalila honor your forebears with their appearance tonight, do they not?"

The traders all bowed, several of them looking at us with open admiration.

"I've seen illustrations of such garments," one of the older women said. "But I've never seen them worn. They're even more elegant than I imagined."

Evie beamed.

"It's all thanks to Princess Evangeline," I murmured. "She created them."

The woman smiled at the princess. "Even in the desert we have heard of the crown princess's genius for design."

Evie flushed with pleasure as others crowded in around us, exclaiming at the dresses and joining the conversation with the traders. I could see Prince Frederic in the distance, looking at his wife with pride. When we had arrived, the traders had been standing alone, an invisible barrier separating them from the rest of the crowd, but our arrival had swept it away.

There might be those who thought dress design too frivolous an interest for a future queen, but Evie wielded clothes as warriors wielded weapons and diplomats wielded words. Tillie had been right when she said Evie's passion was far from useless.

I stayed mostly quiet, content to be nothing more than a model for the outfit, understanding that it was doing the work more than anything I could say. Eventually I grew hungry and thirsty, though, looking with increasing longing toward the refreshment table along one wall.

Evie finally noticed and whispered for me to sneak away. The constantly changing crowd had finally thinned, most of those wanting to examine the unique dresses having had a chance to do so.

I smiled my gratitude and slipped through the crowd, making my escape. I sighed with relief when I downed a whole glass of some sort of unfamiliar juice. I had never tasted anything so refreshing.

Are you finished preening like a peacock, then? Puss leaped onto the table and surveyed the delicacies laid out.

"Get down," I said. "Do you want to get hair through the food? And don't give me attitude just because I attracted more attention than you for once."

I expected Puss to take offense, but he merely looked amused.

You may have been too distracted to notice, but I have been attracting as much interest as any dress. There are still some in Lanare who have yet to see a talking cat.

"Don't you get tired of it?" I asked, thinking of the crowd pressing in around me.

Humans are tiresome creatures in many ways, Puss meowed calmly, *but I cannot blame you for being impressed by my presence.*

I selected a promising looking ball of pastry and stuffed it in my mouth. "Mmm…" I licked my lips. It was just as delicious as it looked.

I glanced up as I wiped icing sugar from my mouth and accidentally locked eyes with Taylan across the room. He was glaring at me with so much fury I actually stumbled back a step. His eyes narrowed as he realized I'd seen him, and he looked away stiffly.

But his gaze only traveled as far as the knot of people still around Evie and Tillie.

I swallowed. The dresses had made a positive impact on most of the Lanoverians at the soiree, but the very fact they had been so well received must have further enraged someone who hated the desert traders as much as Taylan did.

I reminded myself that there was nothing he could do at a royal function. Maybe it was even a good thing for him to get so angry. He might be pushed into betraying himself in some way.

But I found my feet drifting sideways toward one of the long windows that stood open, letting the fresh night air into the ballroom. The windows gave partygoers access to the gardens, and Evie had arranged for decorative lanterns to light the closest section of greenery. Already some people strolled outside, enjoying the moonlight and the freedom from the crush inside.

I stepped out, sighing with relief to be out from under Taylan's view. Drawing in a deep breath, I admired the way the flowers looked in the dusky light. It was just as beautiful outside as inside where great effort had been put into the decorations.

Wandering along beside the windows, I reached the edge of the large rose garden that spread beyond that corner of the palace. Lanterns lined its edge, but darkness lingered further in. I stopped, gazing at some of the nearer bushes, appreciating the way they had been arranged with the blooms slowly progressing from pure white to a deep pink that was almost red.

"Beautiful, isn't it?" asked a familiar voice.

I turned to Xavier with a slight frown. Something was off in his tone. Had he learned something about Taylan since we'd parted ways the day before?

He stood with his back to a lantern, partially obscuring his face, but he appeared to be smiling in the way that had become all-too-familiar in the last weeks.

I frowned, and his expression grew rueful.

"I suppose I can't expect a better reception," he said apologetically. "So let me begin by offering my most profuse apologies for my unconscionable behavior."

He bowed deeply, an elaborate gesture that was no doubt intended to look contrite. My thoughts went blank.

"What in the kingdoms have you done now?" I asked. "Considering the past behavior that you haven't felt was worthy of any apology at all, I'm truly afraid to know."

He straightened, looking confused.

"Pardon?"

I rolled my eyes. "Oh, come on. Surely you're not going to try to play innocent now."

"I…" He looked lost for words, a first in the time I'd known him.

I sighed. "Don't you think there are more important things to worry about than you and me, anyway? The traders arrived just in time, and Evie made a good impression with these gowns, but the whole situation is still teetering on the edge."

"Yes." He latched on to my words, bowing again. "Allow me to congratulate you on your stunning appearance. I'm delighted that you made it to the capital and have been so warmly welcomed."

"Delighted that I made it to the capital?" I stared at him. "What are you talking about?"

He frowned. "Should I not be pleased for you?" he asked cautiously. "I know I wasn't any help, but I'm still…"

I snorted. "Is this some ploy for sympathy? I'm not going to thank you again, whatever you say."

"Thank me?" This time he was the one staring at me, and I rubbed my head where a headache was fast developing.

What had gotten into Xavier? He was frequently infuriating, but tonight he seemed to have lost all sense.

"Forget it." I turned away from the roses. "If you don't have any news for me, I'm going back into the party."

I strode away without waiting for a reply.

"Kali!" he called after me, but I ignored it. It had already been a long evening.

Walking quickly, I didn't look where I was going, merely hurrying down the line of windows, passing the full length of the ballroom. Something strange was going on with Xavier, but was I really surprised? From our very first interaction he had been capricious. My chest tightened, and I continued walking, unable to bear the idea of returning to the stuffy air inside.

Had I been fool enough to forget our first encounter? Had I started to trust the Kuralani prince? I ground my teeth together. I was in danger of letting my emotions get the better of my good sense.

No matter which way I looked at it, Xavier spelled danger. Now that my services as a model were complete, I had no purpose here at the Lanoverian palace. It was time for Puss and me to be on our way. I needed to go somewhere where I would stop running into him every time I turned around.

A distant call of my name made me speed up. Only when the light faded so much that I couldn't see the ground in front of my feet clearly did I look up. I'd gone past the end of the windows and was about to step past the circle of light provided by the last lantern. I stopped and turned back. It was time to reclaim my headspace from the troublesome prince who had taken up residence there.

"Kalila." The oily voice saying my name shocked me into full awareness.

My heart rate picked up as I saw Taylan standing between me and the ballroom.

"I thought I heard someone calling your name," he continued, stepping toward me.

Instinctively, I stepped back, but I stopped myself after one step. I didn't think it was a good idea to let him drive me into the darkness.

I put up my chin. "What do you want?"

He stepped even closer, his nearness making my skin crawl.

"How dare you?" he breathed, the quiet anger more terrifying than shouting. "How dare you parade around as if you're better than the rest of us? As if your ancestry is something to be proud of."

I willed myself not to show my fear. "I am proud of it."

"Is destroying our kingdom—stealing from us in broad daylight and calling it trading—not enough for you filth? Are you determined to rub our noses in it?"

With sudden clarity I realized this vitriol had clearly been building for a long time, probably with Tillie as its focus. But my sudden arrival had provided a safer target than the princess.

There was no point trying to address his comments. He was clearly too far gone to listen to any reason.

I tried to brush past him, but he grabbed my arm with his left hand, pulling me to a stop. I whirled around, trying to wrench myself free, only to see his right hand pulling back in preparation for a blow.

I flinched away, my free arm flying up to shield my head. But his fist never reached me.

My eyes flew back open to see Taylan frozen in place, his raised arm held in Xavier's firm grip. The prince's furious eyes were locked on the other man, steel in every line of his body, and no trace of his usual lazy charm in sight.

I stared at him, trembling as much from relief as the aftermath of the fear. Whatever strangeness had hung around Xavier earlier in the evening had disappeared. He looked achingly familiar and safe, and I had to refrain from flinging myself at him.

With a single movement, he pulled Taylan violently sideways, breaking his hold on me. I staggered backward as Xavier let go of Taylan's arm and gripped the front of his shirt, lifting him completely off the ground.

"Don't you ever touch her again," he said in a deadly tone that made me tremble even though I wasn't the one pinned beneath his fiery gaze.

Taylan swallowed, his eyes wide.

Xavier shook him roughly. "Do you understand me?"

"No," Taylan stammered. "I mean, yes."

Xavier's eyes narrowed, but he flung the other man away from him. Taylan stumbled slightly, taking a moment to regain his balance. When he did, he took several hurried steps backward before stopping and pulling his clothes straight.

Seemingly buoyed by the small distance between them, he gave Xavier a glare of hatred before transferring his gaze to me.

Xavier growled. "Don't even look at her."

Taylan's eyes flicked back to Xavier. "You'll be sorry for this," he hissed. "Both of you."

"I don't think they will," said Xavier's voice, although his mouth hadn't moved. "You'll do well to take note. Don't come near Kali again."

Another tall figure stepped forward, the same menace in his pose as Xavier, like a coiled spring, ready to strike. My mouth dropped open as I looked between the newcomer with Xavier's face to Xavier himself. He didn't even turn to look at his twin, both of them directing the full force of their attention at Taylan.

With a gulp, Taylan turned and fled into the night.

CHAPTER 16

"You're...you're Xander," I stammered.

The newcomer looked over at me, his expression lightening to one of amusement. "Were you expecting someone else?"

When I just stared at him blankly, he shook his head. "Now that I come to think of it, I don't think I told you my name when we met previously."

Xavier's head whipped around to stare at his twin. "You've met Kali before?" He was clearly surprised, but I caught a hint of tension lurking beneath the words.

Xander seemed to catch it as well, his eyes narrowing slightly as he looked from his twin to me.

"Yes," he said slowly. "But only once. Some time ago."

Xavier relaxed slightly, his brow creasing as if he was working something through in his mind.

"Wait!" I cried, grasping what I should have realized sooner. "That was you earlier by the roses, wasn't it? I thought you seemed strange!"

"By the roses?" Xavier asked slowly, his brows rising.

"Rather, I should say I thought *you* were acting strangely,

Xavier." I chuckled. "I had no idea your twin had arrived in Lanare, so I thought it was you."

"Did you now?" Xavier gave his twin what could only be described as a suspicious glare.

Xander laughed, though. "It was certainly an odd conversation. I wasn't sure if I was going mad or you were."

"So does that mean," I said slowly, piecing it together in my mind, "it was you that first time, on the road to Tarka?"

"To Tarka?" Xavier jumped on my words, looking at his brother. "You were there when Kali was attacked?" He sounded disapproving.

Xander looked regretful. "I only arrived afterward, I'm afraid. And then I failed—rather spectacularly—to be any help at all."

I put my hands on my hips, my old indignation flooding back. "That you did! Now that I understand what's going on, I'll accept your abject apology after all."

A hint of humor showed in Xavier's bemusement. "If Xander turned up this evening and started apologizing, it's no wonder you were so confused."

My lips twitched. "It certainly seemed very unlike you," I said gravely.

"Wretch," he said with a smile that made my heart leap strangely.

Xander looked between us again. "Clearly I should have caught up on what's been happening here before wading in."

"But what did you do on the road?" Xavier asked him indignantly. "I've been racking my brains all this time, trying to work out what I'd done to turn Kali against me."

Xander grimaced. "I told her I'd go into town and bring her back her bag—or at the very least some proper clothes." He looked at me apologetically. "Did you wait for me for long?"

"Hours! I was furious when I realized it had all been a waste and I had to traipse into town looking a total mess anyway." This time I was the one giving an apologetic look to Xavier. "But that wasn't what really made me angry. I was actually worried something must have happened to you. Only then I saw you standing with the townsfolk, relaxed as anything, laughing at me with your eyes, without even a trace of guilt. That's when I got furious."

Xander threw back his head and laughed loudly. "Rek always said you'd get into trouble, laughing at the world like that, Xavier. He'll be pleased to hear he was right."

Xavier smiled reluctantly, shaking his head as he looked at me. "I could tell you recognized me, but you were Kuralani, so I thought you recognized me as the prince. That's why I was so confused earlier when you claimed not to have known. I could tell you were upset about it, but I thought you were just worried that I might refute your claim to a title."

"Claim to a title?" Xander looked at me curiously.

"Oh yes," Xavier said casually. "She's Lady Kalila of Kuralan here."

"Of Kuralan?" Xander frowned.

"It's the cat." I sighed. "He insists I have a claim to some honorary title from my desert nomad bloodline, although the traders don't acknowledge any titles. But since I'm from Kuralan, he keeps introducing me that way. And then Xavier encouraged it." I glared at Xavier while his brother looked at him with a raised eyebrow.

"I thought I was helping you," he protested. "I thought your concern about being called out was why you were so against me from the beginning. Now that I know you had a legitimate grievance, everything makes much more sense."

"Yes, it does," I agreed. "I thought you very capricious, not being the least sorry for leaving me in the lurch like that one minute, and then helping me the next."

"Thanks, brother." Xavier gave Xander a look, and Xander began to back away slowly.

"I should be going," he said. "I still haven't greeted Prince Frederic."

Xavier nodded agreement with this statement, but I hurried after Xander. "I'll come, too."

I carefully didn't look at Xavier's crestfallen expression. I had thought I was in trouble before, but everything had changed in the light of the evening's revelations. And although I hadn't yet processed it all, I had a sinking certainty I was in even greater danger from Xavier than I had been before.

"Are you all right?" I asked Xander. "Now that I know you weren't in Tarka at all, I'm guessing something must have happened on your way back to waylay you."

"I am sorry about that. I had just received some intelligence and was on my way to follow it up when I met you. I thought it could wait while I circled back to the town, but urgent news reached me before I got to Tarka. Since it was time sensitive, I had to leave immediately. I was sorry to abandon you, but you were in good health, and had that intimidating cat to assist you. I couldn't risk taking the time to go back when it was only a matter of clothing." He glanced at his brother. "I trusted Xavier would help you get everything sorted out when you eventually made it into Tarka."

Xavier grunted, but he seemed to understand what his brother was referring to, even if I didn't.

"It came to nothing, I assume?" Xavier asked. "If you're back here now."

Xander sighed. "It may have been more than nothing, but it wasn't what I hoped."

I frowned between them, but neither offered me an explanation.

We reached the row of windows, and I stepped into the ballroom flanked by identical princes. Far more eyes than I was comfortable with turned to look at us.

"It's been an exhausting night," I said. "I'm going to bed."

"I'll walk you to your room," Xavier said quickly.

I shook my head. "No, I'll be fine. I'm sure Taylan is still running after the scare you two gave him."

Xavier's face darkened. "I'll be talking to Frederic about him, regardless of whether he's involved with the caravan. He went too far tonight."

"Involved with Caravan Cobolt? That worm?" Xander looked at his brother with interest. "I really have missed a lot."

I slipped away with a softly murmured good night. I could feel Xavier's eyes on me, but he accepted what I'd said and let me flee into the palace corridors alone.

I didn't sleep well. Every time I started to drift off, I got flashbacks of Taylan looming over me, or felt the phantom sensation of his grip on my wrist. As soon as those thoughts jerked me out of potential sleep, Xavier pushed his way into my mind in their place.

Once again, he had been there to put himself between me and danger. All this time, he had been arriving just when I needed him. But I had pushed him away, believing he couldn't be trusted after abandoning me once and then ignoring it. Except, now it turned out he'd never done so.

He might laugh at me in a way that made my blood boil, but he had never actually done anything to make me doubt him. Quite the opposite.

The confusion that had burned in me earlier in the evening after my bizarre conversation with Xander hadn't disappeared, it had merely transformed. Before I had been unable to work out what I thought of Xavier. Now it was fear of my own emotions that kept me awake.

Without the protective barrier of his apparent capricious unreliability, I had to admit I was entirely susceptible to his charm. Even when I thought him untrustworthy, how many times had my breath caught, my heart beating fast? How would I react when I saw him again now, knowing that from the moment we'd met, he'd only acted to protect and assist me?

More frightening than the memories of Taylan were the imaginings that crept in when I tried to relax my mind. Imaginings where Xavier took me in his arms and pressed his lips to mine.

I sat upright, shaking myself. Everyone back home in Karema knew the twin princes were troublemakers, far too charming for anyone's good. Far too charming for my good.

It wasn't beyond the realm of possibility for a commoner to end up with a prince—it had happened here in Lanover, and even back in Karema my own best friend was marrying Xavier's older brother. But Zaria had grown up with the princes, and Prince Tarek was known for being responsible. He had never been one to flirt recklessly with everyone he encountered. Everyone knew he left that behavior to his younger, more carefree, brothers.

Xavier might have proved to have been a steadfast friend to me, but that didn't mean his flirting ways had any deeper significance.

I flopped back down, pressing the pillow over my face and groaning. I was in trouble. Big trouble.

The next morning I slept late, eventually emerging in response to a summons from Evie. She was in her sitting room, Tillie keeping her company, along with their three daughters.

"Kali!" Evie greeted me with a broad smile. "Wasn't it a triumph?"

I forced myself to smile back. "Your creations got the attention they deserved."

"They would have been useless without two such perfect models," she said warmly, and I wrinkled my nose, unsure how to respond.

"But what about Xander returning?" Tillie asked. "That was a surprise. I didn't think we'd be seeing him again."

"I think he got word of what's been going on here," Evie said. "He probably came back to make sure his brother hadn't launched himself into trouble."

Both women laughed while I exploded into coughing, spraying out the water I had just sipped. As I coughed, young Beatrice came over to pat me earnestly on the back.

"Thank...thank you," I managed to wheeze out once I'd regained my breath.

Xander had mentioned something about Xavier getting himself into trouble the night before—but he'd been talking about me. Was Xavier's twin worried that his brother was raising false expectations? Was I the sort of trouble he had a duty to help his brother avoid?

My heart sank. It seemed only too likely.

I tried to remember his exact words, but the conversation was a blur. Xander's eyes had held a kind light, though. It seemed all too likely I was the one he wanted to rescue—before I got my heart broken by his brother. A prince who viewed the world—and those around him—with lighthearted amusement. I would be foolish to take anything Xavier had said seriously.

"It looked like you met him, Kali," Evie said, quite innocently. "Don't they look similar? They're as bad as Iris and Violet, but I'm so familiar with the girls that I have no trouble telling them apart. With the princes, though, I still get confused sometimes. That was one good thing about only having one of them around." She laughed lightly, while I bit my lip.

I didn't feel the same way at all, but I could hardly confess to that. It had been different on that first day at Tarka, but now that I had spent time with Xavier, it was easy to tell him apart from his twin. Even in the dark, when I hadn't known Xander was in the city, I had been able to tell he was unlike his brother.

I frowned, trying to identify the telling difference. But it wasn't any obvious physical characteristic—just something in their air and manner, some essential element that felt different.

I said something vague, and the conversation moved on, Evie and Tillie carrying most of it between them. They must be tired as well after the late night because they both seemed subdued.

Surprisingly, Beatrice remained seated beside me, sitting in prim silence. She seemed even more subdued than her mother, although there was no reason I knew of for her to have lost sleep the night before.

When the twins squabbled over something on the other side of the room, pulling both Evie and Tillie into their disagreement, I addressed Beatrice.

"Are you all right?" I asked the question timidly, aware I was basically a stranger to her.

She looked startled, quickly pushing a false-looking smile onto her face.

"Of course." But her eyes dwelt wistfully on the twins who seemed to have resolved their dispute with equal fervor to how they had started it.

"It must be nice to have cousins the same age," I said. "I always wished for cousins, or a sister of my own."

She heaved an enormous sigh. "I wish I had a sister."

I raised an eyebrow. "But you all live here in the palace. Aren't Iris and Violet as good as sisters?"

She looked away. "Yes, of course. Never mind."

I frowned from her to the twins on the other side of the room.

"Do you not get along?" I asked hesitantly.

Her eyes flew to mine, wide with concern. "Oh no, no! Of course we do. They're my best friends."

I nodded enthusiastically, hoping to calm her concerns. Did she think I might spread a rumor around the palace that there was a rift between the younger generation of princesses?

But although she looked relieved at my easy acceptance of her reassurance, she soon fell back into melancholy again. Surreptitiously, I looked from her to the twins.

Taking a gamble, I spoke again. "It can be hard to feel like the odd one out."

She squeaked, looking up at me with startled eyes.

"How did you know?"

I smiled. "Experience?"

Her eyes widened. "Do you have twins for best friends, too?"

I laughed. "No. But I know what it's like to feel like you don't quite fit in."

She sighed. "It's not that they exclude me or anything. It's just that they're so close to each other. I know it's not their fault. They can't help it—of course they're closest to each other when they're twins. I just sometimes wish…"

"That you weren't the only one who was different?"

She gave me a slow smile. "Yes, exactly."

"But what if it's good to be different?" I asked, determined to cheer up the young princess. "Just look at your mother."

Beatrice turned her eyes on her mother, her brow creasing in confusion. "What do you mean?"

"Do you think she might have sometimes felt out of place as a seamstress who became a princess?"

Beatrice blinked as if the idea had never occurred to her.

"I know you've only ever known her as a princess," I said, "but it must have seemed very strange at first. But she didn't reject the part of her that was different—she still loves designing clothing." I nudged her with my shoulder. "Did you see what she made for your aunt and me?"

As I had expected, Beatrice's face lit up, her eyes gaining animation. I didn't think a daughter of Evie's could be entirely unaffected by a beautiful dress.

"They were beautiful, weren't they? She was so happy with how they turned out."

Beatrice looked at her mother with love in her eyes, and I

marveled at how much older she seemed than her seven years. I supposed it was the effect of growing up a princess.

"Well, last night, your mother's dresses helped bring people together," I said. "I'm sure you're old enough to know there's trouble going on at the moment, and last night your mother used the thing that makes her different to help Lanover."

"She did?" Beatrice gazed at her mother again, wonder in her face.

"You can't do anything about being different from the twins," I said, "but maybe you would feel better about it if you work out what it is that makes you unique—and then work out how you could use that to help people."

"Do you really think I could be like Mother one day?" she asked.

"Of course! It might not be designing dresses in your case, but I'm sure you'll do something even more amazing."

"I'd like that." She glanced back up at me. "You're nice."

I flushed, inordinately pleased at the childish praise. "Am I? Thank you."

"Sorry for being so sad," she said. "I'm just upset because Father is leaving. I don't like when he's away—and I don't like how it makes Mother sad too."

"Prince Frederic is going somewhere?" I asked, surprised not to have heard any word of it.

"Yes." Evie stepped over to join us. She hesitated, glancing at her daughter. "Beatrice, why don't you go and play with the twins?"

Beatrice gave her a knowing look. "I know you just want to talk without me."

Evie laughed. "Of course you do because you're very smart. But you're still too young to be included. Your turn will come. Go on, now."

CHAPTER 17

*B*eatrice pouted out her lower lip before laughing and running off to join Tillie's daughters. Evie affectionately watched her go.

"She's always trying to weasel her way into Frederic's strategy meetings. She's far more interested than her older brother."

"She seems very mature for her age."

"Yes, we're very proud of her." Evie smiled after her daughter. "We just hope her brother catches up at some point."

"Boys are always like that, aren't they?"

We both laughed.

"Poor Frederic was given the Christening gift of responsibility," Evie said with a grin. "So he doesn't quite know what to make of his mischievous son. He tries his best, though."

I stared at her in horror. "What sort of horrible Christening gift is that? You must be joking!"

She snorted. "I only wish I was. And poor Cassian got loyalty. You can imagine how Celine lords it over them. She's the youngest, and she can shoot fireballs from her hands."

"Fireballs?" I stared at her.

"That's a whole other story." She chuckled. "If I start telling you stories about my youngest sister-in-law we'll be here all day."

"If Prince Frederic is leaving again, does that mean they've had word of Cobolt?" I asked in a low voice, remembering the more important point.

Evie grimaced. "The opposite. He's going because they haven't been able to find a trace of them."

"Still?" I frowned. "How is that possible?"

"Exactly. The northern section of the kingdom has been thoroughly searched at this point, and we don't think they're here. We've sent word to all the other kingdoms, and everyone is keeping a close eye out for them. The traveling merchant caravans are furious—they consider it as much an attack on them as on the desert trader caravans—so they couldn't have made it north beyond the border without being spotted."

"You think they've gone south, then?" I asked.

"They might have pushed down into the jungle," she said, "but our main fear is that they managed to take sail."

"I thought all the harbors were closed to them."

"They are," Tillie said, joining us. "But there are beaches with deep enough bays to allow a ship to get close to shore. It's just on the edge of possibility that they were able to use one of those and ferry themselves out to their vessel using smaller boats."

"Could they have gone across the sea, then?" I asked.

"We've sent word to the kingdoms beyond," Evie said. "Celine is a princess over there, so they're close allies. If they do try to go there, they won't get far."

"It seems more likely they would have headed south," Tillie said. "Their desert trader disguise and camels make Lanover the easiest place to hide, despite the current search."

"So Frederic is sailing south?" I guessed.

Evie nodded. "With a ship full of troops. He'll head for Largo and run the search from there." She sighed. "I wish I could go with him, but I can't leave the children for so long, and we certainly don't want to take them into the middle of this mess. They'll be safer here."

Tillie shuddered. "Can you just imagine what trouble Leo and Luca would get up to if we did take them?"

Evie gave her a look of horror before her brow creased, as if she'd been struck by a sudden thought.

"Speaking of a true troublemaker, Xavier told Frederic what happened to you last night, Kali. I'm so sorry. What a relief the Kuralani princes were there."

I flushed. "I'm all right. They stopped him from hurting me, thankfully." I rubbed at my wrist self-consciously, the sensation I felt there a phantom one rather than actual bruising.

"I'm sorry to have to report that he's escaped," Evie said, watching me with concern.

"Escaped?" I stared at her. "Escaped what?"

"Frederic sent guards to his family's home early this morning, but he was already gone."

"Gone? But where?"

"His family claim they don't know," Tillie said grimly. "They acted shocked at the report of his behavior, and said he fled overnight without their knowledge. The whole family is under investigation now, of course. Given the potential links to the situation with the false traders, we have to be sure they're telling the truth. But so far all they've come up with is a suspicion from one of the younger family members that he went south."

"Don't worry." Evie put a hand on my arm. "Given we're already scouring the kingdom, I'm sure he'll eventually be found and brought to justice. Frederic will have his people look for him in Largo."

"Do you think...do you think I could go to Largo, too?" I asked, seized by a sudden idea.

"Go to Largo?" Evie exclaimed. "Whatever for?"

I spoke quickly, my enthusiasm for the plan growing with each moment. "Now that the soiree is over, there's nothing for me to do here. I want to be back on the road. I know I'm only a foreigner and won't be any use to Frederic in his search for the missing caravan, but I do know what Taylan looks like. I can search for him, at least. And it's possible he has information about the false traders, so if I can find him, it might even end up being helpful to you all."

I looked at them hopefully as the two princesses exchanged a silent look. Here was my chance to get away before my emotions entirely got the better of me and led me to do something inexcusably foolish. It was past time I returned to my adventure.

When they turned back to me, Tillie looked fierce.

"You may be Kuralani, but you're not a foreigner. You're one of the desert people, like me."

I threw my arms around the older woman, surprising us both with the sudden hug.

"Thank you," I said in a thick voice.

"Of course you can go if you're sure you want to," Evie said. "But do you really want to risk running into Taylan again?"

"He caught me by surprise last time," I said with determination. "I won't let him do that again."

"We understand," Tillie said. "Neither of us relish being stuck back here waiting, and Cassian is grumpy as a bear that he isn't being allowed to go as well."

I nodded, relieved. At least they had duties and families here to keep them occupied. If I stayed in the palace, I would soon go stir crazy.

And, perhaps more importantly, getting on a ship and sailing away was the one way I could be sure of getting away from Xavier completely.

"But the ship leaves with the night tide," Evie said. "Can you be ready?"

"Of course. I don't have anything to pack except the clothes you've so kindly made for me."

Regretfully I remembered the lost gold. If Puss had stashed it somewhere, there wouldn't be time to retrieve it before the ship sailed. I wasn't missing this opportunity, though. I would have to find a way to survive without it.

"You poor thing, how could I have forgotten? I'll make sure you have a pack with everything you need." Evie launched into plans after that, soon having the whole thing so neatly arranged that I was left with time to spare before needing to report to the dock.

Puss, who had accepted the sudden plans with perfect equanimity, had disappeared on some final, mysterious errand of his own, and I had already bid a teary farewell to Evie and Tillie, so I decided to do a final tour of the nearby section of gardens. My feet kept wanting to take me to Xavier's door, so I would be better safely out of the palace building.

I wandered around, barely seeing the gardens as I told myself I was doing the right thing by running off without even seeing him. My heart wanted to disagree with my head, but the strength of the pull only made me more determined.

Rounding a corner of the path, I froze at the sight of two identical men walking in my direction. Neither of them were looking up, and they hadn't seen me yet. In a moment of madness, I threw myself into the nearest clump of bushes rather than face them.

My heart beat out a staccato rhythm as they walked closer. What had I been thinking? I should have just hurried off in the other direction. Clearly I was losing my grip entirely.

To my horror, just as they reached me, Xander gripped Xavier's arm, pulling his brother to a stop.

"That's quite a story, Xav."

Xavier met his brother's eyes defiantly. "I'm not the one obsessed with a pointless quest."

"Pointless?" Xander frowned. "You heard what the wise woman said."

Xavier raised an eyebrow. "I heard a bunch of cryptic nonsense that could be interpreted in multiple ways."

"Yes, I know you're determined to think that." Xander narrowed his eyes at him. "You made that clear at the time. Along with your determination to flirt your way through Lanover rather than devote yourself to something more useful."

"Useful? Ha!" Xavier shoved his brother lightly, making Xander glare at him.

I remained frozen in the bushes, my regret grown fiery hot at having become an unwilling observer to the conversation.

Seeing the brothers at odds hit me with unexpected sadness. And despite my own resolutions, it hurt to have Xander confirm my fears about Xavier.

Flirting. Was that really what we'd been doing? Unbidden, a series of images flashed through my mind. Xavier, bending over my hand to press his lips to my knuckles. Xavier, turning his back on me as I hid in the river water, asking if I wanted him to obscure the horse's eyes as well. Xavier, holding my hand firmly in his as he claimed a hurt ankle and asked me not to leave him— an ankle that had been fine the next time I saw him.

Yes, there was no other word for it. I wasn't being unfair. He had been flirting, although I had been resolutely trying not to see it.

Pricks of embarrassment swept over me. Had I looked as foolish to him and others as I felt?

"I mean to see this matter through," Xavier said to his brother, a warning in his tone, and I longed to leap out and defend him. Xander might doubt him, but despite my own initial fears, Xavier had proven devoted to helping the Lanoverians uproot the criminals in their midst.

Xander drew a deep breath, concern on his face. "I hope you know what you're about, brother."

Xavier's face relaxed, his usual smile slowly spreading across his lips. "Don't I always?"

Xander didn't smile back. "Just don't forget what Father said."

"I make it my life mission to forget at least half the things he says," Xavier said lightly.

Xander gripped his arm again, frowning. "I'm serious, Xav. You remember how furious he was when he learned we were planning to sneak away without a proper delegation."

Xavier snorted. "That I couldn't forget."

"Then I hope you also haven't forgotten the condition he set when he eventually let us go?"

"Of course I haven't." Xavier's lips twitched. "It was rather surprising at the time. Who knew Father of all people would command us to marry for love?"

I stifled a gasp as Xander frowned at his brother, his serious expression unchanged.

"That's like you to remember the good parts and not the bad. Father knows enough to obey the wise women's commands—he won't choose brides for us."

"Thank goodness," Xavier said.

"But that doesn't mean we're entirely free." Xander still hadn't let his brother go. "He told us to find someone in the new kingdoms. That was his one condition. Don't pretend you don't remember."

Xavier shook him off, no longer smiling.

My heart leaped painfully in my chest, and I turned blindly to push further into the bushes. I didn't know where I was going or what I was doing, I just needed to get away.

"What was that?" Xander's voice already sounded more distant than before.

"It must have been an animal," Xavier replied before I burst out of the greenery on the other side, screened from their view by the large bushes, and ran for the palace.

CHAPTER 18

*B*ack in the palace, I was swept into a whirlwind of activity. The trip was being planned on such short notice that there was a constant stream of people hurrying down to the docks, either to board the ship or deliver supplies. I dragged Puss to join the next group leaving, eager to be away from the palace as quickly as possible. Xander's confirmation that Xavier's interest in me could never have been anything more than flirtatious had killed any desire to linger for further farewells.

Puss didn't even complain about the speed, giving me such a knowing look that I didn't dare question his forbearance. Karema was landlocked, so when we reached the dock, the sight of the ocean hit me at full force, distracting even my spiraling emotions.

"It's…enormous," I gasped, staring at the water disappearing into the distance.

Surely you didn't think it would be small? Puss gave me an odd look.

"No, of course not. But…I can see why they call the desert the Sea of Sand. It's just like this."

"A desert like the ocean?" A passing sailor gave me a strange look. "What can you be thinking, miss?"

"It's the size of it," Frederic said, stepping up and joining me with a warm smile. "I know what she means."

"And that distant swell of waves looks like the dunes," I added, pointing toward the horizon. "It smells completely different, though." I drew in a deep breath. "I caught hints of it before, but it's so much stronger here."

Puss smacked his lips. *It's nice and fishy.*

"Shall we board?" Frederic gestured up the gangway. "The captain assures me he'll sail with the tide regardless of who's on board." He laughed with the assurance of someone who knew he wasn't in any danger of being left behind.

Puss scrambled unceremoniously up my dress, draping himself across my shoulders with an exaggerated expression of disinterest. I stepped out over the water, my courage buoyed by the knowledge that Puss disliked having nothing but a thin plank between us and the ocean even more than I did.

"It's good to know we have a bold captain," I said.

Frederic laughed. "That we do."

"I learned it all from your sister," said a deep voice, its owner bowing to Frederic.

When he straightened, the prince clapped him on the shoulder with a friendly grin.

"This is our captain, Tom," he said to me. "Tom, this is Kali, a last-minute addition to our number. And the impressive feline around her shoulders is Sir Puss."

I examined the striking man of around thirty with curiosity, while he looked back at Puss and me with equally curious eyes.

"Which sister is that?" I asked him. "I understand Frederic has rather a lot of them."

Frederic laughed. "Far too many of them."

"I had the good fortune to know Princess Celine when we were both a lot younger," the captain said.

"Most people would count association with Celine in her youth to be *mis*fortune," Frederic said with a grin.

Tom grinned back. "And yet, here I am, about to captain a royal vessel south. I'm the youngest captain ever to do so, don't you know?"

"It's a well-deserved appointment." Frederic turned to me. "You mustn't be concerned, Kali. We're in good hands with Tom."

"Your trust is greatly appreciated." Tom bowed even more deeply. "I look forward to speaking with you further, Kali—and even more so with your fascinating companion. But for now you must excuse me. There is still much to see to if we're to catch the tide."

"Of course," Frederic said. "I'll take Kali to her cabin."

I like him, Puss said as soon as Tom had walked away.

I twisted, trying to get a good look at his face. He almost never responded to people that way.

"I'm glad to hear it." Frederic gestured for me to cross toward the door that led below deck. "I'm afraid we've crammed the ship as full as she'll hold, so there's no question of anyone getting any space to themselves until we reach Largo."

"You don't need to worry about me," I said quickly, climbing down the ladder on the other side of the door.

"The females on board have been assigned two of the cabins," he said. "But we've had to hang some hammocks along with the existing bunks."

"I'll take a hammock," I said. "I've only read about them in books, and I've always been curious to try one."

"That's the spirit." Frederic pulled open a plain wooden door. "I hope all the other non-sailors aboard will have a similar attitude."

I stepped into the small, square room, Puss jumping down as I did so.

I will find a sleeping space of my own, he said, stalking off down the narrow corridor.

Frederic watched him go with alarm. "Should I have made special arrangements for him?"

I shook my head. "Don't worry, he wasn't upset. I suspect he's off to establish dominance over any rat catchers the sailors host on board. Cats have been making themselves comfortable on board ships forever, haven't they?"

Frederic smiled. "That they have. And you'll be all right as well?"

"Perfectly comfortable," I assured him, ushering him off before turning back to examine my new temporary home in more detail.

My pack had already been deposited inside, along with a number of others, although there was no sign of their owners. I removed the blanket I'd brought with me and placed it in one of the hammocks. Standing back, I examined the hang of material and decided to use the window of privacy to best advantage.

Grabbing the side of the hammock, I tried scrambling inside, making the attempt in a rush. The hammock twisted wildly, dumping me onto the wooden planks of the floor. Scrambling back up, I tried again, moving more circumspectly, and this time I managed to get inside. I had to wriggle around considerably before I got into a comfortable position, though.

Rolling out, I tried again and again, improving my technique until I could do it without disgracing myself. I had just climbed out again when a lurching motion sent me staggering across the room. I grabbed onto a nearby bunk, anchoring myself as I peered toward the one, circular window. The glass was so frosted with age and seawater that I could see nothing out of it.

The door creaked open, and a head poked in.

"Hello," the young woman said cheerfully. "You must be Kalila. I'm Carina. Is it your first time on a ship?"

I nodded, wondering if it was so obvious.

"We're setting sail," she said. "So you won't want to stay down here. It's much nicer up on deck." She grinned. "At least until you've seen whether you get seasick."

"We're allowed up there?" I asked.

"Of course! Come on!" She led the way, chattering the whole time. From her talk, I soon learned she was an old hand at shipboard life, being maid to the First Mate's wife. "We don't normally have so much company," she told me, and I gave her an apologetic look.

"You mean you normally have more room."

She laughed. "The excitement and company are worth it, I promise. This will be a far more interesting voyage than most."

"I would have thought it was always interesting on the ocean," I said as we came above deck and the breathtaking expanse of water hit me all over again.

Carina seized my hand and squeezed it. "I can see you feel just like me! There's no better life than on the ocean."

A wave of queasiness hit my stomach, and I winced. "Let me see if I get seasick before I decide how I feel about that."

She laughed. "Hurry over to the edge in case. And look out at the horizon. That helps."

I obeyed, gripping the wooden rail in tight hands and staring fixedly at the distant line where sea and sky joined.

The ship's pitching increased as we maneuvered out of the harbor. My stomach roiled with it, but as we hit the open ocean and the rhythm of the swell and roll steadied, my stomach settled.

Drawing a deep breath, I smiled. It seemed the ocean and I were going to be friends after all.

"Feeling better?" asked a sympathetic voice behind me, making my hands tighten around the rails again in shock.

Slowly I turned, my eyes widening as a tall figure strolled easily across the moving deck to join me at the rail.

"What are you doing here?" I gasped.

Xavier raised an eyebrow. "Kali, I'm hurt! If you didn't know I was coming, why didn't you say goodbye?"

I turned away from the smile that lurked around his lips and from the bright, determined look in his eyes that belied the casual expression.

A minute of silence passed as I tried to unscramble my shocked thoughts. I had run for the ship the moment the opportunity arose, thinking I was escaping Xavier's constant presence. But instead, I had just ensured we were both trapped in an even more limited environment. There would be no escaping him on the ship.

"I wonder what calamity I'll need to rescue you from on the ocean?" he asked in a teasing voice. "I tremble to think of the possibilities."

"Maybe I'll rescue you," I snapped, and he chuckled.

"Please do. I welcome any and all efforts from such a beautiful rescuer."

I snorted. "I'll make sure to let you fall to your death next time if I don't happen to be looking my best."

He turned, leaning back against the rail, so he could look at me more comfortably.

"What nonsense is this? You always look your best, Lady Kalila."

I raised both brows. "Lady Kalila? That's a bit much, especially from you."

When he merely grinned at me provocatively, I looked back out at the ocean. "But what are you doing aboard?"

"The same as you," he said promptly.

"What? Looking for Taylan?" I turned back to him, despite my earlier determination to keep my eyes on the waves.

"Of course," he said. "We know what he looks like which is more than can be said of the others who've joined Frederic to search for the missing caravan."

A sudden suspicion gripped me. "Just when did you decide to join the group going south?"

He pursed his lips in an exaggerated expression of thoughtfulness, although his eyes didn't leave mine.

"Hmmm…it's hard to pinpoint it exactly. Maybe three or four hours ago after hearing an interesting piece of news from Princess Evangeline."

"Three or four…" My mouth dropped open at his effrontery. "You're joking!"

"Am I?" He smiled at me, his eyes dancing.

"You…You're…" I humphed and spun away from the rail, hurrying for the other side of the deck, his soft laugh floating after me.

That night in the hammock, I decided to do everything in my power to avoid the prince for the rest of the voyage. He seemed determined to continue his willful flirtation, so it was up to me to stop the nonsense.

But it soon became clear that avoiding Xavier was much easier said than done. The only place I was free from him was my cabin, and my stomach wasn't easy enough with sea life to permit me to spend all day and night shut below deck. My patience wouldn't have stood for it for long, either. While I liked the rocking of my hammock, being below deck during the day made me itchy. I longed for the fresh sea breeze and endless horizon.

Puss was no help either. He had taken to life aboard ship with ease and rarely stopped by to see me.

My favorite place was near the prow of the ship, leaning against the rail, my face toward the ocean. Unfortunately, that made me all too easy to find.

"Do you think they're out there somewhere?" Xavier asked,

appearing at my side as he so often did. He mimicked my pose, looking out toward the water. "On the ocean like us?"

I wrinkled my nose. "What an unpleasant thought. And I was so enjoying the peace."

"My apologies." He turned to look at me, but I kept my gaze firmly forward. "I wish we had time to stop at the islands. I'd love to show them to you. Xander and I visited earlier in our trip. They're beautiful—all yellow sand, turquoise waters, and green trees."

I couldn't help a soft sigh of regret. "Never mind. There's enough beauty here for me." I swept my gaze across the deep blue of the distant water, the brilliant bright blue of the sky, and the green, foamy waves that split around the prow of the ship. "Look! The dolphins have even joined us today."

Several sleek, gray bodies broke from the waves, leaping into the air as they easily kept pace with the boat.

"Enchanting," Xavier said in an unusually soft voice, and it took all my willpower not to look sideways at him.

My rigid posture seemed to amuse him, though, and he chuckled. "I'm beginning to get nervous," he said, leaning forward with his elbows on the rails. "The voyage has been too quiet. When are you going to get into trouble?"

"I can stay out of trouble for several days at a time," I said stiffly.

"Can you?" He gave me a wounded look. "But if you do that, what good am I?"

I finally cracked and turned to glare at him. "Are you forgetting that you're even more of a reckless adventure seeker than I am? I'm waiting for *you* to get into trouble."

My eyes strayed back over the deck behind us, traveling up the tall central mast to the distant circular platform near its top where one of the sailors kept watch.

"Admit it," Xavier whispered in my ear, his unexpected nearness and the brush of his breath against my skin making me freeze. "You're dying to try climbing the mast."

"I don't know what you're talking about," I managed to say, wondering how he'd read my mind.

He leaned slightly back, although his voice stayed at the low, intimate volume. "You can't hide it from me."

Understanding broke over me at the bright spark in his eyes. It took one adventurer to recognize another.

"Have you already done it?" I gasped, spinning all the way around to look directly at the mast.

It loomed high over the rest of the boat, crisscrossed with ropes, sails, and yardarms.

"On our way to the islands. Xander and I raced." He smiled with satisfaction. "I won."

"You raced? Are you mad?"

"You tell me." He grinned at me wickedly. "You're the one thinking of doing it."

"Of course not," I said firmly. "I wouldn't be so reckless."

But my eyes betrayed me, sneaking back to the mast again. The ocean was beautiful, but with unceasing good weather and no role to play on the ship, it did tend toward monotony.

"Do you really dislike it so much?" Xavier asked, examining my face.

"Dislike what?" I frowned at him.

"Your own nature. I know you said your parents disapproved, but don't parents always?"

"Not just my parents." I sighed. "Everyone in Karema disapproved."

"Not everyone," he said with a cheeky grin. "I was in Karema, even if we didn't know each other yet."

I rolled my eyes. "Irrelevant. Everyone I knew was always chiding me for wanting adventures. Recklessness is selfishness," I quoted.

Everyone thinks those unlike them are selfish. Puss appeared from nowhere, leaping up to balance on the top of the rail. *But if we were all meant to be the same, we wouldn't all be so different.*

"Careful!" I cried, looking at him in alarm.

He gave me a superior look. *I don't fall.*

"Sir Puss is right," Xavier said. "Not understanding what motivates another person doesn't automatically make that person wrong. It's possible to have different priorities from someone else without one or the other of you being selfish and wrong."

"But sometimes people are selfish and wrong," I objected.

Puss hacked out a rough laugh. *All the time. But not because they're different from each other. It's just as possible to be cautious and settled and wrong as it is to crave new, fresh experiences and be wrong.*

"Then how am I supposed to know?" I said.

Xavier leaned back on the rail, his brow creasing as he considered my question. "I suspect that takes a lifetime. I certainly seem to understand myself and others better as my experience grows."

I raised a disbelieving eyebrow. "You self-reflect? I don't believe it."

He grinned. "Even, I, the notoriously carefree prince, have occasionally been known to self-reflect. Not as often as Rek, of course. I wouldn't want to lose my reputation."

"I don't think there's any danger of that," I muttered.

He grinned happily. "I don't like to disappoint. Especially you, Kali."

I looked away, my eyes passing unseeing over the deck. Xavier was utterly impervious to every attempt to push him away.

Distracted by the man at my side, it took a moment for my mind to register what my eyes were seeing. I started, leaning forward and staring across the deck. Xavier was instantly alert at my side.

"What is it? What did you see?"

I turned to him, the blood draining from my face. "Taylan. I just saw Taylan."

CHAPTER 19

"*W*here?" Xavier was all business, his eyes sweeping the deck, not an ounce of disbelief in his voice.

"He disappeared from sight as soon as I got a good look at him. But I'm sure it was him."

"Come on." He grabbed my wrist and pulled me behind him across the main deck, making for the afterdeck at the stern of the ship where the captain stood by the wheel.

He didn't break stride, tugging me up the stairs that led to the wide deck and not stopping until we stood before the captain and Prince Frederic, who was keeping him company.

"Kali just saw Taylan," he announced.

Frederic exclaimed. "Here? On board the ship?"

I nodded. "I don't know how it's possible, but I'm sure it was him."

Frederic and the captain exchanged looks.

"There are a lot of new people on this ship," Tom said. "And I've never seen the man. He could easily be hiding among the delegation for all I know."

"A bold venture!" Frederic's lips twisted. "But, to be honest, my memory of his appearance is vague at best. I couldn't swear he hadn't managed to swindle his way into the ranks of my people either."

"I would recognize him," Xavier said in dark tones. "I took special note."

"There's only one thing to be done, then." Tom reached for a nearby bell and began ringing it in a loud, strident pattern of clangs.

In an astonishingly short time, people began pouring out of the two doors that led below deck. Sailors, guards, even the cooks appeared, Carina in their midst.

"What's happening?" I asked.

"That's the call for all hands on deck," Frederic explained. "We'll bring everyone up, and the two of you can look at every face."

You'd better have some of the sailors make sure the delegation members know the meaning of the bells, Puss said, having followed us at a more sedate pace.

"Don't worry," Tom said. "They know their jobs. They'll bring everyone up."

The mass of people milling on the deck were calling questions, so Tom shouted for order. Within a surprisingly short time, he had everyone in ragged lines that ran the length of the deck.

Feeling highly self-conscious, I joined Xavier and walked the length of each line, carefully examining each face. The various ship's inhabitants looked back at us with curiosity or annoyance, but nowhere was the familiar face I had glimpsed earlier. I held on to hope until we reached the end of the last line.

"He's not here," I said, my voice shaking.

What would everyone think of me now? I had disrupted the entire ship over an anxious hallucination. Xavier didn't show a moment of doubt, though.

"Send some of your men below deck to search," he told Tom.

"Already done," the captain replied. "They left as soon as you'd checked them, back at the beginning of the line."

Xavier nodded his thanks, and another tense wait began. But when the men climbed back on deck, they were shaking their heads.

"Everyone's up here," one of them said, approaching the captain.

My shoulders slumped.

"I'm sorry," I said in a small voice. "I was sure I saw him."

"Don't be sorry," Frederic said kindly. "You had a traumatic experience at his hands, so it's understandable you'd be jumpy. And it's good to keep my people alert. A drill will have done them good."

"Thank you," I said, although his graciousness made me feel even more guilty.

I looked around for Puss, meaning to ask if he had seen anywhere on board where a person might hide themselves, but he had disappeared. I grimaced. I should have thought to ask him at the beginning. If Taylan was aboard, surely Puss would know.

"We'll continue to keep an eye out," Xavier told me softly when the crowd dispersed, many of them sending me surreptitious looks.

"I must have imagined it," I said.

"Maybe." He rested his hand lightly under my elbow, steadying me as I climbed back down from the afterdeck. "But there's no harm in being cautious."

I hesitated, looking up at him. "Thank you, Xavier."

I hoped he wouldn't ask why because I didn't want to voice my gratitude that he had believed me so completely—and continued to do so. I still felt foolish about the whole thing.

"There's nothing to thank me for, Kali," he replied in a low voice.

Thank him after we catch that man, Puss said in tones of distaste. He was sitting on the main deck, as if he had been waiting for us the whole time, although I hadn't seen him there earlier.

"Exactly." Xavier smiled, switching effortlessly from the intense moment to his usual carefree manner. "The cat is always right."

Cats generally are. And I even more so than regular cats.

"He's modest, too," I muttered, and Xavier sniggered.

Cats have no need for modesty.

"I'd noticed," Xavier said with another laugh. "But you will help me watch over Kali, won't you, Sir Puss?"

Naturally I shall do so. Puss began to clean one paw.

It was only after Xavier had left to consult further with Frederic that it occurred to me to wonder at Puss's calm acceptance of Xavier's request. Last time he had said something similar, Puss had responded by laying claim to me.

I went below deck feeling uncomfortable for multiple reasons. Puss hadn't been around much lately. Was he up to something?

Outwardly, the voyage continued as smoothly as it had before the incident, but I struggled to enjoy it as I had before. I jumped at every shadow, constantly imagining prickles in the back of my neck, as if eyes were on me.

Instead of standing at the rail, I took to pacing up and down the deck, soon walking with sea legs as confident as any experienced sailor. But even that movement wasn't enough. I longed for something to drive out the restless, itchy discomfort that constantly plagued me, even above deck.

I watched the sailors clambering up and down the shrouds—the name I had learned for the rigging that held the mast in place—whenever they changed lookout shifts. If I was honest, I was becoming more and more obsessed with the idea of trying it myself. I had always been good at climbing, and I was sure I could manage it.

Finally one afternoon, as we sailed closer to Largo, I peered up at the lookout platform to find it empty. It was the first time I had seen it without the usual ever-present sailor. Concern pricked at me, a heightened version of the feeling that had been lurking around me constantly. What had gone wrong in the shift change? We were never without a lookout.

Some back part of my brain suggested reporting it to the captain, but I was seized by a sense of urgency. Now was finally my chance to go up myself. I would just go to the first platform and check that my nervousness was pure fancy. Once I saw the seas were clear for myself, I might finally be able to shake off this feeling. Then I could go to the captain if no proper lookout had appeared.

I kicked off my flimsy shoes and raced to the bottom of the closest shrouds. Ratlines stretched between the ropes, made of wooden slats at first, but further up replaced by thin pieces of line.

I had spent my childhood clambering around both the inside and outside of my father's mill, but the angled rope ladder was different from anything I'd tried before. The rocking of the ship didn't help either, and several times I lost my footing and was only saved by the firm grip of my hands.

I had just gotten used to the technique needed to ascend safely when the lower wooden slats ran out. The rope bit into my bare feet, and I looked down uncertainly at my discarded slippers. But with a shake of my head, I turned back toward the sky. Such insecure footwear would be a danger on a climb like this.

Gritting my teeth, I pushed on, knowing the true challenge was still above. I kept my eyes firmly fixed upward as I rose higher and higher, careful not to look down at the deck which shrank away from me at a surprising rate.

Distantly I heard a shout and wondered if the official lookout had returned and noticed me. I ignored the call, not looking for the source. I wasn't going to listen to anyone telling me to climb down. Already I could feel the thrill of the challenge racing through my blood, driving away the itching fear I felt on deck. Up here there was nothing but me, the sky, and the mast, and all that was needed to keep me from falling was my own strong arms and legs.

A gust of wind plucked at my skirts, tangling them with the shrouds. I stopped and pulled them free with one hand, hiking them up between my legs and tucking them securely into my waist. If I'd been more considered, I would have borrowed a sailor's outfit before attempting the climb.

Staring upward, I saw the approaching futtock shrouds—ropes which joined the regular shrouds to the edge of the wooden platform that the sailors called the top. I swallowed nervously. These lines angled outward, and I had watched the sailors clamber up them, climbing the underside at a forty-five degree angle as if it was as easy as climbing the regular, inward-angled shrouds.

Despite my determination to conquer the challenge I had set for myself, I didn't fancy the fall to the deck below—or if the ship hit a big enough wave, tipping the boat, I might end up in the ocean itself. But now that I'd made it this far, I noticed that the top—a similar platform to the lookout higher up—had a hole positioned right at the top of the ratlines I was climbing.

I almost cried with relief at the sight of it. That must be the mysterious lubber's hole I had heard one sailor mention with disdain. I didn't care what he thought, though. I was a land lubber, and I would happily use the option to avoid climbing the futtock shrouds.

The reaching fingers of my right hand found the sturdy support of the wooden platform just as the ship lurched over a particularly big wave. My fingers slipped on the wet boards, only my grip on the rope with my other hand keeping me from sliding off the lines altogether.

My hand gripped so tightly it cramped as my fingers strug-gled to find purchase again. I waited this time, timing the swell and dip of the ship before I grabbed the platform with both hands and pulled myself up through the hole.

Collapsing onto the wood, I grabbed a rope wrapped around the mast and clung to it, relieved to be off my feet for a moment. Taking steadying breaths, I looked upward. There was still a long way to go to the lookout platform.

I'd told myself I'd only go this far, though. There was no need to go higher. The sailors made it look easy, but I had already experienced for myself that their ease was deceptive.

I gazed out across the ocean instead. Even from here I had a better view than down on deck, and I would soon be able to ease my mind. Maybe I would even manage to shake the lingering concern entirely.

But as I gazed into the distance—first toward the shore and then out to the deeper ocean—I frowned. Was that a smudge on the horizon? I squinted at it, but even from my higher vantage point I couldn't be sure what I was seeing. Uneasiness gripped me as I looked up at the empty lookout post and then down. Despite the earlier shout, there was no sign of anyone else climbing up to join me. It hadn't been the returning lookout after all.

Was the smudge some sort of danger? An approaching bank of storm clouds maybe?

I could go down and sound the alarm, sending a more experienced sailor up in my place. But I had already sounded a false alarm once, and I couldn't face doing it again. I had to go higher and get a better look before I said anything.

Pushing myself up to my feet, I reached for the new set of shrouds that anchored on the wooden top and stretched up the rest of the mast. Driven now by a new urgency, I barely felt the bite of the ratlines on my soles.

Moving more quickly than I had lower down, I raced upward. I resisted the urge to look out toward the horizon as I climbed.

Better to focus on not slipping. When I reached the lookout platform it would be safe to look.

The higher I got, the more the ship seemed to rock, each fresh wave sending me swaying wildly. My stomach lurched in response, but the wave of energy from the distant cloud pushed the seasickness away, overpowering it.

In what seemed an impossibly short amount of time, I reached the lookout platform. Hauling myself through the same hole as the one in the top, I drew in several shaky breaths. But I didn't collapse this time. I had a purpose now.

Gazing across the ocean, I held my breath, wondering if the black smudge would be gone.

It was still there. Larger than before, it spiraled upward. Now that I could see it more clearly, it was nothing like a storm bank.

"Smoke!" I screamed, the wind trying to whip away the word.

I grabbed a rope and leaned out, peering down at the deck. "SMOKE!"

CHAPTER 20

Faces turned toward me from across the deck. I looked for the captain at the wheel, meeting his eyes across the distance and pointing out toward the ocean.

"Over there! Something is burning!" I shouted.

Tom called something I couldn't hear, and sailors lurched into motion in response. Two of them raced for the shrouds I had used, clambering upward at an astonishing speed. For once even they made use of the lubber's holes, ascending all the way to the lookout platform in record time.

"There," I said at regular volume, pointing again. "That's smoke, isn't it?"

"Aye, that it is," one of them said grimly. "And there's only one thing can be burning all the way out here."

I gulped. "Another ship?"

The man who had spoken had already disappeared back into the hole, but the other one paused to nod, his face ashen. He swung his feet through the hole and then paused to frown at me.

"Do you need help getting back down, my lady?"

I shook my head. "I can manage. Don't wait for me."

He disappeared without acknowledging my words, but he didn't head back down to the deck. When I carefully lowered myself through the hole after him, I saw him clambering out along the yards, adjusting the sails in response to the shouted commands coming from below.

Peering down, I realized more sailors were swarming upward, coming not for me but for the sails. Pulling myself back onto the lookout platform, I decided to hold tight until they'd finished their work. I didn't want to send either myself or a sailor flying from an accidental collision.

Shouts and cries floated up from the length of the ship, and I gripped the nearest ropes with white knuckles as the vessel lurched, the wind catching the newly adjusted sails and altering our course.

My eyes fixed on the black smoke, now directly in front of us. We were traveling further out to sea, at an angle from our original course, in order to reach it.

Finally our new course was set, the sails all adjusted, and the sailors descended again. I peered through the hole, examining each yard carefully. No one else remained aloft.

Some sort of altercation seemed to be happening down on deck, however. I sighed as I recognized Xavier. He appeared to be arguing with Frederic who had a tight grip on his arm, preventing him from beginning the ascent.

I slipped through the hole. He must think I'd gotten stuck since I hadn't reappeared. I needed to show him I was fine.

Descending with less speed and more care than I'd ascended, I took my time getting down. By the time I reached the wooden slats of the lower lines, my muscles were trembling with exertion, my fingers almost numb from gripping so hard for so long in the wind. I ignored the discomfort, though, since my nostrils were picking up the acrid sting of smoke.

When I got close to the deck, strong arms wrapped around me, pulling me safely down the last couple of feet. For a brief moment I let myself relax into Xavier's hold, trembles spreading through me.

But as soon as I'd recovered my breath, I pushed away from him.

"I'm fine," I said firmly. "I just didn't want to get in the sailors' way."

He shook his head, wordless for once, and my lips twitched.

"Weren't you the one encouraging me to try the climb?" I asked. "I'm sure you said—"

"I'm sure I said nothing of the kind," he replied firmly.

I shook my head sadly. "Now you're losing your memory as well. You'll be as boring as Rek before you know it."

Xavier froze, a horrified look crossing his face before he broke out in a laugh.

"You wretched girl."

I grinned at him. "You can't take risks if you're not willing to let other people take them, too."

His arms shot out and wrapped around me, pulling me close as he buried his face in my hair.

"You're right, of course," he murmured. "I'm just not used to being on the other side."

"What are you doing?" I asked in a shaky voice, terrified of how much I liked the feel of his strong arms around me.

I pushed away, and he reluctantly let me go. His eyes latched on to mine, making my heart beat as raggedly as it had up on the mast.

But a gust of wind blew a band of smoke across us, making us both cough violently.

"Ahoy!" Someone outside the reach of the smoke shouted loudly, and I staggered over to a clearer looking patch of rail.

Outside the direct cloud of smoke, I mopped at my streaming eyes and peered across the water. Another wooden vessel, half the size of ours, sagged in the water.

Its sails were already gone, and the main mast had snapped,

smashing part of the deck and trailing in the water. The whole ship listed toward the side, pulled down by the wooden pole. I suspected it wouldn't be above the waterline much longer.

Bright spots of light drew my eye, flames still burning in pockets across the deck, somehow finding fresh fuel among the already blackened wood. I scanned the deck for human figures, but I could see no movement.

"Ahoy!" a ragged voice cried again, and I swung my gaze down to the water.

The swelling waves were dotted with debris, some of it burning in small patches of orange. But among the pieces of wood, canvas, and various other flotsam were moving figures.

I collapsed against the rail. Survivors. There were survivors. Our rescue attempt wasn't in vain.

Sailors rushed forward to line the rail. Several of them were busy tying the top of rope ladders with their most secure knots before throwing the length of the ladder down the outside of the ship. The ladders dangled down into the water, and the swimmers began to move toward them.

Many of them were clinging to wood or other floating pieces, kicking weakly and making slow progress. How long had they already been in the water? Thank goodness it wasn't ice cold here, as I had heard it could be in some parts of the ocean.

Some swimmers were without flotation assistance, so our sailors flung ropes to them with something attached to the end that bobbed on the top of the water. The swimmers latched on to them thankfully, the sailors on board hauling them in by means of the rope.

When the first swimmers neared, a number of our sailors responded to a direction from the captain, swarming over the edge of the rail and descending the rope ladders. When they reached the bottom, they hooked one foot on the side and swung out, so that they hung off the side of the ladder, leaving the way free for the swimmers to climb.

Anyone who seemed to lack sufficient strength to pull themselves upward was aided by a sailor who helped guide them up the ladder. It was a long process, and the sailors were replaced as they themselves grew tired. The afternoon light faded, the dusk of twilight replacing it as people continued to be pulled from the water.

Those of us merely gaping at the process launched into action when the first of the victims heaved themselves over the rail and onto our deck. Grabbing blankets from a pile that had appeared behind me, I handed them out, wrapping each one securely around the shoulders of a rescued swimmer. Most of them appeared to be sailors, but some must have been passengers, including a few women who Carina and I swept away to our cabin.

Safely inside, they stripped off their wet clothes and replaced them with borrowed clothing from the women on board our ship. Most of them cried throughout the process, either silently or loudly, but no one chided them.

The oldest of the women recovered first.

"I must go and see if my husband made it on board," she told me with burning eyes.

"Your husband was on the ship with you?" I asked.

"He's the captain. I saw him in the water, but he won't climb up until everyone left alive has been rescued. I have to find him."

I nodded, taking her arm and helping her out of the cabin and back toward the deck. She shuddered as we walked, clearly near the edge of her physical capacity, her determination the only thing keeping her upright.

When we reached the group of dripping people still clustered on deck, her face lit up, and she rushed for the wet man talking to Captain Tom, Prince Frederic, and Xavier.

He turned as she called his name, relief sweeping over his face. He held out his arms for her and she fell into them, tears streaming down her face.

"We saved as many as we could," he murmured into her hair, and she nodded against his chest.

I met Xavier's eyes, my own full of questions. He stepped slightly back from the group, gesturing for me to join him.

"What happened?" I asked quietly. "Has the captain explained it? Does he know what caused the fire?"

"They were attacked," Xavier said grimly.

"Attacked?" I stared at him in horror. "But...who could have attacked them all the way out here? Who would attack them anywhere? I've never heard the Four Kingdoms has a problem with pirates."

"They don't." His jaw clenched. "From what Frederic said, this is a first."

"Wait..." My eyes widened. "It wasn't..."

"That's what we think," he said. "It looks like Cobolt have indeed been out here on the ocean with us."

"But...it makes no sense!"

"Doesn't it? Unfortunately it makes too much sense. They were traveling south when this ship hailed them. It's a usual practice in these areas, two passing ships stopping to exchange greetings and news of approaching weather and such things. But Cobolt didn't want to be seen. They boarded this ship and stripped it of all valuables. Then they set it on fire and left everyone to burn."

My hands flew to my mouth as my stomach turned over. "But that's...horrific! I know they're criminals, but how could they do such a thing?"

Xavier shook his head wordlessly, his eyes hard. I tried to wrap my mind around it.

"They didn't succeed, though. Witnesses survived. So what were they trying so desperately to hide?"

"That's the strange thing," Frederic said, breaking away from the two captains and approaching us. "There's nothing obvious in the captain's report. The only thing that stands out is that they were traveling south. We're close enough now to Largo that their bearing makes it clear they were headed even further south. But there's nothing beyond Largo."

"Perhaps that's why they were going there," Xavier suggested. "They're planning to hide in the wilderness, and they didn't want their hiding place discovered."

"Perhaps." Frederic gave a frustrated sigh. "But there's nothing further south but impassable reefs and desert. Why make it their final destination? What do they intend to do with all the gold and goods they stole?"

We both looked at him wordlessly. There were no answers to his questions, at least none that made any sense.

"We'll make straight for Largo now, of course," Frederic said. "We're too far behind them to have any hope of catching them, and we were already filled to capacity. With so many new people, we need to get to shore fast."

"But you'll send ships from Largo to search?" Xavier asked.

"Of course." Frederic frowned. "And we'll search the surrounding areas by foot. They may have made landfall not far south of the city with the intention of working their way north again. It's the most logical course."

Someone called his name, and he hurried away, leaving me alone with Xavier again. He drew me over to the rail, examining my face in the moonlight.

"Cobolt didn't succeed because of you, you know." He brushed a strand of wet hair out of my face.

I couldn't remember when it had come loose, but in the process of helping the survivors, I had become quite damp. I couldn't even feel the cold, though. My heart was thumping so fast I felt flushed all over.

"I didn't do much," I said.

"Yes, you did. The lookout had become ill and hadn't reported it. We would have sailed straight past the disaster if it wasn't for you."

I looked away. "I shouldn't be praised for something that happened by chance."

Xavier reached up a hand to cup my face, his warm fingers brushing my skin before falling back to his side.

"But how many girls would have attempted such a feat? You've been told you're reckless, that your desire to take risks is wrong, but if you weren't that way, a lot of people would have died today."

"I…" I stared at him, trying to make sense of his words.

They sounded strangely familiar, echoing back to me in my own voice. I had told Beatrice that her mother used her unique qualities to make a difference to people. Is that what I'd done today?

How much easier it was to say the words to someone else than to believe them about myself. But I couldn't deny that my rash decision to climb the mast had been one small part of saving a great many lives.

"Does it matter what other people think?" Xavier asked, his voice low. "I think you're incredible."

I pulled away, pressing my damp hands to my hot cheeks. "Please stop. I can't…I don't…" I shook my head and stumbled backward while Xavier watched me, confusion on his face.

"Kali," he said, reaching for me, but I shook my head.

"Today has been…overwhelming. I can't."

I turned and fled, glancing only once over my shoulder. He watched me go, a crease between his eyes.

I didn't look back again. The moonlit deck was too drenched with emotion, the energy surge from the rescue bouncing from person to person. I couldn't let him say things he didn't really mean—my heart couldn't take it. I needed to breathe. I needed to think.

And we needed to find the murderers who had left all these people to die. Xavier and I might only have a small part to play, but that search was where we needed to focus our attention. We couldn't let the moonlight trick us into playing games that would only lead to heartbreak and distraction.

PART III

THE FORTRESS

We sailed into Largo Bay the next day, the bright sun burning overhead in a clear sky. The smell of smoke still lingered around our ship, and the captain had ordered a series of signal flags raised that must have alerted the harbormaster to the basic situation.

We were berthed in the center of the quay and greeted by a large contingent of people, including a bevy of local doctors. I didn't even have to disembark to see the city was already abuzz with shock at our arrival and the attack.

I'd passed a fitful night wrapped in a blanket on the hard floor of our cabin since I'd given up my hammock to one of the rescued ladies. Everyone on our ship looked worn and exhausted, the aftereffects of the previous day catching up with us.

I hung back, wedging myself in the prow of the ship where I was out of the way, letting the sailors work efficiently to unload the unexpected extra passengers. The local Largoans took over as soon as the survivors stepped foot on the dock, sweeping them away in a constant stream that moved deeper into the city.

Prince Frederic had been one of the first to disembark, directing the flow of people and talking with an older, responsible looking man who I suspected was the harbormaster. At some point another man approached, his clothes proclaiming him a local noble.

"That's the earl of Largo," Xavier said, strolling up to join me. "The governor."

"I hope there's not too much panic in the city," I said. "There must be a lot of ship traffic in and out of this bay."

Xavier nodded, his face lacking its usual animation, concern etched across his forehead.

"I'm sure Frederic will be doing everything possible to reassure them. We have no reason to think this is the beginning of a general problem with pirates. The captain overheard some talk among their attackers, and he seems confident the robbery was secondary to their desire to eliminate witnesses."

I shivered. "They're fortunate they didn't just run them all through on the spot."

Xavier's arm moved, as if he meant to put it around my shoulders, but when I flinched, he let it drop.

"It's easier to leave someone in a hostile environment to die than it is to kill them with your own hands," he said. "It would take a very hardened person to slaughter that many people in cold blood once the initial struggle was past."

"As it turned out, it's fortunate they have some limit to their villainy," I said softly, "although I can't bring myself to view them any more lightly."

"Nor should you. Whoever these people are, they've shown themselves to be callous and cruel in the extreme. The sooner they're caught, the better."

I drew a deep breath, straightening. I preferred to think about future action rather than dwelling on the horrors of the past.

"In that case, we should be thinking about our own role in the search."

"Taylan." Xavier's voice held a hard note that made me shiver again.

I realized that his eyes had barely left the gangway since he had first come into my sight.

"Are you watching for him?" I asked, struck by a sudden thought.

Xavier nodded. "If he somehow eluded us, he'll need to disembark at some point."

I bit my lip, trying to ignore the fluttering in the region of my heart at this sign that Xavier still believed in what I'd seen, despite the lack of evidence.

"I assume you haven't seen any hint of him."

"Unfortunately not. Although now would be a bad time for him to show his face. That crowd looks to be on edge, and if anyone was apprehended right now with suspected ties to the attack, they look ready to fall on them in a frenzy."

I looked across at the rapidly growing crowd pressing around the edges of the dock and shuddered.

"We want him brought to justice, not attacked by a wild mob."

"Don't worry." Xavier pulled his eyes from the stream of people still using the gangway to give me a reassuring look. "The crowd aren't the only ones gathering."

I looked again, and this time I caught the flash of uniforms pushing through the crowd as guards arrived in the wake of the governor.

"I'm sure the moment Frederic stepped ashore, he sent for the governor's guards to swell those of the harbormaster," Xavier said. "He's been helping his father for years now and is an experienced ruler. He won't let the situation get out of hand."

I nodded, relieved to hear it.

"So what do we do next?" I asked, glad to have our own personal mission to focus on in the face of so much chaos. The last thing I wanted was to be a burden on Prince Frederic with everything he had to manage.

Puss strolled across the deck, leaping onto the rail beside us. He was watching the growing crowd with an intense expression.

"Where have you been?" I asked. "I haven't seen you since before I climbed the mast!"

Don't tell me you needed my help in fishing people out of the water. A shudder ran the length of his body, finishing at his tail.

I grimaced. I could hardly be surprised that Puss had absented himself given how wet I'd ended up in the process. And I hadn't even been one of the ones going over the side of the ship.

It's hot, Puss said, shaking his fur.

The long ginger strands no longer looked luxurious, instead appearing like a heavy burden in the muggy air of southern Lanover.

"I'm sorry," I said sympathetically. "Would you like me to trim your fur for you?"

What?! Puss leaped straight into the air, as if someone had skewered him with a hot poker. He would have toppled over into the harbor below if he hadn't performed an impossible twist in midair, landing on the deck of the ship.

"It was just a suggestion," I said in a small voice while he glared at me with a face of wrath.

No one touches my fur, he meowed, and I nodded vigorously while Xavier tried to hide his laugh behind a cough.

"Do you mean to help us look for Taylan, Sir Puss?" he asked.

Naturally. Puss shook himself off, giving me a final glare before strolling over to jump onto the rail closer to Xavier.

"Great, now you're even going to steal my travel companion," I muttered, making Xavier look at me with a hint of his usual humor.

"I wouldn't dream of doing anything so ungallant."

You have no say over who I do or don't travel with, Puss said, *so don't make promises you can't keep.*

Xavier looked at him in surprise. "Don't tell me you've taken that much of a liking to me!"

Don't worry. Puss looked at me, his expression softening the slightest bit. *I'm not finished with the miller's child yet.*

"Miller's child?" Xavier looked at me with interest. "Your father was a miller?"

I nodded. "In Karema. Now my brother runs the mill."

"The brother who left you behind as a child?" A displeased note crept into Xavier's voice, and I was seized with concern for Bernard. What if Xavier asked his father to give the lease to someone else? My brother had been absent for most of my life, but he was still my brother.

"It was my father who sent him away," I said. "It's not Bernard's fault."

"Then why did he cast you out as soon as your parents died?" Xavier asked, the hard note still in his voice.

I shook my head, surging forward to lay a hand on his arm, looking up at him with concern.

"No, no, he didn't do anything of the kind. Of course he didn't. He told me I was welcome to stay with him, and I'm sure he would have treated me well. But he was little better than a stranger by that point. I had no desire to stay."

Xavier looked down at my hand, his eyes flying quickly back up to mine. I flushed and pulled my hand away, stepping backward again.

"I'd always wanted to leave, anyway, so I saw it as my opportunity. Please don't get the wrong idea about Bernard."

"The wrong idea," Xavier said slowly, looking at me with a creased brow as if trying to read a deeper meaning in my words. His features suddenly tightened, and he straightened. "Of course I wouldn't take any action against your brother. Is that what you were thinking?"

I looked away, too embarrassed to meet his eyes.

"Kali." He shifted, putting himself in my eye line again. "How can you think I would misuse my position so? Your brother holds the lease and has committed no crime, as far as I'm aware."

"I'm sorry," I said in a whisper.

Xavier continued to examine my face, his brow creased. After a moment, he stood back with a sigh.

"Apparently Xander's appearance wasn't enough to convince you I'm not a capricious royal, acting according to the whim of the moment."

"No, no." I stared up at him in horror. "Of course you would not…I mean I would not…" I got lost in a tangle of my words and fell silent.

A slow smile spread over Xavier's face as he observed my confusion. "I see I'll just have to make even more of an effort to convince you."

I bit my lip, aware my whole face was flaming. But before I could think of anything to say, a horrible hacking noise made us both start. We turned in time to see Puss cough up a hairball.

I made a disgusted face, but Puss looked up at us, completely unfazed.

If you're done talking nonsense, we have a job to do.

"Do you have any idea where to start looking?" I asked hopefully. Puss had a way of knowing the location of people and places he had no business knowing.

"We should search the ship," Xavier said. "He may still be concealed somewhere, planning to disembark under cover of night."

The ship is empty, Puss said with absolute certainty. *We must seek him in the city.*

"Are you sure?" Xavier asked doubtfully.

Puss turned a cold look on him, and I spoke quickly.

"He might be a little infuriating, but I've never known Puss to be wrong. If he says Taylan isn't on board, then we don't need to waste our time looking here."

Xavier still hesitated before gazing out over the city and nodding. "Very well, then. We start our search in Largo."

"What about our packs?" I asked, looking at a single file line of sailors who were unloading an incredible number of bags, parcels, and crates, piling them haphazardly on the dock.

"They will be taken care of," Xavier said. "They'll be delivered to our rooms at the governor's mansion."

"The governor's mansion?" I stared at him. "Am I supposed to stay there?"

"Of course." He gave me an amused look. "Why would you be bothered by a mansion? Have you already forgotten that you just came from a palace?"

"Yes, but that was different," I said uncomfortably.

"Was it?" Xavier chuckled. "You have some strange ideas, Kali of Kuralan."

If you're going to start talking nonsense again, I'm leaving.

We both hurried to apologize to Puss, and I gestured for him to lead the way off the ship. But when we approached the gangway, he scrambled up my dress as he had when we came aboard, leaving me to carry him across the thin stretch of water.

"The water can't get you all the way up here," I couldn't resist whispering.

That's what you think, he muttered, looking down at the ocean with distaste.

"You seemed to like the ship," I said. "It's surprising given your feelings about the ocean."

Sailors are sensible creatures, Puss said. *They dedicate their lives to keeping the water* out *of their vessel.*

I laughed. "I guess that's one way of looking at it."

By the time we stepped onto solid land, the governor's guards had succeeded in getting the crowd under control. Xavier slipped away for a quick word with Frederic before returning to my side. I tried not to feel self-conscious at his presence. I had intended to look for Taylan myself, with just Puss for company, as usual, but somehow Xavier and I had become a pair. When had I agreed to look for Taylan with him? I couldn't quite work out how it had happened, but the arrangement seemed too established for me to protest now.

Xavier gestured toward one of the streets beyond the dock, looking at me with a disconcerting twinkle in his eyes.

"Well? Shall we begin?"

I hesitated for a moment before nodding. He was only asking me to do what I already intended to do—look for Taylan. That's all it was, and I would just have to keep that firmly in the center of my mind. We were looking for Taylan.

CHAPTER 22

"You said you had an idea where to start?" I asked Xavier as we moved away from the chaos of the dock.

"Taylan's family are wealthy and have extensive connections across the kingdom—including branches of the family in every major city. The ones in Lanare are claiming they have no idea where he's gone, but he doesn't seem the sort to run off into the wilderness with nothing. Even if his family are telling the truth, there's a good chance he'll go to one of their connections in Largo for assistance. He's probably hoping they haven't heard yet about his disgrace and flight."

"Do you have a list then?" I asked.

He nodded. "I thought we'd start with the most closely connected and work our way down."

"Do you think they'll tell us anything, if we ask?"

"If he really was on the ship with us, he would only have arrived just before us. I'm hoping the disruption of his sudden appearance will be hard to hide if we turn up on their doorstep."

"That makes sense. And if they don't know of the happenings in Lanare, they won't have any reason to hide him, anyway."

So where is this first location? Puss asked, walking past us to take the lead.

"You don't already know?" Xavier asked in a teasing voice.

Puss didn't turn, just stalked silently ahead.

Xavier exchanged an amused look with me and consulted a piece of paper in his hand.

"If the directions I've been given are right, we just need to cut through the market, and we'll find it on the other side."

Puss made an abrupt left turn, and I followed obediently, letting him lead us into a large open-air market that brimmed with delicious smells and colorful sights. In every direction people passed by dressed in a range of styles and materials. I even saw some of the full-covering robes of the desert traders.

Breathing in deeply, I hummed appreciatively. "Something smells amazing!"

Xavier glanced at me, looking torn. "The food sold at the stalls here is incredible. I'd love to introduce you to it, but time could prove crucial."

"No, no, of course we should keep moving," I said quickly. "Finding Taylan and helping Frederic is far more important than my stomach."

"Where's Puss?" Xavier asked suddenly, looking around our immediate vicinity. "I thought he was right in front of us."

I looked up, scanning the crowd for the tell-tale ripple. "He's over there." I pointed a distance ahead of us where the crowd were opening ranks and then closing again in a straight line, as if someone unseen was walking through.

Xavier followed the line of my finger and shook his head. "How does he do that? He's not even waist high!"

I shook my head. "I long ago gave up trying to work out the mysteries of Puss."

"Hurry! We should catch him." Xavier grabbed my hand and tugged me through the crowd.

I stumbled after him, trying not to think about the strength and warmth of his fingers wrapped around mine.

We're just looking for Taylan. We're just looking for Taylan. That's all this is. I repeated it over and over in my head. My rapidly beating heart didn't seem to be listening, though.

Thanks to Xavier's confidence at pushing through the crowd, we reached Puss before he exited the market on the other side.

He only acknowledged our reappearance with a single backward glance before starting down a branching street. We hurried to keep up, Xavier muttering to himself as he examined the paper in his hand.

"Are we going the right way?" I asked him.

He gave me a rueful grin. "I hope so? I've been to Largo before, but I didn't make a study of the streets. We're in Sir Puss's hands here."

"His paws you mean," I said, making him chuckle.

A warmth spread through my chest, and I swallowed. When had his amusement stopped irritating me and started bringing me pleasure instead?

We're just looking for Taylan. This doesn't mean anything else. I repeated again, my inner voice growing more feeble.

Puss stopped in front of a large gate set in a high wall. Showing above it was the top of what looked like an extensive mansion.

"This looks promising." Xavier rapped loudly on the gate.

After only a moment's silence, it creaked loudly as a man in a crisp uniform pulled it open and gave us both a haughty look.

"What business do you have here?" he asked.

Xavier bowed. "Allow me to introduce us. I'm Prince Xavier of Kuralan, and this is—"

"Kali," I cut in quickly. We were in a new place, and there was no reason for the foolish business of my supposed title to spread any further.

Xavier gave me a quick look but didn't attempt to correct the introduction. Looking toward Puss, he attempted to continue with his introduction, but the servant cut him off.

"Your Highness!" He bowed deeply. "This is an unexpected honor. The family is not accepting visitors at the moment, but in your case…" He trailed off and peered back over his shoulder, looking torn.

"Don't tell me," I muttered to Xavier out the side of my mouth. "They're looking to make trade connections across the desert, so it's not so easy to turn away a Kuralani prince who turns up on their doorstep."

He gave me a satisfied look, and I realized he'd already been bargaining on that fact when he made his plan. I shook my head, impressed. I would have been wandering blind trying to find Taylan on my own.

A low rumbling sound made me glance down to find Puss giving me a piercing stare. Although I hadn't spoken aloud, I gave him an apologetic look. I wouldn't have been completely blind with Puss by my side.

"It seems promising that they were told to deny any visitors," Xavier whispered back.

The servant turned back to us, apparently having made up his mind.

"If you would like to step inside, Your Highness." He pulled the gate wide and gestured invitingly.

But when his eyes traveled from me to the cat sitting at my feet, his brow creased, an expression of distaste flitting across his face. Xavier immediately halted, frowning from the man to me. He was clearly about to speak up in my defense.

But something about Puss's behavior made me shoot Xavier a warning frown and a quick shake of the head. His expression tightened, but I tipped my head toward Puss, widening my eyes in silent communication.

Puss would normally have stalked through the gate before

either of us could make it there, but he hadn't moved. Instead he was giving me a look that clearly meant *stay at my side*.

Xavier hesitated, but I waved for him to go on.

"I'll stay out here with Puss," I said. "Go."

Still he hesitated, but eventually he heaved a sigh and followed the servant inside. As soon as the gates closed behind him, I turned to Puss, hands on my hips.

"What was that about? Why didn't we go with Xavier? Taylan might be in there right now!"

Puss stood and walked away from the gate, following the line of the wall. *Come with me.*

I followed, glancing back at the gate with reluctance. "Xavier will expect us to be waiting for him. Where are we going?"

Puss didn't reply, leading the way around the enormous property, down a side alley, and out the other side. The wall continued all the way around, but on the other side, a smaller, less elaborate gate gave access to the rear of the property.

"Do you think Taylan is in there and might try to run?" I asked, wondering why I hadn't thought of it.

It seems a logical assumption, Puss meowed calmly.

Strolling back to the alley, he positioned himself just around the corner out of sight. I trailed behind.

"I suppose it might be a long wai—" I started to say when a creak, like an opening hinge, cut off my words.

Gasping, I peeped around the corner.

"There really is someone coming!" I exclaimed quietly.

You're surprised? Puss also stuck his head around, watching the gate swing all the way open.

He whisked himself back at that point, and I did the same. But he only waited for a count of five before moving forward again. The gate had already been closed, and someone was hurrying in the opposite direction.

"It's him," I gasped. "It's really him!"

Come, then, Puss said.

I looked at the closed gate and then back at the man walking briskly away from us.

"But Xavier…"

Is not here. Do you wish to lose this opportunity?

I grimaced. "No, of course not. Let's go."

Stepping out briskly, I started after Taylan, pulling up the hood of my light cloak to obscure my face.

Taylan seemed confident he'd escaped his pursuers, however, since he didn't glance back once. Instead he was intently focused on something in his hand and the path ahead of him, clearly moving with a purpose and not just fleeing the property blindly.

"Where is he going?" I muttered to Puss, but the cat didn't answer.

Several times I had to break into a light jog to keep up, and my uneasiness grew the further away we got from Xavier. How long would he be with Taylan's family? What would he think when he came out and found us gone? If only there'd been a way to send him a message.

I didn't have much free thought to question my decisions, though, given the pace Taylan set. Was he trying to reach somewhere under a deadline? A spurt of excitement ran through me. Was it true he was in league with the missing caravan? Was he going to meet them?

At last we reached what seemed to be the edge of the city, the buildings less closely clustered together and less well kept. Taylan stopped outside one particularly woebegone looking example and hesitated, consulting the object in his hand which I could now see was a piece of paper. Its appearance, and his expression as he looked at it, reminded me forcibly of Xavier, hurrying through less than familiar streets with directions in hand.

Had Taylan been following directions to this place? Perhaps provided by his Largoan relatives? I melted back into the heavy shadows around the rundown property on the other side of the road, Puss disappearing even more effectively beside me.

Taking a deep breath, Taylan straightened his back and reached out to open the door. Before he could touch it, however, it swung open.

For a surprised second, he stood facing two men, both with heavy packs slung across their backs. They looked back at him with equal astonishment.

"What is this?" one asked in a threatening growl.

Taylan fell back several steps before gathering his courage.

"I came in search of you. I see I was just in time."

"In search of us?" the second man asked, stepping forward with an ugly expression on his face.

Taylan held up both his hands placatingly. "I want to help you!"

"Help us?" The first man looked at the second one and laughed roughly. "And what help do you think we'd be in need of from the likes of you?"

I frowned. Who were these people? This interaction was going nothing like I'd imagined.

"You're Cobolt," Taylan said eagerly. "The tip on where to find you cost a lot of money—evidence of just what I can bring to your cause. My family has wealth and connections that you could only dream of."

The first man's eyebrows rose. "Our cause? And what do you imagine that to be?"

Taylan's bearing lifted, his manner becoming animated. "You're the ones with the courage to do something about the desert scourge plaguing our kingdom."

"Desert scourge?" the second man asked slowly.

Taylan nodded eagerly, stepping forward. "Not everyone in Lanover is as blind as our foolish king. We can see the so-called desert traders for the vermin they are, stealing from the kingdom's hard-working merchants."

"Vermin?" the first man repeated, something in his voice setting every hair on my arms on end.

But the second man gave a contemptuous laugh. "So much righteous anger over a matter of business. Did your woman leave you for one of these desert rats or something?"

I was at just enough of an angle to see part of Taylan's profile, but even without a clear view, I could make out his shock at the idle words. The report from the Lanoverian royals had said nothing about Taylan having a family of his own, but was it possible he really had loved a girl who had chosen a desert trader? It would explain the level of uncontrolled vitriol.

Before I could consider the possibility further, his face spasmed, his eyes bulging wide and the breath surging from his lungs. I looked down to see a sword hilt protruding from his middle, held in the hand of the first man.

Taylan looked down at it as well, a gurgle sounding in his throat as blood poured from the wound. For a horrifying moment, he hung there, suspended on the blade. Then the man lifted one boot and shoved him off, leaving his body to crumple lifelessly in the dust of the road.

I slammed both hands over my mouth, holding back the cry of horror and distress. What had I just witnessed?

"The thing about vermin," the murderer said, calmly cleaning his blade, "is that they eat the weak. You should have thought more carefully about who you wanted to get into bed with."

"Really, Gage?" the second man asked in an impatient voice. "We should have found out which of our contacts gave him the information on where to find us."

"We'll just deal with all of them when we get back," Gage said, unmoved. "There's no time for it now. If we don't move quickly the caravan will leave us behind. They won't wait—not when we have only four days before the emperor's deadline for returning."

The second man grunted, looking down at the body and chuckling. "He miscalculated. Thinking he'd found an ally in his hatred."

He shook his head, chuckling again, while I struggled not to throw up. How could they treat murder and death so callously?

These are the people who left a whole boat to drown, Puss whispered so quietly I could barely make out the words.

The reminder of his presence steadied me, and I managed to suck in a couple of shaking breaths.

"What just happened?" I whispered as the two men took off down the street. "This must be a dream."

Come! Puss said sharply. *There's no time to be lost.*

"Time? What do you mean?" I stared down at him.

He raised his eyebrows. *Don't you want to see where they're going?*

"I..." I carefully kept my eyes averted from the grisly sight in the middle of the road, trying to pull my thoughts together. "They said they're going to join their caravan! You want us to follow them?"

My mouth said the words, but my legs weren't listening, firmly locked in place. I closed my eyes and took several deep, calming breaths. If I wanted these people brought to justice for their crimes, then they had to be found. Gage had said they were leaving the city. This might be our only chance.

 *L*ike Taylan before them, the two men from Cobolt didn't seem to have any fear of pursuit. Even so, I hung back further than I had while following Taylan, sticking to the shadows as much as possible. I was not only driven by fear after their casual murder, but also by the environment. On the outskirts of the city there was much less traffic to hide my movements.

Had the men separated from the caravan to seek provisions or intelligence? Or had they had some other, more sinister, intention? Since they were unlikely to chat to each other about it, I had no way of finding out. It wouldn't matter, though—not if I could bring back information that would allow Frederic's guards to capture the whole caravan.

As I moved, part of my mind went back over their brief conversation. They had mentioned an emperor, but all the kingdoms on both sides of the desert—and even across the sea—had either a king, a queen, or a sultan. No one had the conceit to style themselves as emperor.

Was the false caravan from somewhere else, then? But where? There was nothing between these kingdoms and the eastern two kingdoms but desert. And beyond Ardasira and Kuralan were mountains so high they couldn't be crossed.

Was *emperor* some sort of code word, then? Or an ironic title for the leader of their criminal gang? That seemed the most likely explanation, if a little odd. But if he wasn't with them, where was he? Did they have a hidden base of operations somewhere? It would have to be well hidden if it had remained undiscovered all this time despite being large enough for the entire caravan.

The man called Gage and his companion moved at a fast enough pace that I was out of breath keeping up. They were heading east, toward the desert, as I had expected, given their stated intention of joining the rest of the caravan. So many camels and people couldn't be easily hiding in the city.

But I had expected them to move northeast, angling toward the start of the route that led to the closest oasis. Each caravan had their own routes through the desert, utilizing the hidden oases, known only to them, but there were also public oases used by all, and the one closest to Largo was one such. Every route into the desert made for that one first.

The two were heading sharply southeast, though, as if they intended to enter the desert and head south. But south of Largo was only the sea. The desert continued unbroken to the southern coastline of Lanover, and there were no known oases in the section south of Largo. Not that anyone had any interest in going there since there were no settlements to trade with either.

Neither man faltered, however, seeming certain of their path. I began to wonder how long I should keep following. There would be no way to hide myself in the desert, and I didn't want to risk losing myself in the short stretch of wilderness between this part of Largo and the sand.

When I ducked across a large gap and into the shadow of the last visible building, I stopped. Puss halted at my feet, staring ahead at the retreating men with narrowed eyes.

They are definitely heading south.

"Do you hear the rest of the caravan?" I asked hopefully, knowing how keen Puss's senses were.

He gave a soft growl. *They are beyond my reach. I suspect they are on the fringe of the desert.*

I sighed. "That's what I feared. I don't think we can follow so far. And it would do us no good, anyway. I can't arrest the whole caravan alone. By the time I got back and reported their position, they would have moved on, disappearing into the desert. I'm better off going back now and making the report as soon as possible."

I took Puss's silence as agreement, turning back toward the city.

"Do you think Xavier will still be at that merchant house? Should we go there first?"

Again Puss gave no opinion, so I did my best to retrace my steps. I had been so intent on not being seen while tracking my quarry that I would have failed at the task without Puss's assistance. But with his unerring sense of direction, we easily found our way back to our starting point.

We arrived to find the gate closed and no sign of Xavier. I hesitated, eyeing the solid wood of the gate.

"Should I knock and ask for him?"

Puss lifted his head into the slight breeze, gazing at the top of the wall. *He's no longer there.*

I nodded acceptance of his judgment, well past the point of questioning how he knew such things.

"Where should we go then? To the governor's mansion? Xavier said that's where we have rooms."

I just hoped they'd let me in if I arrived without the prince. The guards on the gate might not think me a legitimate part of the delegation.

We should go to the ship.

"The ship?" I frowned at Puss. "Why would he be there?"

He will be looking for you. Puss said the words without a trace of uncertainty. *And he knows you've never been to the governor's mansion and are uncomfortable about lodging there.*

I started slightly at his referencing the very thing that had been on my thoughts. "So you think he'd go to the ship?"

It's the only place in Largo that is familiar to you.

I considered the matter. "I can see the logic of that. And even if he's not there now, he may have left a message with the sailors."

It was easier to find my way back to a major landmark like the docks, especially given the route led through the market. Once again I resisted the urge to stop at the market stalls. The caravan was well ahead of us, and a little extra speed wouldn't allow us to catch them now, but I still felt a sense of urgency. I couldn't dally just for the sake of my stomach.

I reached the royal berth at the dock to find the ship strangely quiet and deserted after the earlier bustle of activity. The gangway was still in place, though, so it couldn't be completely emptied.

I looked around for Puss, thinking he would want to be carried across, but there was no sign of him. I spun in a circle, staring around me. He had been beside me just a moment before.

"Puss?" I called. "Puss? Where are you?"

There was no reply.

"That wretched cat!" I muttered. "Where has he gone now at such a moment?"

I considered turning back to search for him first, but if he'd chosen to go off on his own, there was little likelihood of my finding him. My eyes caught on a familiar figure standing at the railing of the ship.

Xavier was gazing further left, where the docks ended. Had he seen Puss?

I ran over the gangway and across the deck to join Xavier.

"Can you see him?" I asked breathlessly, putting my hand on his arm without thinking.

He froze beneath my touch for a single breath before

launching into sudden motion. Spinning, he swept me into his arms and buried his face in my hair.

"Kali! Where have you been? I've been searching everywhere!"

"Sorry." I struggled unsuccessfully to free myself. "Were you worried?"

"Was I worried?" He pulled back with a rough laugh, examining my face. "Of course I was! You just disappeared in the middle of a strange city—one with an unknown number of cutthroats at large."

I shivered at his words, an image of Taylan's end flashing in front of my face.

"What is it?" he asked, still gazing down at me. "What happened?"

"I…" My voice shook, so I started again. "I'm fine. It wasn't me. But…but Taylan is dead."

"What?" Xavier jerked me back, putting me at arm's length so he could see me more clearly. "What are you talking about?"

"Oh Xavier," I wailed, my earlier resolution to be strong cracking and crumbling. "It was awful. He just crumpled like… like…" I gulped, losing my words completely in the stream of tears.

He pulled me close again, holding me firmly against him, allowing his calm and strength to flow through into me.

"But you're not hurt?" he murmured urgently into my ear.

I shook my head wordlessly, and he breathed out, some of the tautness leaving his muscles.

"Thank goodness for that." His embrace somehow tightened. "I thought…" He didn't finish the sentence.

As my tears slowly subsided, the hysterical tinge leaving my thoughts, I stiffened. What was I doing? What was Xavier doing?

I made an attempt to pull away, but he just held on tighter. My brain told me to try harder, to show him I meant it and pull free, but instead I sagged back into the strength of his arms. I had been strong while I had to be, but I wanted to let someone else provide the strength for a moment. Surely that wasn't so wrong?

But the tickle of Xavier's breath moved down from the top of my hair, his head bending until his mouth rested near my ear. The soft feel of his breath against the skin on the side of my neck made me shiver.

"Don't ever do that to me again, Kali," he whispered. "If anything happened to you, I would…"

"Would what?" I couldn't help asking, the words slipping out on a breathless whisper.

"Do something drastic," he replied in the same low murmur. "Something I might regret. You're very important to me, Kali."

He pressed a kiss just below my ear. I gasped, my whole body stilling as my thoughts whirled hopelessly out of control. What was happening?

Xavier chuckled quietly at my reaction, the sound almost reluctant. "I wasn't going to say anything in the midst of all this. It didn't seem like the right timing. But it's hard to stay in control around you, Kali."

"I don't…I don't understand," I managed to gasp out.

He finally moved his bewitching lips away from my skin, pulling back and looking at me with eyes that trapped me just as effectively.

"No," he said with an affectionate smile, the laughter in his eyes again. "You seem determined to misunderstand me—you have since the moment you walked into Tarka." He laughed again. "What a sight you were! A bedraggled mess, but with such a light of determination in your eye. You were striding into battle, regardless of the state of your armor. I knew in that moment that you were a kindred spirit."

"You don't know anything about me," I said in faltering tones, trying to resist the breathtaking intensity of his expression.

"Nonsense," he said with a disapproving look. "You're the daughter of a miller from Karema—an orphan with no one to call family except a talking cat and an older brother who's a stranger. You love adventure—something you inherited from your desert nomad mother. You care about the truth, even when it's not to your advantage. You don't want to take things you haven't earned, but when the position is reversed, you're happy to help others, even if they've done nothing to put you in their debt. You climb masts on a whim and have no hesitation in chasing down a man who attacked you. In short, you're just my sort of woman, Kali of Kuralan."

"How…how do you know all that?" I asked weakly.

He grinned. "Because I've been chasing you since that first moment I saw you. Haven't you noticed by now?"

"I…" I gulped, terrified at the rush of joy that was spreading through me. "I don't know what you could possibly mean, but—"

"What I could mean?" He gave me an incredulous look. "Surely you've learned something about me in all this time as well? Whatever else could I mean except that I want you to marry me?"

"Marry you?" I stared at him in shock.

"Of course." He gave me an affectionate shake. "I love you far more than is sensible, my darling Kali. And I have every intention of chasing you for the rest of my days, so please have pity on me and stop running."

"I heard you in the garden with your brother," I blurted out, making his brow crease, the amusement dropping from his face. "I know your father's requirement that you bring back a bride from the Four Kingdoms. You can't marry me." I sought around desperately for an explanation for his mad words. "You've just gotten carried away because I didn't flirt back with you. You can't be used to that."

He stared at me in stunned silence before breaking down into laughter, his shoulders shaking with more amusement than my words could possibly warrant. I tried to pull away again, but he stopped laughing, still not letting go.

"I promise I'm not so easily swayed by any woman who doesn't show me interest. I have met the occasional such person before." His eyes danced. "Just one or two, of course, given my irresistible charms."

I snorted. "Irresistible? Hardly!"

I bit my lip when my voice wobbled tellingly on the words, and his eyes dropped down to linger on my lips. My breath caught, and I struggled to keep my expression under control.

"Oh really?" he asked, a playful acceptance of my challenge in his voice. "You say you didn't flirt back, but that's not quite how I remember it. Are you sure you're so entirely unmoved?" He pulled me closer again, dropping his face toward my ear. "Even when I do this?" he whispered, brushing a kiss against the skin behind my ear.

Despite my resolution to remain unmoving, I shivered, and he laughed, a rough, gravelly sound in the back of his throat. "What about when I tell you you're the most enchanting woman I've ever met? And that even the constant presence of that infernal cat isn't enough to put me off?"

His words snapped me out of it, and I pulled back hard enough to tear myself from his hold.

"Yes, Puss! Where is he? Have you seen him? He was right with me, but he just disappeared."

Xavier groaned. "See what I mean? How can you think about that cat at a moment like this?"

"I'm worried about him," I said defensively.

Xavier gave me a wounded look. "Really? Is he not able to take care of himself?"

I pursed my lips, not meeting his eyes. "I suppose he is…"

Xavier took me briskly by the upper arms, looking down at me sternly. "I refuse to consider Sir Puss until you give me an answer. Surely you don't mean to keep a prince waiting!"

I groaned. "Exactly! You're a prince! How can I marry you?"

"How can you not?" he asked and pulled me forward, pressing his lips down firmly over mine.

For a second I stayed rigid, too shocked to move, and then I melted against him, unable to resist the effect of his warm lips and firm hold. I could only fight my heart for so long.

When he finally raised his head again, he had a satisfied look. "You can't possibly say no now."

I leaned back and shoved him lightly in his chest. "That was cheating!"

He grinned. "Who said I played fair?"

"But seriously, what will your father say?" I asked. "You can't just pretend you're not a prince."

"Father will just have to cope," Xavier said calmly. "He told us to marry for love, and he can't think I'm going to walk away from you and just fall into love with some other girl."

I flushed, unable to continue resisting his words.

"He didn't approve of Rek and Zaria at first either," Xavier continued, and I started at the mention of my friend.

He looked down at me with a curious expression that slowly changed into one of recognition.

"Wait a minute!" he said. "I thought there was something familiar about your name from the beginning! You're the friend Zaria kept talking about. The one we were supposed to meet at her betrothal but who ran off instead."

I smiled guiltily. "Yes, Zaria is my best friend. I didn't mean to run away, but..."

"But your father died, didn't he?" Xavier's arms tightened around me again. "And you didn't want to be grieving at her celebration. See, I told you that you're more considerate to others than yourself."

I rolled my eyes before frowning. "But Zaria performed a great service for the kingdom. Of course your father approved the marriage. Are you sure—"

"I'm sure I don't care what Father says." Xavier looked down at me with serious eyes. "I can walk away from Kuralan if that's what it takes. I'm serious, Kali."

I buried my face in his chest, unable to cope with the emotion on his face.

"Don't look at me like that," I said in a muffled voice. "I can't think straight when you look at me like that."

"Shall I just do this instead?" he asked in a wicked tone, his head dipping toward my neck.

"No, no!" I pulled myself back quickly, putting him at arm's length. "I don't want to see you barred from your homeland, though."

He smiled. "I don't want to see you unable to ever return home, either. Don't worry, we'll find a way to convince Father. Maybe if we find this caravan for Frederic, Lanover will be so grateful they'll take you in as a citizen."

"The caravan!" I pulled myself free completely, my eyes widening. "Taylan! What am I doing?"

Xavier looked at me with narrowed eyes, as if checking to see I wasn't going to fall apart again at mention of Taylan. "You said something about him being dead, but surely that isn't possible. Are you sure he didn't spread the rumor so he could disappear?"

"No, I'm telling you I saw it with my own eyes!" I quickly outlined what had happened and everything I'd seen and heard.

"He was murdered! And you were there?" Xavier pulled me in for a quick hug before letting me go again. "So he wasn't ever working with them? We were wrong on that one."

"But not wrong that he'd contact them," I said. "The whole thing makes no sense, though. From the way they talked, Taylan miscalculated, and they aren't enemies of the desert traders but must actually be desert traders, after all. But if they are, Taylan isn't the only one to have misunderstood the situation. How could there be a whole caravan of desert traders no one has ever seen?"

"Maybe it's only those two scouts who are traders?" Xavier suggested. "A group of thieves could have hired two rogue traders as guides for the desert."

"Perhaps," I said. "Although they responded very strongly to Taylan insulting desert people—a strange response if they're traitors to their people themselves."

Xavier sighed. "We can't make sense of it without further information. We need to get to Frederic and tell him what's happened. He needs to send people after the caravan."

I groaned. "But how will they ever find them?" I brightened. "I saw some desert traders in the market. Are there some caravans here who could go after them? If anyone had a hope of tracking them through the desert and catching them, it would be the traders. And they have more reason to want them captured than anyone."

Xavier ran a hand through his hair, looking toward the docks. "Frederic is meeting with caravan representatives who are already here in the city, but unfortunately there aren't any full caravans here at the moment. We believe several of the ones who were in the southern part of the kingdom are moving here at speed, but I'm not sure when they'll arrive."

"Even if they arrive tomorrow, it might be too late." I sighed. "Is there really nothing we can do to go after them immediately?"

"We'll tell Frederic, of course, but he's not going to order anyone out into the desert. It's too dangerous for that, and he would never require anyone to go to their death. He'll be as frustrated as we are, but he'll make the sensible decision and wait for the caravans to arrive."

"Sensible…" I murmured the word, meeting his eyes. "Maybe sensible isn't what's needed here?"

His brows quirked together. "What do you mean?"

"Isn't that what you were talking about before? Sometimes the kingdoms need the kind of people willing to act in the moment—

the kind of people willing to take risks if that's what the situation requires. Maybe right now, what Lanover needs is someone a little reckless." I gestured between us. "And here just happen to be two such people."

"You want us to go after them ourselves?" Xavier's mouth dropped open, but a spark of excitement entered his eyes. "Just the two of us?"

"Well, I hope Puss would come, too." I scanned the dock, trying to catch sight of him.

Of course I would, why else am I here? he asked from my feet, making me jump.

"Puss!" I screamed. "How did you get there? Where did you go?"

There are some things no one should have to witness, he meowed, giving us both a look of distaste.

I flushed, glancing at Xavier and then looking back at Puss. "You don't mean…Surely you couldn't have known he was going to…"

Have I appeared slow before now? he asked.

"Puss!" I squealed again.

Xavier threw me an amused look. "Never mind that. But what do you mean, Sir Puss? Are you saying you agree we should go after Cobolt? Is that why you came to the kingdoms?"

I could see confidence fill him at the idea that Puss was here for just this purpose. The possibility provided a foundation for Xavier's own instinctive preference. But, perversely, my hesitation grew in pace with his enthusiasm. Was I leading Xavier to his death? I couldn't be responsible for that.

I specifically chose to travel with someone willing to set off into the desert, didn't I? Puss asked, not exactly answering Xavier's question.

Xavier grinned at me. "There you go. Sir Puss has sought out two of exactly the sort of reckless people as are needed."

A throat cleared behind us, and we all spun to stare at the captain. He gave us a slow smile.

"I believe there are three such reckless individuals present. And I have a much better idea than setting off into the desert."

CHAPTER 24

*E*verything happened in a whirl after that. Tom assured us that with his ship berthed and waiting to eventually return the royals to Lanare, he had no immediate duties. Even so, I was reluctant to put someone else at risk. But once he explained it all, I couldn't turn down his proposal.

"No one goes along the southern coastline of Lanover," he said, pointing out the region he meant on one of the maps in his cabin. "That's because there's nothing of value down there. No towns, no cities, no resources. Just desert and a coastline riddled with dangerous reefs."

"And then you found out there were kingdoms on the other side of the desert," Xavier said with a knowing look.

The captain—who insisted we call him Tom—grinned back. "As you both know, with the chance of reward comes those willing to take risks. Some of the younger captains and navigators have been starting to test the route eastward. The reefs really are deadly, though. No one has made it through with a ship of any size. And without room to carry cargo, there's no point facing the danger."

"But we don't need to take cargo," I said slowly, his plan becoming clear.

"Precisely." He looked back and forth between us, his face turning serious. "I've made the journey—or part of it anyway—but I won't underplay the risks. Even an experienced navigator and captain can end up tearing out the bottom of their boat. And there's no passing ships to rescue anyone in trouble in that region. If we go down, we'll be on our own."

"We would be even worse off in the desert," Xavier said. "And we'll make much better time on the ocean. My only concern is overshooting them completely. Even assuming they'll be following the coast, we don't know how far inland they'll travel."

"Actually, I've been thinking about that," I said. "From their conversation, I'm convinced they have a base somewhere and are returning to it. And it must be in the desert if they're heading south and need four days to reach it. Princess Tillie has been researching the old empire, and we have a theory. We think there must be ruins of old cities buried in the desert."

"Old cities?" Tom stared at me.

I leaned forward against the table where he had spread the map. "Think about it," I said, warming to the topic. "An empire would have had many cities—ones we would never find if they don't happen to lie on caravan routes. But if you think about the kingdoms now, many cities are built on the coast. It's a logical place to build given the access to ocean trading, so it makes sense the old empire would have done the same. There may not have been reefs back then—for all we know, they appeared when the High King turned the land to desert."

"So you think these criminals have set up a base in ancient ruins?" Xavier asked.

I nodded. "How could they have built structures of their own in the middle of the desert? I think it's likely their base is on the coastline, so we should be able to see it from the sea."

"In that case, it's settled." Tom briskly rolled up his map. "I'll fetch my navigator."

"Your navigator?" Xavier and I exchanged looks. Someone else was going to risk himself for our wild theories?

"We can't possibly do it without him," Tom said. "He's the one who's been along the route with me before. I'll only be a moment."

He disappeared out of the cabin, and I watched him go, my mind racing with all the possible consequences of our hasty decision.

Arms slipped around my waist, and Xavier leaned down to put his forehead against mine.

"Such a troubled face, my lady! Aren't you a little excited to be setting off on an adventure?"

I groaned, pulling back. "I'm too excited! That's the problem. It makes me doubt my decisions. Doesn't it do the same for you?"

He pulled me back in close. "I've learned to trust my instincts."

"If half the stories about the royal twins are true, don't they generally lead you into trouble?" I grumbled.

I felt his chuckle through his chest. "They might lead me into trouble—but rarely into trouble I wasn't seeking. And right now, I'm far more interested in the fact that I have a moment alone with you. I can think of far more interesting ways for us to spend the time than worrying."

He bent his lips slowly down toward mine, his eyes teasing me as he did, daring me to respond.

I screwed up my nose and pushed him back. "This is hardly the time for that."

"Don't you have any pity, my lady?" he asked plaintively.

"Don't call me that," I scolded him. "You know it isn't true."

I keep telling you it is true, Puss said, making us both jump.

"How long have you been there?" Xavier asked.

The whole time—unfortunately. Or have you forgotten I came in with you?

Xavier and I exchanged guilty looks while Puss pointedly returned to cleaning his paw.

The cabin door opened, and Tom appeared, a younger man following behind. He had the same light of enthusiasm in his eyes as Xavier and Tom, so I could see it was no use questioning if he was sure he wanted to participate.

"Captain says we need to leave immediately," he said. "I'll just need a bit of time to organize some basic provisions. It should take no more than thirty minutes, which is good since the tide is running in our favor right now. Can you be ready by then?"

Xavier nodded. "I've already checked, and our packs haven't been unloaded yet. Other than collecting them, I only need to write a letter to explain the situation to Frederic." His mouth quirked to one side. "I'm just sorry Xander isn't here. He'll be furious he missed such a chance."

The grin that all three men exchanged made me groan. "What am I getting myself into setting off with these three mad men?"

Don't worry, Puss said, winding around my ankles. *I'll be there, too.*

I smiled down at him, rolling my eyes. "Why does it make me even more nervous that that's actually reassuring?"

We sailed out of the bay only twenty-five minutes later. We were in a much smaller boat than the ship that had brought us from Lanare, but she flew before the wind. The captain and navigator cheerfully wrangled the sails, directing Xavier and me to help whenever a task could be completed without previous experience.

"Once we've found the base," Xavier said cheerfully, his face set into the wind and his brow furrowed against the glare of the sun on the water, "we'll sail back and report the position to Frederic. Some of the caravans will hopefully have arrived in Largo by then, and they can set out across the desert in force."

"I just wish we knew why Cobolt are doing it," I said. "Why set the kingdom against the desert traders if they have at least some ties to them? And what can they do with all that stolen gold if they're living out in the middle of the desert?"

No one had any answers. Even Puss was silent, apparently deeply uncomfortable at being out on the ocean in such a small vessel.

Our initial passage went smoothly since the seas around Largo Bay and Banishment Island—the southernmost isle—were well mapped. It was only as the distant coastline turned sharply eastward, leveling out to form the southern edge of Lanover, that a new light of tension and concentration entered the eyes of both Tom and the navigator.

Tom took his place at the wheel, and the navigator stationed himself in the prow, sounding line in hand. I eyed the leather marks tied at regular intervals along its length. I didn't want to bother either of them with questions, so I had to satisfy myself with guessing that they were used to show how deep the water was without the line having to be pulled back up and measured.

"I want one of you starboard and one port," Tom directed. "If you see white water—anything that looks like agitation around an obstruction just below the surface, call it out. I'd rather be warned of something I know is there than miss something."

His eyes kept flicking between a rough map, covered in incomprehensible marks, and the ocean in front of us. I had no idea how he could make any sense of it and was only glad I wasn't behind the wheel.

"Shouldn't we slow down?" I asked hesitantly, unable to keep the single question in.

"We don't want to go too fast," Tom said, his eyes on the ocean, "but we don't want to go too slow, either. Speed will prevent rolling and keep our direction stable. That will help us keep on track. The path through is tight in places."

Time blurred after that. It moved terrifyingly slowly in places where the water foamed and spat over barely submerged reefs only an arm's reach from our boat. At other times it sped up, hours passing as my eyes strained to watch the unchanging expanse of water, the reefs moving past unseen beneath the surface and the tension of the watch turning my back and neck into knots of tight muscle.

We dropped anchor every night despite our desire for speed. Tom insisted it was too dangerous to proceed in the darkness, and neither Xavier, Puss, nor I had any desire to protest. Puss barely moved the whole journey, curled up in the tiny cabin, out of sight of the water.

Our food was served and eaten cold, usually in hand while we stood with our eyes on the water.

When the distant coastline changed, endless yellow sand replacing the previously unbroken jungle, Xavier asked if we could move in closer to shore.

"We don't want to miss seeing any structures they may be sheltering in."

But Tom refused. "The reefs are even thicker further in, and we're not familiar with the route. We have to follow the marked route if we don't want to end in disaster. Many captains have contributed to mapping it out."

Xavier reluctantly agreed, and I was transferred duties, staring at the distant land instead of the sea in front of us. While I had grown to hate the swell of the waves, so deceptively calm on top and so endlessly treacherous, it turned out the unchanging sand was even worse. Within hours I was having to blink to drive away false images of blurry structures looming from the sand, as the distant heat haze combined with my brain to play tricks on my vision.

I was standing staring at the shore when Xavier cried a

warning a half-second before the navigator repeated it. Tom exclaimed, and the boat lurched violently starboard, away from the shoreline.

I staggered, reeling across the deck. The starboard rail loomed in front of me, and for an awful moment, I was sure I was going overboard, straight into the water. But a strong arm caught hold of me just as a loud crunching sounded and the boat righted itself suddenly, sending me slamming into Xavier's chest.

He only just managed to catch us both, preventing me from falling to the deck. We stood frozen in position for a moment, my heart hammering and my breath rasping in and out of my mouth. He was also breathing hard, and his other arm came up to encircle me, holding me close.

But Tom and the navigator launched into action, Tom shouting and gesturing as the navigator ran for the port side where I had been standing. Their movement jolted us into action, and we hurried after him, all three of us peering over as we tried to assess the damage.

"It's a long scratch," the navigator called over to Tom. "But it looks like we got lucky this time. It hasn't punched through."

Tom sagged slightly over the wheel. "I knew we picked a thick-hulled boat for a reason. Back to your places!"

We all jumped to obey, Xavier racing back to his usual station on the starboard side.

For almost an hour, we were all unusually alert, the restless energy of the moment of crisis only slowly draining away. But all too soon, the shore began to blur again, the sand turning indistinct, and my eyes imagining stone structures where there were none.

I blinked, rubbing at my eyes and shaking my head to clear it. But when I opened them again, I could still see a shape rising from the sand, like an enormous fortress, though far in the distance.

"Does…does anyone else see that?" I asked in a shaky voice.

I didn't take my eyes from it, so I didn't know if they were looking until Xavier gave a wordless cry of excitement.

"I'm not imagining it, then?" I asked.

"That building must be enormous," Tom said in a tone of respect. "How is it still standing, way out here in the desert after countless generations?"

"We've made good time," Xavier said, a dangerous light in his eyes. "We must have beaten the caravan here. Do you think they've left their base unprotected? Surely there can't be too many more of them out here?"

"You want to go ashore?" Tom sounded doubtful.

"Look at that thing." Xavier met my eyes. "That's not just a rough base in some broken ruins. It's an actual fortress. The desert trader caravans aren't equipped to lay siege to a fortress. We need to get in before the people of the Cobolt caravan return, and this base is back at full strength. It might be our only chance to catch them in a weakened state. Once inside, we can gather intelligence. At the least, we can conceal ourselves and open the gates when the Lanoverian troops arrive with the caravans."

"Are you sure?" Tom asked, his gaze resting uneasily on Xavier.

Of course we shall do so. Puss stalked on deck as if he hadn't been cowering below minutes ago.

Tom sighed and shrugged. "It's your decision. But be warned, we'll be sailing back. We have to report this find."

"Agreed," I said. "We have to get word to Prince Frederic as fast as possible. Just make sure you don't sink yourselves on the way! We'll be counting on you to get those forces here sooner rather than later."

Xavier agreed, and Tom and the navigator huddled in a quick consultation before beginning to adjust the sails. We maneuvered around to face the shore and made our slow way toward it. The navigator made even more use of the sounding line as he felt a route through the reefs to where the water lapped against the sand.

As soon as the water was shallow enough, Xavier and I prepared to jump off, our packs held above our heads. I held out an arm to Puss, but he ignored me and clawed his way up Xavier to drape himself over his shoulder.

Xavier looked startled, turning to me with a question in his eyes.

I suppressed a smile. "You're taller."

Xavier snorted but also refrained from laughing aloud.

"Are you sure about this?" Tom asked one last time. "You'll have no backup, likely for days."

Xavier grinned at him. "We'll just have to make sure we don't get caught." He vaulted over the edge of the boat and splashed down into the shallow water.

CHAPTER 25

After wading fully ashore and watching the boat disappear back out to sea, we turned to face the fortress. Now that we were on land, it was further away than it looked.

"It'll be sunset soon," Xavier said. "We should wait and approach in the dark."

In that case, we'd better position ourselves behind that dune, Puss said. *Unless you want to be seen by anyone looking out a window.*

We hurried to follow his suggestion, sitting side by side on the sand, out of eye line of the fortress. Xavier talked about his childhood, making me laugh with the stories of the antics he and Xander got up to with their sister and Zaria. The crown prince, Tarek, was sometimes a comrade in mischief and sometimes a parent figure. He sounded well matched with my responsible yet fiery friend, a thought that brought me great pleasure. I couldn't wait to see her again and congratulate her in person.

Xavier also coaxed me into telling my own stories—both about my childhood and the years after Zaria left the palace and joined me in our own mischief.

When it finally started to get dark, he took my hand, interlocking our fingers and squeezing gently. "I'm glad she found you after she left. What happened to her was terrible."

I smiled, enjoying the warmth of the contact.

"What about you, Puss?" Xavier asked in a coaxing voice. "You must have plenty of stories from the Palace of Light."

Puss shot him an unimpressed look, but Xavier wasn't abashed.

"What about the horse you mentioned. Arvin, wasn't it? Surely you have stories about adventures with him."

No one who met Arvin would want to go on an adventure with him, Puss meowed caustically. *And cats do not get up to* mischief. His whiskers twitched. *Are you suggesting I'm a dog?*

Both Xavier and I laughed, trying to hide the sound behind coughs. Puss regarded us both with narrowed eyes. *I believe it's dark enough to be moving now.*

We just laughed harder.

He was right, though, as he generally was. We slung our packs onto our shoulders and set off across the sand. A rocky patch just above the waterline provided an easier walking surface until the dark square of the fortress loomed over us, blocking out the moon and stars.

The vast complex was set some way back from the shoreline, and the main entry seemed to face into the desert. We trekked across the sand to reach the smooth stone of the back wall, marveling at how worn it was. And yet somehow it was still standing.

There were neither doors nor windows at ground level, but higher windows dotted the expanse of the wall. Even though I knew they couldn't see me in the darkness at the base of the wall, it still felt like hundreds of eyes watching my every movement.

We picked left at random and worked our way around the structure, looking for a door. We found none.

On the opposite side to the sea, we discovered vast wooden

gates. There was no latch on the outside, however, and they didn't even stir at our attempts to maneuver them open.

"The stone is one thing," Xavier marveled, "but how are wooden gates still in such good condition?"

"There really must be people living here." I ran my hand over the gate. "And they can't have arrived recently. It's as if someone has been maintaining this place all along."

"All along?" Xavier stared at me. "Are you saying you think there's been someone here since the empire fell and the gardens transformed into desert? How could that be possible?"

I flushed. "It doesn't seem likely—I'm just saying that's what the condition of the building suggests."

Puss made a rumbly purring sound, as if pleased with the conversation.

"Do you know something about this place, Puss?" I asked, staring at him. "Is this where you've been wanting to come this entire time?"

Puss merely walked on, continuing our circuit of the structure. With a loaded exchange of glances, Xavier and I followed him.

On the final wall, we found a much smaller wooden side door, and with both of our combined efforts, we managed to prize it open.

"We've damaged the latch." I examined it but could see no easy way to fix it. "If someone finds this, they'll know someone's come in."

Xavier sighed. "It can't be helped now. And we couldn't have stayed out there in the desert for days, anyway. We don't have any shelter, and we didn't bring nearly enough water."

Reluctantly I nodded and trailed him into the fortress. He had already removed two small lanterns that had been attached to the outside of our packs, lighting them both and handing one to me.

I held it up to see a large antechamber, the walls made of the same gray stone as the external wall. It had once had a long strip of carpet and tapestries on the walls, but they had mostly rotted away, everything coated in a thick layer of dust.

Xavier coughed, waving a hand in front of his face to try to clear the dust his feet had disrupted. "What was that about people still living here?"

I grimaced, putting a layer of material over my mouth and nose to filter out the dust. "It doesn't look like it, does it? I must have been wrong."

Humans. Puss walked past us, apparently unbothered by the thick air. *Always judging by appearances.*

He used his nose to nudge open the door on the other side of the room which had been standing ajar. We hurried after him, holding our lanterns ahead of us, my heart pounding as I considered what we might find on the other side.

It was another long hallway in similar condition to the room we'd just left. We walked down it, staying near the wall so as to avoid the rotted line of carpet up the middle.

"This must have been an impressive place once upon a time," I said, my eyes roaming over the ruined splendor.

"There are no signs of a struggle or of damage other than what's been caused by the passage of time." Xavier stuck his head through a side door, holding his lantern through to illuminate the room beyond.

I peered over his shoulder and saw an ancient dining room, the wood of the table and chairs in much worse condition than that of the main gate or side door.

"When was the last time someone ate in this room, do you think?" I asked.

"It must have been a long time." Xavier's eyes were alight with the thrill of discovery. "How long do you think it's been since someone other than us set foot here?"

"What if there's really no one here?" I met his eyes nervously. "We could be bringing everyone across the desert for nothing."

I wouldn't call this nothing, Puss said in a matter-of-fact voice.

"They'll find our dead bodies if there are no supplies here," I said, naming my worst fear.

Xavier stepped to my side, cupping my face in one hand. "Don't worry. A structure of this size must have had an internal water source. We'll find it."

"If it hasn't dried up in the countless generations since anyone used it," I muttered before nodding and resuming the search. Giving up hope didn't serve any purpose.

"Kali, come look at this one," Xavier called from further down the corridor.

I hurried forward to look through the doorway he was standing in. When I saw what was inside, I gasped and stepped into the room.

It must once have been a dressing room of some kind since a number of shoulder height frames displayed outfits of impossibly ancient material. But it was the style of the dresses that shocked me. Every single one of them was a variation on the outfit Evie had made for me to wear to the soiree.

"Incredible," I whispered, the full reality hitting me for the first time. "There really was an empire in the desert lands once, and this was one of their fortresses—an entire small city contained in the one structure. It's…almost unbelievable."

"But you were the one who believed it was possible," Xavier said, a note of pride in his voice. "You were the one who worked out this could be here."

I shook my head. "I just never imagined something like this!"

I touched a corner of the draping material on the nearest outfit, and the material crumbled to dust beneath my fingers. I jumped back before the rest of the outfit disintegrated as well.

"Don't touch them," I said unnecessarily. Neither Puss nor Xavier seemed to have had the same impulse.

I sighed, looking at the beautiful dresses that had been dulled by age and could never be worn again. "I wish Evie could see these. She would be fascinated. There are more variations than shown in the pictures of the book."

"Maybe she can come here one day and see for herself," Xavier said, indicating we should keep searching.

I lingered at the door for a final glance, my lantern held out. Had any of my own ancestors lived here and worn one of those dresses?

I shook myself, trying to dislodge the foolish thoughts. Countless people must have lived in the old empire. Of course these dresses wouldn't have belonged to my own ancestors.

"It's this place," I whispered. "It's such a strange atmosphere, it makes the oddest thoughts seem natural."

Hurrying after Xavier and Puss, I kept to the corridor after that, careful not to enter any of the rooms. We made it across what I estimated to be nearly half of the fortress before Puss froze, sending a warning look back at us.

Xavier immediately extinguished his lantern, and I rushed to do the same, leaving us illuminated only by a thin stream of moonlight through a nearby, dirty window, high up in the wall.

A shuffling sound reached my ears, and despite my intentions to throw off the unsettling feeling of earlier, I shrank closer to Xavier. He put an arm out, as if to shield me, and I shamelessly hid behind it.

I could feel the tension in his frame, but neither of us moved again, poised waiting to hear any further sound of movement. The light trip of footsteps preceded the appearance of a small figure, the height of a child.

The golden skin of her face and arms was hard to see in the dim light of the hallway, and she wore dark clothes. But her eyes stood out starkly, widening as they peered into the shadows where we lurked.

I had to suppress a rising giggle. From her appearance, you would think we were the unknown terror, lurking in the deserted fortress.

Mreeow. Puss ambled forward into a patch of clearer moonlight.

The girl gasped, staring at him, transfixed. He strolled up to her and butted against her leg, purring with satisfaction.

"Look at you!" she murmured, her words accented but understandable. "I've never seen a handsome creature like you around here."

Mreeow, Puss said again, as if pleased with her praises.

I stared at the picture they created, too shocked to speak even if I hadn't been trying to hide. What was happening? Had Puss come under some strange enchantment in this forsaken place? I had never seen him act so much like a cat.

"If you come with me," the girl said, "I'll find you a treat."

Puss's purrs deepened, and he rubbed his head against her legs again. The girl bent over and picked him up around his middle, carrying him awkwardly, the bulk of the unnaturally large cat overspilling her arms. She looked delighted, though, despite his weight, and he continued to purr as if he'd suddenly discovered the meaning and joy of life.

The girl scurried away, further into the fortress, no longer interested in figures that moved in the shadows. We waited in frozen silence until all sound of her passage had ceased.

"What," I said slowly, "in all the kingdoms, was that?"

"Have...have you ever seen him like that?" Xavier asked, seemingly equally shocked despite his shorter acquaintance with Puss.

"Uh uh, never." I stared down the corridor although they were long gone from sight. "But...who was the girl, Xavier? She can't possibly be living here on her own. Where would she have come from?"

"There are people here after all." He hadn't moved from his defensive stance in front of me. "And they have Puss. We'll have to move much more carefully."

Neither of us said anything about it, but both of us reached for the other, linking hands and not letting go as we crept after the girl, our lanterns left unlighted. But as we got deeper into the fortress, the moonlight grew stronger as the windows became less dirty. We even discovered an internal, open courtyard, the regular doors and windows opening into it providing extra moonlight.

Xavier stopped by one of the doors. "If I had to guess, I would say the water source is in that central courtyard. It's probably a spring of some type."

"We have enough water for now," I said. "We can wait to get a better idea of what's going on here before we risk going out in the open like that."

After a moment's consideration, Xavier agreed, and we continued forward. The dust had disappeared by that point, and the old, rotten carpet had been stripped from the floor, leaving plain, worn stone.

We were both moving so slowly that at the sound of footsteps, we easily whisked ourselves through the closest door. Leaving it slightly ajar, Xavier peered back out to the corridor while I turned slowly to examine the room.

With a gasp, I tapped at Xavier's back, not taking my eyes from the room. He shook his head, though, not changing position. Whatever he was seeing was equally shocking.

When the footsteps receded, he finally turned, freezing as soon as he took the room in properly.

"There are definitely people here," we both said at the same moment.

"That was an adult woman who just walked past," he said. "She looked like she was carrying a basket of clean laundry."

"And this room is definitely lived in." I eyed the fresh looking sheets and soft blanket on the bed. "We're fortunate there wasn't someone in here!"

We progressed even more slowly after that, sneaking our way through the section of the fortress closest to the front gates. To all appearances, it could have been a building inside any of the Four Kingdoms. Only the absence of the accents and familiar details of home differentiated it from Kuralan. It certainly looked nothing like the creepy, deserted ruin we had first entered.

Given the hour, we didn't encounter many other people, but a cozy kitchen still contained the remains of a warm fire, and we were able to find enough fresh bread that a small portion wouldn't be missed. The only people we did pass were three women and another two children. Neither were the girl we had first seen, however, and we caught no sign of Puss. They were all dressed in an ordinary style of clothing that would have passed in the streets of any town in Lanover, the colors mostly drab browns and creams. They might live in a magnificent building, but their lives looked far from luxurious.

We spent at least half the night searching before the exertions of the day overcame me.

"We have to rest," I whispered to Xavier. "I'm going to make a mistake otherwise."

"Where do you want to go?" he asked. "Back outside?"

I shook my head vigorously. "From the dust, these people don't use some portions of this place. We should be able to find somewhere in the unused section."

He frowned, looking back the way we had come. "I think we should keep going. It looks like they're living in the central portion, so I suspect there's another unused area just beyond here."

I agreed, leading the way forward again. His prediction was proved right as the dust levels grew again. When the crumbled carpet reappeared, we walked along it this time, obscuring any footprints we might leave behind on the dusty stone sections beside it.

Eventually we'd gone far enough to feel safe, so we stopped at the first empty room we found. The absence of either carpet or furniture meant lowered levels of dust, although it was still a far from welcoming environment. But we had brought blankets, at least, which we laid out on the ground.

"I can take the first watch," Xavier said. "I don't think we should both sleep at the same time."

Reluctantly I agreed with this assessment. I just wished I wasn't leaving it to him to go first. But I didn't think I'd be able to stay awake if I tried.

"Make sure you wake me," I said sternly. "Don't try anything heroic. You have to get some sleep."

"Yes, my lady," he said meekly, and I pushed him lightly in the shoulder.

He caught my hand in his, using it to pull me close. Wrapping me in his arms, he rested his chin on the top of my head and sighed. I rested my cheek against his chest and mirrored his sigh.

"Do you think he's all right?" I asked softly. "I keep thinking of how he looked when she carried him off. What have they done to him? And how?"

"He's from the Palace of Light," Xavier said in a bolstering tone. "Of course he'll be all right."

Naturally I will be just fine as soon as the two of you stop that unnecessary display, a familiar voice meowed.

CHAPTER 26

We leaped apart, my hand flying to my chest. "Puss! Where did you come from?"

He gave me an incredulous look. *I just walked through the doorway. Where else would I have come from?*

"But...what happened to you? You turned into a...well, a regular cat!"

A regular cat? Puss's eyes bulged as he looked at me. *You think that's how a regular cat behaves? Have you met any self-respecting cats?*

"Was it all an act, then?" Xavier stared at him in fascination. "But *why?*"

I should think that was obvious. Puss strolled over to a central place on the laid-out blankets and lay down. *Were you planning to spend days creeping around trying to see what's going on here?*

Xavier and I exchanged a look.

"Well," I said, "I suppose, yes, we were..."

Unnecessary. This is a community that usually holds about eighty people. Fifty of them are out with the so-called Caravan Cobolt, and most of those who remain are children, along with a few women and one man.

"You learned all that already?" I asked, sitting beside him.

Naturally. I was also fed some choice morsels for dinner and discovered that the one man who remains here—the self-styled emperor—has given a deadline for the return of the caravan. And that deadline is tomorrow.

"We already knew that," Xavier muttered rebelliously.

Did you know that the children here all hate him? And the women likely do as well, to a lesser degree, although they hide their emotions better.

"If they hate him, why do they let him call himself their emperor?" I reached out a daring hand and scratched Puss behind one ear.

He leaned into my hand. *According to the child you saw—an accommodating girl who explained everything to me—these people have been living in this fortress since the High King overturned the empire and left it a wasteland. The other inhabitants fled into what is now Ardasira and Kuralan or took up a nomadic lifestyle, but the ancestors of these people were the most fiercely loyal to the High King. They were the ones who stood against the third brother from the beginning, and they had already fled to this fortress on the coast. Here they were protected from the destruction. Even the building itself was protected from the passage of time.*

Xavier raised an eyebrow. "Whatever protection may once have existed seems to be running out—faster in some parts than others from the look of it."

"If they're running around Lanover stealing and murdering everyone they meet, then their descendants have stepped out of the High King's protection," I said fiercely.

Precisely. Puss stretched himself out. *The abundant gardens in the inner courtyard are now barren. The nearby seas no longer provide fish, and the nearest jungle is empty of game. Even the people themselves have dwindled, their numbers declining rapidly in recent generations. But those who remain have survived by being intensely devoted to their shared history and to their leaders—who they believe to be the remaining true line of rulers.*

"And so they're blindly following this current emperor," I said in disgust.

"Not the children," Xavier said thoughtfully. "So there's hope for change."

Do you plan to sit around here for twenty years waiting for it? Puss asked caustically.

Xavier chuckled. "Hardly. It's just a thought. Cobolt has committed atrocities, but perhaps not everyone bears equal responsibility for them."

"We can worry about that when they're facing justice," I said. "For now, there are only two of us and a great many more of them."

Puss gave a warning rumble in the back of his throat, and I quickly corrected myself. "Three of us, I mean."

"If the caravan is coming back tomorrow, we have to do something." Xavier paced across the room, sending up little eddies of dust. "It sounds like we should tackle this emperor. Given the honor guard left behind, we shouldn't have too much trouble."

Puss growled. *Just because they are women and children doesn't mean they're weak. And they may not like the man himself, but they are devoted to what he represents. Would you hurt them to get to him?*

"No, of course not," Xavier said quickly. "We'll just have to find him when he's alone."

There's only one time when that occurs, Puss meowed.

"Did that girl really tell you all this?" I asked doubtfully. "You just revealed your enchanted nature to her, and she started telling you all their weaknesses?"

Puss gave a contemptuous sound that was half yowl, half growl. *Of course I did not. What do you take me for?* He grinned. *The poor girl was in great need of a companion, and I merely proved an appealing one. She was more than eager to explain to her new pet all about her life in the big castle.*

"So that was the reason for the act!" Xavier cried, as if that was the part of the whole business that had most been weighing on him. "Very stealthily done, Sir Puss."

I must return to her now, he said. *Before she wakes and finds me missing. But tomorrow, at the midday meal, come to the large banquet hall. The emperor feasts there alone each day.*

"He would," I muttered, thinking of his grandiose title and the things that had been done in his name.

Kali, you should wear your gown from the soiree, Puss added, making me stare.

"My dress from the soiree? But naturally I didn't pack that!"

Haven't you looked through your whole pack? Evie seemed a reasonably reliable girl to me.

"Do you mean you asked her to pack it?" I asked, digging through my pack. It was true that down the bottom had been a couple of fancy gowns that I hadn't needed on board the ship and therefore hadn't touched.

Sure enough, hidden beneath them was the aqua silk of the soiree outfit.

"Unbelievable." I pulled it out.

Don't get it out here, do you want it all dusty before tomorrow? Puss gave me a long-suffering look, and I quickly shoved it back into the pack.

"It's a good thing it doesn't crease," I muttered, as he stood and stretched, wandering out of the room without any further farewell.

I stood, but Puss didn't return.

I gave Xavier a sad look. "I want to give you a goodnight hug, but I feel like if I do, Puss will instantly reappear to make a disgusted remark."

Xavier laughed. "In that case, lie straight down and go to sleep. Morning will be here all too soon."

With a reluctant final glance at him, I lay down on the hard floor and wondered how much Puss had already known about this place before we came. And how was I going to sleep after his revelations?

The next thing I knew, Xavier was crouched beside me, shaking me gently awake. I sat up abruptly, looking from Xavier's face to the room's one window.

"That's daylight," I said accusingly, and he chuckled.

"Don't worry, sleeping beauty, it's only dawn. There's still plenty of time for me to sleep." He leaned in daringly and stole a kiss, his lips gone before I had time to realize they were there.

We both looked expectantly toward the door, but Puss didn't appear. Xavier looked back at me with a wicked twinkle in his eye and leaned in close again.

I laughed and evaded him. "No, you don't! You must be exhausted. Lie down and sleep!"

"Yes, my lady," he said meekly, his eyes lingering on my face in a way that made me blush.

But within moments of laying his head down on a rolled jacket, his breathing deepened, the even breaths indicating he had been more tired than he was letting on.

I stationed myself by the slightly ajar door, where I could listen for anyone coming down the corridor. Refreshed by the sleep, despite the hard floor I had used as a bed, I thought back over everything that had brought us here. The more I thought on it, the clearer it seemed that Puss's hand had been involved in leading us here from the beginning.

I was convinced Taylan had reached Largo on our own ship, and Puss had spoken with certainty about his not being there after he disembarked. Did that mean the cat had known Taylan was there the whole journey and hadn't revealed his hiding place to us?

A surge of anger quickly died. Taylan hadn't been in league with Cobolt from the beginning. It was only after arriving in Largo that he received the information on how to find the false traders—information that must have been procured at his request by his cousins.

Leaving him free had allowed me to follow him to the false traders. Of course, it had also led to his murder, but even Puss couldn't have known that would be the outcome. He didn't know the future.

But he had sent me back to the ship where not only Xavier but Captain Tom also waited. Had he always intended us to come by boat?

I massaged my head. And he had told Evie to pack my new outfit. It was all too big to properly comprehend.

"If this was all your plan, Puss," I whispered, "what comes next?"

No one answered.

I woke Xavier before the sun reached its peak, although I changed into my gown before I did so. He woke quickly, leaping up and giving me an admiring look.

"Did I tell you that night how stunning you look in that?" he asked in a deep voice.

I flushed. "No, I don't think you did. We had more important things to talk about."

He pulled me closer. "Are you sure? I can't seem to think of anything more important right now…"

He leaned down slowly, his eyes devouring my face before he gently pressed his lips to mine.

Really? You're worse every time I see you, Puss said from the doorway, making us jump apart again.

"You do that on purpose," Xavier said in wrathful tones.

I don't know what you're talking about, Puss meowed loftily. *I merely came to check you were ready. Come with me.*

"I thought we were supposed to meet you at the banquet hall," I said.

I don't leave things to chance, Puss said, making me narrow my eyes as I followed him down the corridor.

"Does that mean you're responsible for my meeting Xavier?" I asked, struck by the discomfiting thought that Puss might be behind Xavier's and my connection as well.

Do I look like a godmother? he asked in horrified tones. *It's not my job to facilitate true love.*

"So you're saying our love is true and acknowledged by the Palace of Light?" Xavier asked promptly.

Puss glanced back at him with a forbidding expression. *I believe I already said I'm not a godmother. I have quite enough to do with them already, and I won't be pulled into any such business. Ask yours, if you want to know.*

"I will," Xavier said, and Puss froze, fixing him with a suspicious look.

But don't you go calling one now. We don't need any of their interfering here.

I laughed. "Don't worry, Puss. We won't let anyone steal your glory."

Puss humphed, but he also turned back and resumed walking, his tail twitching with satisfaction. I suppressed a smile and followed.

He led us confidently through the inhabited parts of the fortress, somehow leading us up empty staircases and down deserted corridors, so that we ran into no one.

"I really wish I knew how he does that," Xavier muttered, and I silently agreed.

We eventually reached a small room that contained only two doors. Puss crossed to the second one, turning to give me a pointed look when I didn't immediately join him.

"Is that the banquet hall through there?" I whispered.

Puss nodded, his own voice quiet as well. *I will go through first. Xavier you follow after a minute or so. I recommend you draw your sword before you do.*

Xavier obediently pulled it free.

Kali, you remain here.

"What?" I gasped, glaring at him. "You want me to just wait here?"

For now. You will know the right moment to appear.

"I'll know the right moment to appear?" I sputtered, only just remembering to keep my voice lowered.

Puss turned to Xavier with a pointed look, and he leaped to open the door for the cat, giving me an apologetic smile as he passed.

"Traitor," I muttered. He was much too pleased about leaving me back here in safety.

Puss strolled through the door as calmly as if he was merely going for a morning walk. He gave no indication that we needed to close the door behind him, so Xavier left it open, and we both peered through at the room beyond.

A large hall stretched out in front of us, dominated by an enormous wooden table. Its surface had been polished until it shone, and a whole row of silver candelabra ran down the center, although there was plenty of light from the many windows which gave a sweeping view across the ocean.

Dishes had been laid out across one end of the table, enough to feed a whole party of people although only one chair was occupied. At the head of the table, a man sat with his back to us, only the top of his head visible above the elaborate chair.

The only other people in the room were two children, a girl and a boy, who stood at attention, one on each side of the table. Their eyes were glued on the man, clearly awaiting any commands. Xavier snorted softly beside me, clearly unimpressed with a man who used children as servers.

Puss made his slow way across the room, capturing one child's attention and then the other. Their eyes widened, and they exchanged panicked looks. The man didn't respond, presumably too absorbed in his meal to notice the cat.

When Puss finally reached the table, he didn't hesitate, leaping gracefully onto its surface. The man cursed, jerking back in his chair.

"What is this?" he cried, leaping to his feet.

"It's…it's Jessie's cat," the boy said in a voice that was suppressing either fear or anger. After Puss's comments the night before, I couldn't be sure which.

The man stared at Puss, but Puss paid him no attention, too busy examining a nearby plate of steamed fish.

Mreeow, he said, crouching down to tear at the fish with his teeth, exactly like a regular cat would.

"How does he do that?" Xavier asked in an admiring whisper.

The man, whose posture had been tense, slowly relaxed.

"Well, well," he said. "I didn't realize any of the old rat catchers were left alive. But you're a magnificent beast. A cat fit for an emperor indeed."

He picked Puss up off the table, and the cat purred. The man laughed and sat back in his chair, Puss now across his lap. He looked toward the boy.

"You may tell Jessie the cat is now mine."

The boy gulped. "Yes, Your Imperial Majesty."

"Your Imperial Majesty?" I whispered. "Seriously? From a child? While he's dining alone? Has he looked at this place lately?"

Xavier put a calming hand on my arm, giving me a warning look.

"I think that's my cue," he said.

Holding his sword in a casual manner that belied the tension I could see in his muscles, he strolled into the room.

Again, the children were the first to see him. Both of them leaped back, the girl screaming. The emperor surged to his feet, whipping around to see what had startled them.

The action should have sent Puss flying, but somehow he scrambled up the man's side, draping himself across his shoulders as he usually did to me. The emperor seemed too shocked at Xavier's appearance to even notice the cat was still there.

Xavier stepped closer, and the man growled.

"Stop! Whoever you are, and however you came here, I command you to stop in the name of the emperor!"

Xavier stepped forward again. "I know no empire, and I acknowledge no emperor."

Now that he had turned, I could see the self-titled emperor clearly for the first time. But he was far too distracted to see me, lurking just outside the room. He had the same golden skin and sleek black hair as Xavier and I did, although his resemblance to me ended there. Where I was short, he was tall, his shoulders broad and his brow pronounced.

For all his assumed authority, he hesitated at the appearance of an unexpected man with the bearing of a soldier. But when Xavier took yet another step forward, he launched into action. Throwing himself sideways, he snatched at the girl and pulled her in front of him as a shield.

I expected her to scream and fight, but she accepted his actions meekly, although her face turned ashen.

Xavier immediately stopped, the air around him seeming to crackle with tension.

"Are you a coward, emperor?" he asked in a soft, yet deadly voice. "You must be one if you hide behind a child."

"I am the emperor," he said, "descended in a direct line from the grandfather of the three brothers. I have authority here, and you will not challenge me." His eyes flicked sideways to the boy, who received whatever silent signal he'd sent, fleeing the room.

Xavier hesitated, glancing at Puss. But Puss didn't respond, still lying calmly across the emperor's shoulders. I could see Xavier's frustration, and his longing to act, but the entire scene was so surreal that it was impossible to trust the man at the center of it. He seemed all too likely to take an action that we would consider unhinged in the extreme.

A chorus of voices and pounding feet sounded just before the boy burst back into the room, people streaming through behind him. A small collection of women came first, followed by a crowd of children, all shouting angrily.

I barely had time to feel relief that someone had come to protect the girl when I registered their actions. Far from challenging the emperor for his unconscionable action, they bunched themselves between Xavier and his target, facing Xavier defiantly, their bodies providing a larger shield than one frail girl.

Xavier fell back a step, clearly as much at a loss as I was. Puss had been serious when he said these people's loyalty overrode their personal feelings toward the man himself.

My eyes sought the cat, just visible above the gathered crowd due to the emperor's height. Puss was looking straight at me, his eyes seeming to beckon me forward. I gulped. This was the moment Puss had been waiting for?

Shaking my head in bewilderment, I stepped out into the room. At first no one noticed me, so intent were they on Xavier. But then a child looked up, followed by another.

Both of them screamed, attracting the attention of everyone else, and soon the whole room was shouting or screaming, as if I was their childhood nightmare come to life instead of one ordinary girl.

Several of them turned to look at something on the wall, its position having previously obscured it from my vision. I wanted to look, but I also didn't want to take my attention off the screaming mass of people.

Out of the corner of my eye, I saw Xavier turn to look, however, a strange stillness coming over him as soon as he did.

"K…Kali…" he stammered.

I turned my head, my eyes latching on to an enormous portrait on the left wall. A strange, cold sensation washed over me, and for a second, a ringing in my ears drowned out the shock of the crowd.

It was a painting of me.

CHAPTER 27

I blinked and blinked again. With the first moment of shock gone, I could see the differences. The woman in the portrait was clearly older, her face lined where mine was not, and her outfit—though similar in style to mine—was a deep purple. Her cheekbones were a slightly different shape as well, and my nose turned up slightly more than hers did.

Still, it was an unsettling likeness. My eyes drifted to the man painted at her side, her hand placed on his arm, and I sucked in a second shocked breath. Bernard. Or an older version with some of the same subtle changes as between the woman and me.

"Who are those people?" I asked, but my quiet voice was lost in the loud hubbub that had followed the screaming.

Behold! Puss shouted, his voice reverberating around the room and bringing instant silence. *Her Imperial Highness, the Empress Kalila, true heir of the last great emperor.*

"Impossible!" the emperor shouted. "Who said that?"

He was looking in all directions, trying to identify the culprit. Everyone could see that Xavier hadn't spoken, and it had clearly not been the voice of a child or a woman. But even though Puss was draped over his shoulders, he never suspected the cat.

"It was the emperor himself!" one of the women shouted, a strange, martial light in her eyes. "He spoke from the painting to name his true daughter." She turned to me and threw herself to the floor at my feet. "Your Imperial Majesty!"

The rest of the women and children dropped in her wake, the floor a sudden carpet of people. Only the girl gripped in the emperor's tight hold remained upright.

With the barrier between us removed, her eyes met mine, her own wide and scared. But although no words were exchanged, a light came into hers, bringing life where before there had only been resignation.

Without warning, she sprang into violent motion, flailing within the man's grip so intensely that she broke his hold and sprang free.

"What are you doing?" he shouted, his face burning with rage. "Protect your emperor!"

"We serve the true heir!" one of the women said. "We serve the Empress Kalila."

"Wait, I'm not—" I started to say, but Puss gave me such a fierce glare that I subsided.

The man wasn't finished, however. Drawing a dagger from his belt, he leaped toward the nearest woman, grabbing her hair and using it to pull her up toward him while she screamed and tried to wrench herself free.

Xavier leaped toward them, his sword up, but he wasn't the only one to spring into motion. The ginger bundle across the emperor's shoulders turned into a whirlwind of fur and claws, scratching at the man's face and throat.

He screamed, dropping his dagger as he clawed at the cat clamped to his head. Staggering backward, he crossed the room, blind to everything but his struggle with Puss.

"Watch out!" I screamed, but he was cursing too loudly to hear any warning.

Colliding with one of the tall windows, he smashed the

ancient glass, wobbling once before toppling through the opening and out of sight.

"Puss!" I picked up my skirts and ran toward the broken window.

Xavier caught me around the waist just as I leaned dangerously out of the jagged opening, peering down. On the distant sand below, the body of the self-styled emperor lay crumpled and still.

I could see no sign of a cat, however. Had the emperor landed on top of him?

"Puss!" I screamed again.

There is no need to deafen me, said a cranky meow. *A hand would be much more welcome.*

I gasped and turned slightly to see Puss standing on a small ledge just below the window, not so much as a hair out of place. Laughing and sobbing at the same time, I carefully reached through the pieces of broken glass still clinging to the frame.

Puss took a flying leap and scrambled up my arm and into the room. I caught him and clutched him to my chest, burying my face in his fur despite his growls of protest.

"I thought you were dead," I said in a trembly voice, and he stilled, allowing me to pet him for a moment.

When I pulled my head up and sniffed, he gave me a stern look.

You may put me down now.

"Cat, you can speak!" A girl stood staring at him.

"Jessie?" I asked, on a guess.

She nodded without taking her eyes off Puss. "Do you belong to the empress?"

I laughed. "I think I belong to him."

She frowned but relaxed when Puss spoke. *Naturally I belong to Empress Kalila. Is it surprising that an empress would have a talking cat?*

The girl shook her head vigorously, and I glared at the shameless cat. He merely began to wash one of his paws.

I expected the crowd around us to be shocked and traumatized at the sudden and unexpected death of their ruler. But the mood in the room was growing more and more celebratory. The people crowded around me, stopping just short of actually touching me as they exclaimed and cried and promised loyalty.

The entire spectacle made my skin itch, but every attempt to protest was drowned out. Before I knew it, I was seated at the head of the table, many voices insisting I eat.

Finally giving up, I decided on my first command as empress.

"Someone fetch some more plates. Everyone will sit and eat. There is plenty of food for all."

"Really?" Jessie asked. "Are you sure?"

I glared at her. "Are you questioning your empress's orders?"

Her eyes grew wide, and she shook her head even more vigorously than she had done last time, running to a seat half way down the table and plonking herself into it.

"Admit it," Xavier breathed in my ear, leaning over me. "You enjoyed giving orders at least a little bit."

I laughed, but several women nearby drew in shocked breaths, their eyes lingering on Xavier's nearness to me.

I searched for the right thing to say, not wanting to see them turn on him next. "You may relax," I said, in my most regal voice. "This is Prince Xavier of Kuralan, my betrothed."

They all drew back respectfully, giving curtsies in Xavier's direction. I heard the words *prince* and *betrothed* travel down the table which was already filling with women and children.

"You know, it's a great relief to hear you say that," Xavier said conversationally. "You never officially accepted my proposal earlier, and I was starting to fear you were only using me for my good looks."

I narrowed my eyes at him, muttering threats as he laughingly took the seat at my right hand.

"I really need to tell them that I'm not their new ruler," I whispered to Puss who had leaped up onto the arm of my chair.

Are you sure about that? he asked quietly. *Or have you forgotten that Caravan Cobolt is due to arrive this afternoon? You might want to save any confessions until after your own reinforcements arrive.*

"But I can't keep lying to these people," I hissed. "Not like this!"

Who said anything about lying? Puss returned to the fish he had earlier abandoned. *Don't you listen to a word I say? How many times have I said that you're descended from emperors? The proof is right there on the wall. That is the emperor and empress most famous for having three sons—you're descended from the middle one.*

"Descended from the middle son? Are you telling me I actually have royal ancestors?" I gasped.

I've only been telling you that since the beginning. Puss glared at me, clearly not appreciating the interruption to his meal.

I looked at the portrait again, trying to absorb the information that my ancestor had been an emperor. But so many generations had passed since then. Did my distant lineage really have any meaning? Given the time involved, even the resemblance seemed unnatural.

I turned back to Puss. "How is it possible that I look so much like the ancient empress? That isn't how family likenesses usually work."

Puss gave me another impatient look. *Surely you don't think it a coincidence? The High King's plans don't rely on chance. I have no doubt he was laying the seeds to reclaim the Fortress long before he assigned me my mission. Do you think it beyond him to ensure a descendant was born at the right time with the right appearance?*

I gaped at him. Was Puss saying the High King was responsible for how I looked? That from the moment of my birth, he had intended me to claim my place as empress here?

"But...I can't rule these people. That's ridiculous!" A sudden thought occurred to me, and I struggled to keep my voice at a whisper. "I'm not the true empress anyway! My brother is older than me. Shouldn't he be the emperor?"

He already abdicated, Puss said glibly.

"Abdicated?" I stared at him in growing wrath. "Are you telling me Bernard knew why you wanted him to cross the desert?"

Of course not, Puss said, just as calmly. *That would hardly have helped my case. But he clearly stated he had no intention of ever setting foot in the desert, let alone beyond, and that he relinquished all claim to his mother's heritage.*

I eyed him suspiciously. "That doesn't sound like an official abdication."

Puss growled in impatience. *Does anything about this situation strike you as a formal legal process? The empire is gone. There is nothing left to rule that warrants any title at all, and there is no institution or army to pass judgment on succession. The only thing that matters is that the man wearing the crown did* not *have a true claim to it. I will use any tool necessary to make these people recognize that truth. Even if it means turning you into their new ruler.*

"I might be a closer heir than their previous emperor," I said in increasing desperation, "but I have no training or experience in leadership."

"You don't have to remain their ruler," Xavier said in a whisper. "I think the High King only intended you to free them. But I think Sir Puss is right, and you'll have to play the role of empress for a short while. We're going to have to tread carefully before this Gage returns."

He had spoken the final sentence a little too loudly, and the name spread in whispered ripples down the table.

"Of course they will all recognize our true ruler," one of the women said to another, but her voice was uneasy.

"Do you believe Gage will accept it?" the woman replied. "No more than his brother did." She nodded toward the window.

His brother? I exchanged worried glances with Xavier.

"He won't let the others get close enough to see her face," the second woman said. "He'd rather drive a blade through her heart, the blackguard."

My stomach roiled as the image of Gage doing exactly that to Taylan danced before my eyes.

"We'll protect her," one of the children said fiercely, and fear shot through me.

"No, no," I started to say, but Puss's soft growl cut me off. "What am I supposed to tell them, then?" I whispered to him in my most irritated voice. "Since you're the one masterminding everything, what's your plan to get us out of this situation?"

My task is complete, he said. *I have delivered the miller's child—the true descendant of emperors—to the Fortress.*

"What?" I stared at him.

You are empress here. You may direct your people as you see fit.

"I may…what?" I stood up, wrath on my face, and every other person in the room except Xavier also leaped to their feet.

"Oh, never mind," I said hurriedly, sinking back into my chair. "Please, all sit down."

Puss gave me an infuriatingly knowing look and returned to his fish.

"That cat," I muttered quietly. "That mangy, good-for-nothing, flea bitten—"

Xavier cut me off. "If Sir Puss won't help us, we need another plan. And we need one fast."

I looked down the table at the line of women and children, the young ones all chattering excitedly as they helped themselves to the array of dishes on offer. An hour ago, I'd been a fugitive in an unknown fortress, and suddenly I was a ruler with people depending on my judgment to determine whether they lived or died. It was too much.

"You can do this," Xavier said softly, his gaze catching and holding mine. "Remember to follow your instincts. You have better ones than you think."

I drew a deep breath and closed my eyes, trying to think. Follow my instincts? What were they saying?

I expected them to be telling me to run far away and hide, but instead a fierce determination was rising within me. A desire to stand and face my enemy head on. But that was foolishness. I had seen Gage, and he would trample me into the ground in seconds. I wasn't like Xavier. I wasn't tall and muscled, trained to wield a sword. And even if I was, I couldn't face the whole force of Caravan Cobolt, not even with Xavier's assistance.

And yet, still my instincts said to stand and face him.

Face. My eyes were drawn to the portrait of a face unlike, and yet also strangely like, mine. What was it the woman had said? That Gage wouldn't let the others in the caravan get close enough to see my face. If that was true, then facing them was exactly what I needed to do. I needed to find a way to show myself to them.

I beckoned down the table to the two women from the earlier conversation, and they both leaped to their feet and hurried to stand beside me.

"Do you know who in the caravan will stay loyal to Gage?" I asked. "There must be some who won't be swayed by seeing my face."

"Traitors any one of them," one of the women said fiercely, and the other nodded.

I inclined my head, trying to look as regal as possible. "And yet, I am sure their numbers exist. I need to know how many and if you know who."

The two women exchanged a look, their brows furrowed in such identical looks of concentration that I concluded they must be sisters.

"I would say ten," one of them finally announced. "And we

know them well enough. The others have wives or sisters here, or they went with the caravan reluctantly. We couldn't gainsay the emperor's orders, but it was hard to understand how lying and stealing was in keeping with the old ways."

"He said it was part of a bigger plan," the other said, "but it never sat right with me."

"A bigger plan?" I frowned. "What bigger plan?"

"To unite the desert peoples under their ruler again." This time both women smiled, clearly in agreement with this part of the old emperor's plot.

"The desert trader caravans you mean?" I asked. "They acknowledge no ruler except the caravan heads."

"Exactly." Both women nodded.

"But if the kingdoms turned against them, they would see the need to unite," Xavier said. "And that's when the supposed heir planned to reappear, a Fortress refuge at his command with a treasury full of gold."

I blinked. "Did he think that would work? The traders treasure the freedom their nomad life brings them."

"They couldn't maintain that life if the trading networks were closed to them, though," Xavier said. "The desert is too dead for that. In dire circumstances, it's possible they would welcome a homeland of their own, if only to provide a ruler who could negotiate with King Leonardo on their behalf. It's at least possible it would have worked. But only as long as they didn't realize their so-called emperor had engineered the entire situation."

"Naturally none of us would have betrayed him," one of the women said. "Not until we realized he'd been betraying us all along, claiming a throne that was never his. He said he was the only living heir. It's the only reason we followed him."

"And most of those with Caravan Cobolt will feel like you?" I asked.

They nodded, speaking over the top of each other to assure me it was so.

"What are you thinking?" Xavier asked, a crease in his brow.

"Don't worry," I said. "If this plan works, I don't need to put myself in danger."

"If it works." Xavier grimaced. "I don't like the sound of that."

"Dust!" The shout came from the window.

I twisted around to see one of the children had snuck away from the table to peer down at their old ruler's body. His eyes were now trained on the horizon, though, as he craned to see at an angle.

"It's the caravan!" Other voices took up the cry, as everyone surged around me, some wringing their hands while others took up fighting stances.

"Silence!" I shouted, and instant stillness fell. I took a deep breath. "If they're already nearly here, then we need to move fast. Are the front gates locked and barred?"

Several heads nodded.

"Is there any way to open them from the outside?"

The same heads shook from side to side.

My mind raced as I thought through the various angles. "Who knows the location of the side door?"

It wasn't in a part of the Fortress they used, and there had been no footsteps in the dust near it, so I wasn't surprised when the women all exchanged confused looks.

Only Jessie stepped forward, a nervous look on her face. A smile spread over my face. Here was an explorer at heart, like me.

"Take several people with you," I said. "Including some adults. The latch has been broken, and Gage may know of the door's existence. Use furniture—whatever you can find—and secure it."

She nodded, swelling with pride at being assigned the task.

I'll go with her. Puss jumped down from the table. *In case she loses her way.*

I hid my smile. Puss would never confess to feeling any affection toward the girl, but his actions spoke for him.

"And what of you?" Xavier asked.

"We need that portrait." I pointed at the wall. "So we'll need a ladder and several strong adults."

The remaining women launched into action, several running from the room while the others gathered near the wall, looking up at the portrait with its heavy frame and murmuring plans for transporting it.

I joined them. "Where's the best place to stand on the walls—somewhere visible from in front of the main gate?"

"There's a walkway all around the top of the Fortress," one of the women said. I wished I knew their names, but there was no time to stop for introductions now.

"Yes," another agreed. "If you stand in the middle, anyone at the gates will see you."

I looked up at the heavy portrait. "They'll need to see the portrait too. Can we get a chair up there? Or something else we can prop it up on?"

Once again, people sprang to obey my every suggestion. I grabbed Xavier's arm in the flurry of movement, sagging into him.

He slipped his arm around my waist, supporting me. "What is it?" His whisper was urgent, concerned. "What's wrong?"

"What if this doesn't work?" I whispered back. "All these

people are relying on me. And if I get it wrong, they'll throw themselves into harm's way to try to protect me. It isn't right!"

Xavier's hold tightened. "No, it isn't," he murmured. "But don't let yourself think about it. When this is all over, and everyone's safe, there will be time for thinking about how to keep them all safe in the future. But they've been trained to think this way, and it's not something that can be changed in an instant. So stop thinking yourself, and just follow your instincts."

"But what if they're wrong?" I asked in an even lower voice.

"Trust yourself, Kali," he said. "Who knew you needed to keep climbing that mast? Did anyone tell you to do it?"

"I saw the smoke and knew I had to go up," I said.

"You knew it was smoke?"

I shook my head slowly. "No, I just knew something was wrong."

He smiled and tapped me on the head. "Your brain is a beautiful thing, Kali. Let it do what it needs to do and stop getting in its way."

I laughed and pushed myself away from him. But his confidence was refreshing, filling me with a buoyancy I'd been missing before.

He slipped his hand into mine. "Don't worry. I'll be by your side the whole way."

I squeezed his hand back before pulling myself free and directing the ladies who had returned with two ladders. One of the children had gone to a better vantage point to look for the caravan, and he came racing back into the banquet hall.

"They'll be here in ten minutes, I think."

"Faster!" I yelled, and everyone responded.

Eight people—two on each side—carried the portrait up the remaining stairs to the top of the Fortress.

"Thank goodness the banquet hall isn't on the bottom level," I said as they maneuvered it out the door onto the wide walkway.

A view stretched out in all directions, allowing me to see over the wall and across the desert, as well as back down into the inner courtyard. A waist high stone barrier ran on both sides, but when the wind plucked at my gown, our position still felt insecure.

I paused, letting the rush of energy from the fear fill me, sending my mind whirring even faster than before. I would use it to my advantage.

"Where's Puss?" I asked Xavier. "We need him here!"

"I'll find him." Xavier raced away toward the stairs, and I nearly called him back, feeling his absence from my side.

But I held the words in. There were more important things than my comfort right now.

"Put the chairs there," I directed the two women who puffed their way up the final stairs, chairs in tow.

Working together, we positioned the chairs and lifted the heavy portrait up. I stood back to examine its height.

"You won't be able to see the whole thing," I said. "But you'll see the face and most of the gown. That's what matters."

A third woman put down another chair next to the portrait and gestured for me to sit. Every part of me wanted to be up and moving, preferably pacing. But I forced myself to sit, knowing that if I was going to pull this off, I needed to carefully craft the picture presented to the arriving desert dwellers.

Puss and Xavier still hadn't returned when Caravan Cobolt became visible, the individual people and camels close enough to be distinguished. They were moving at a swift pace, obviously eager to return home after their long journey.

I remained sitting as the leaders of the caravan reached the gate, murmuring last minute instructions to the women beside me.

"Open up!" someone shouted from below, pounding on the wood of the gate.

"What's going on?" another voice called. "What sort of welcome home is this?"

Still we all remained silent.

More of the caravan members had dismounted, and the clump of people at the gate was growing. None of them had looked up yet, though, to see me sitting above them.

I continued to wait as the final stragglers arrived, the camels lowering to sit and let their riders dismount. There were some women among them, but more men—as expected given the absence of men among those left behind.

I glanced at the stairs. Still there was no sign of Xavier and Puss. If they didn't arrive within the next minute, I would need to act without them. Timing was everything.

A ginger streak bolted up the stairs and leaped into my lap. I smiled, patting Puss's fur with a trembling hand.

"Just in time," I murmured.

I'm always on time, Puss meowed.

"Even that time I was stuck in the pit?" I asked quietly, my eyes narrowing.

Puss wouldn't meet my eyes, coughing instead.

"I knew it!" I hissed, trying to distract myself from the tension of stretched nerves and anxious thoughts. I was only half paying attention to my own words, though, most of my attention on the scene before us.

Gage appeared from the back of the crowd, pushing past people as he elbowed his way to the front. Everything in me screamed that it was the moment to act.

"Now," I muttered to Puss and surged to my feet.

He leaped from my lap onto the top of the half-wall.

Your empress welcomes you home, he yowled, his voice booming over the wall.

I stepped forward and held up a hand in a wave, smiling serenely at the crowd below.

Shouts broke out as everyone craned to look upward.

"What is this?" Gage shouted, his face terrifying in its intensity.

"Look to your own portrait to see the truth," I called in my loudest and most commanding voice, pointing at the painting propped up beside me. "Look at it, and then look at me. Your true empress has returned."

A shudder shook the crowd below, rolling across them as their world twisted and shifted.

"What is this treason?" Gage bellowed. "Where is the emperor?"

I met his eyes, holding his gaze unwaveringly. "Go to the ocean, and you can see for yourself."

I didn't like that his body still lay there, but there hadn't been time for anything else, and I was willing to use any tool I had.

Gage cursed, turning to two men who lingered close behind him. He murmured something to them, but we were too far away to do more than guess at his words. I glanced at Xavier, who stood back a couple of steps out of sight.

"The side gate?" I asked, and he nodded reassuringly. It was done.

Several men broke off from the crowd, circling left toward the wall with the side gate. Three others followed Gage as he ran the other way, racing for the ocean. I counted them. Four had gone to the side gate, and three with Gage. Including him that made eight. It was enough.

I ran to the other side of the walkway and looked down into the internal courtyard.

"Quick! Open the gates!"

The messenger poised there waiting for my message sped off. I ran back to my previous vantage point.

It felt like an agonizingly long time, but in reality was only seconds before the gates began to creak open.

"Hurry!" I called. "Get inside. Leave the camels!"

I regretted abandoning the beasts, but it was the best I could do for now. They showed no signs of straying, so we would hopefully be able to gather them soon. For now, I needed to get all the people safely inside.

The gates opened only part way, a woman dashing out from the opening. As people poured inside, she spoke urgently to two of the men still on the sand. They frowned, but after glancing up at me, both nodded. Grabbing at the arms of several more men, they gathered a group and turned on two of the remaining men.

After a short altercation involving shouted words I didn't catch, the two men they had grabbed were unceremoniously deposited in the sand beside the camels. The group who had done it turned back toward the gate, but from my vantage point I caught sight of the men who had gone to the side door returning. They had found it barred and returned to seek fresh instructions.

I leaned dangerously far over the edge, feeling the reassuring grasp of Xavier's hands grabbing the back of my dress as I had known he would.

"Run!" I shouted, waving frantically for the remaining caravan members to get inside.

They obeyed instantly, not pausing to question or even look around them.

The second the last one passed through, the great gates slammed closed again. I breathed a sigh of relief, my legs turning wobbly and weak. I clutched the wall in front of me for support. We'd done it.

A reverberating shout of rage drifted over from the ocean side of the Fortress. I sighed and sank back into my chair.

"Gage found his brother."

I had no idea if there had been any love between them, or if it had been swallowed by ambition and wicked action, but my heart twisted all the same. I knew what it was like to lose what little family you still had.

Xavier held out a hand, and I took it, rising back to my feet and smiling up at him. I had lost my old family, but I had found a new one in Xavier, and I didn't intend to let him go, no matter what his father or anyone else said.

"Do you think your father would accept an empress as a sufficient ally?" I said with a slightly hysterical giggle.

Xavier pulled me close and laughed. "How could he possibly not?"

I shook my head and reluctantly stepped back, gesturing for everything to be carried below. I still had to face the bulk of the caravan, letting them see the likeness for themselves up close.

Another bellow sounded, but I ignored it. What I didn't intend to do was stay to bandy words with a murderer. Our walls were secure, and he was the one adrift in the desert. There was nothing to be gained by further engagement.

The people waiting below, both men and women, swarmed around me, all of them exclaiming as they saw my face at closer range. They all deferred to one man, calling him caravan leader, so I pulled him aside.

"You're sure all of Gage's followers are on the other side of the wall?"

He saluted. "Yes, Your Imperial Majesty."

"You really don't have to—" I sighed, giving it up for the moment. "Never mind that, what about the reverse? None of our people are stuck out there?"

He saluted again. "No, Your Imperial Majesty. It was expertly handled."

I breathed another sigh of relief. Unlike the women who had remained behind, I knew the true crimes committed by this group. But it wasn't my role to sit as judge and sentencer over them. What mattered for now was that those inside the walls were no immediate threat.

The caravan leader watched my face, his own expression slowly changing as he absorbed mine. He was clearly a perceptive man.

"You came from Lanover, didn't you?" he asked.

I hesitated. "Not originally, but I've spent some time there recently."

He grimaced. "Enough time to hear of Caravan Cobolt, I'll be bound."

I hesitated again before nodding.

"Some of us tried to stop Gage from burning and abandoning that ship," he said hurriedly. "But those loyal to him were the strongest fighters, and we were easily overwhelmed."

I raised an eyebrow. "But you greatly outnumbered them."

He sighed. "As our caravan's crimes mounted, many of us began to protest. That's when Gage made it clear those left behind were hostages. The threat was enough to subdue many. Without them, we didn't have the numbers to stop Gage when he torched that ship." A haunted look filled his eyes. "I've had nightmares every night since. So many dead."

I placed a hand on his arm. "Gage killed some of the sailors outright, but rescue arrived in time to save those left to drown."

The man's eyes widened, his frame sagging with relief. "Oh, thank goodness," he muttered.

I decided to take a risk. "Other caravans will be arriving soon, along with Lanoverian forces. If you're serious about your regret, I hope you'll support me in welcoming them."

He met my gaze, and I could see he understood the full import of my words. It was not for me to decide their guilt—that would be something he must negotiate with the victims.

"We will welcome them," he said at last, and I nodded.

"In that case, you should all eat and drink and rest. There will be time enough for everything else later."

Despite my insistence that they care for themselves first, I couldn't stop them from greeting me one by one, each person introducing themselves, including the women and children who had been here the whole time. I did my best to remember them but dreaded my inevitable lapses. There were just too many to remember all at once.

Finally, as night was falling, I climbed wearily back up to the top of the wall. I'd already heard the reports from the children who'd taken it on themselves to stay up there as afternoon watch, but I wanted to see for myself.

It was as they'd said. Gage and his followers had taken the camels, along with all the stolen money and goods on their backs, and disappeared into the desert. It wasn't unexpected, given the report that the caravan's water reserves were running low. They'd need to make for an oasis because the only source of fresh water near here was barred to them.

"It's a pity they were able to take everything with them," Xavier murmured at my side, but I shook my head before resting it on his shoulder.

"Our caravans are coming, and they'll be angry. It's better this way. They'll have an enemy to chase down, and that will soften them toward everyone inside the Fortress."

He chuckled. "When did you learn all this statecraft?"

I smiled up at him. "A very smart person told me I needed to follow my instincts."

"He does sound smart," Xavier agreed with a straight face. "Sultan Khalil should make him an official advisor—probably give him a handsome salary too."

"I'll be sure to tell the sultan that when I meet him," I said gravely.

Xavier laughed and pulled me around to face him. "Will you expect him to bow in your presence, Your Imperial Majesty? I think empresses outrank sultans."

I groaned. "I'm just hoping by the time Frederic arrives here with the caravans, I'll have trained them out of the titles and the bowing. I'm hoping Frederic will accept the Fortress as a city of Lanover. The caravan leader looks like a good candidate for mayor, if King Leonardo agrees. And once they have their camels back, they'll be able to start trade with the rest of the kingdom." I twisted to look down into the Fortress. "Who knows what treasures might be hidden in this place? If nothing else, there will be historians from across the Four Kingdoms, as well as Kuralan and Ardasira, wanting to come study it. Hopefully that will be enough for them to get a proper start on a free life."

"But not with an empress at their head?" Xavier asked with a chuckle.

I put my cheek against his chest. "If I hear *Your Imperial Majesty* from you one more time," I yawned, "I won't be responsible for the consequences."

"Oh really? How very intriguing…Your Imperial Majesty."

"Hey!" I pulled back and swiped at him with both hands.

But he caught them, laughing down into my face before stealing a kiss.

"I like kissing an empress," he said plaintively. "Surely you can't deny your one true love."

"Fine." I gave him a stern look. "You can choose. I can stay here in my rightful place as empress of all the desert, or I can return to Kuralan, marry you, and become Princess Kalila."

"Who wants to be empress of a desert?" he said promptly. "My lady."

I chuckled, my sleepy eyes drooping again. "That's better."

He ducked down, stealing another kiss. "I do like the sound of Princess Kali best of all."

I sighed with happiness and wrapped my arms around him, my eyes drifting shut. "Me too. I was so sure my future lay in adventures across the desert, and somehow, all I can think of now is returning home to Kuralan."

"Traveling can have that effect," Xavier agreed. "But don't worry, you'll get itchy feet again soon enough."

I smiled, not opening my eyes. "As long as you're traveling with me, I'll go anywhere in the kingdoms."

Warm lips pressed against mine once more. "We'll visit them all."

EPILOGUE

"You look perfect," Evie breathed, gazing at me with wide eyes. "A true empress."

I turned to the mirror, flushing at the sight of my pure white gown, designed by the princess herself as a perfect mix between a traditional wedding gown and the ancient gowns of my ancestors.

"You're stunning, Your Imperial Majesty," Zaria said, curtsying deeply.

"Stop that!" I cried, throwing a loose flower at her. "I'm not an empress anymore. I've officially abdicated the position."

Zaria laughed, clearly thinking herself hilarious. She and Prince Tarek had arrived two weeks before, and she was still laughing every time she thought of my unexpected ascension to a higher rank than her own.

"I always knew you were special," she told me when she finally regained control.

"Yes, yes." I rolled my eyes. "You always knew I was royalty." A smile slipped over my face. "After all, you only like to be friends with royals, don't you?"

"What?" She put her hands on her hips.

I chuckled. "Too close to the truth? Where's your other best friend? Prince Navid, I believe that would be."

"He wasn't a prince when we became friends," she protested, making me laugh harder.

"I'm glad to see you so happy," Tillie said, smiling at me affectionately. "Thank you for coming, Princess Zaria. It's nice to see Kali around an old friend."

"But of course!" My friend beamed at the two Lanoverian princesses. "I would never miss Kali's wedding. And Rek would never miss Xavier's. I'm just sorry Sultan Khalil couldn't come himself."

"It's a long journey," Evie said graciously. "Lanover is honored by the presence of Sultana Rabia and her children."

"Don't look nervous, it isn't because he disapproves," Zaria assured me in an under voice as she slipped the final white rose into my hair. "He just couldn't leave Kuralan without a ruler for so long."

I turned to give her a fierce embrace. "I'm glad you and the prince didn't remain behind in his place."

"As if we would!" She hugged me back. "Rek is far closer to Xavier than his father ever was."

"I can't believe this is really happening," I said. "We're going to be sisters."

I looked across at Tillie and Evie who were helping each other to fasten the attendant dresses Evie had designed for the three of them. I had seen what it could mean to share a palace with a sister-in-law who was also a friend, and I couldn't wait.

"You are coming straight back home after the wedding?" Zaria asked, looking at me suspiciously. "Xavier doesn't have a secret plan to whisk you off on an adventure?"

I suppressed a grin. "We both want to see home again. I'm not promising we won't be off on new adventures, but we're ready for a break for now."

"Oh good." Zaria rested her head on my shoulder and smiled

at me in the mirror. "He's going to be so happy when he sees you."

I flushed again, wishing the minutes would pass more quickly so I could be by his side.

"We're going to be sad to lose you, though," Evie said, coming over to join us. "It's been so nice to have you here for these months."

"Thank you for accepting me as an honorary Lanoverian," I said.

"How could we not, now that the Fortress has officially allied with us?" Tillie asked, her eyes alight as they always were when she spoke of the ancient city.

I had learned a great deal about the complicated legal framework of the desert traders in the last few months. They were party to the treaties of the merchant council, but given their geographical limits, they had long ago sworn limited fealty to the Lanoverian crown as well. Evie and Tillie repeatedly insisted it gave me legitimate grounds to call myself Lanoverian.

What mattered more, however, was that the Fortress had now been officially accepted by the desert trader caravans. The Fortress had signed to their treaties and bound itself to their laws. With the backing of the caravans, it had become a semi-independent city-state—the home base that the traders had long been without. I truly believed it would be a beneficial arrangement on all sides.

"Have you convinced King Leonardo to let you go with one of the caravans heading south after the wedding?" I asked.

She smiled beatifically. "We're going with Caravan Adira—Cassian and the children as well. We'll be able to stay at the Fortress for a whole month."

"Your father must be so happy," Evie said, referring to the head of Caravan Adira.

"He's beside himself," Tillie said. "He finally gets to introduce his grandchildren to the caravan life."

"And you'll finally get to see the Fortress for yourself," Evie said.

"Living history," Tillie breathed. "I never thought the trader caravans would have a capital city, but is it any wonder they've assumed joint ownership over the heritage it represents?"

"I'm just glad they were able to recover all the stolen property and return it to the towns," I said. "And I hope it won't be long before the rest of Lanover stops viewing the remaining residents of the Fortress with suspicion. All of those who accompanied the caravan have faced judgment and accepted the punishments given."

"Don't worry," Evie said. "The governor of Largo has come up to Lanare for the wedding, and he said several trade agreements have just been signed between Largoan merchant families and the Fortress."

"Really?" I spun to look at her in delight. "You're sure?"

She laughed. "You abdicated, remember? And it's your wedding day! You don't have to think about trade treaties today."

I turned back to the mirror, smiling ruefully. "It isn't easy to shake the sense of responsibility over so many lives. But now that they have a mayor from among their own people, they'll be fine. I know they will."

"Of course they will." Zaria handed me a bouquet of trailing white blossoms. "Since the caravans defeated Gage and his followers, there's no one left to try to control them."

"And now your betrothed awaits." Evie gave me a gentle shove toward the door.

I moved eagerly, having to hold myself back from running through the corridors of the palace. But when we arrived at the doors of the enormous throne room, I stopped to take a nervous breath. I could hear the murmur of the crowd even through the heavy wood.

I didn't hesitate for long, though. Xavier waited for me on the other side, along with a future more bright than any I had imagined in all those years spent dreaming of adventures.

Xavier wrapped his arms around me with a contented sigh, surveying the crowd that was still deep in celebration despite the late hour. He pressed a kiss against the top of my head, and I leaned back against him.

"A perfect day," I said, and he murmured agreement.

An identical face to the one behind me approached through the crowd, and I straightened, smiling at my new brother.

Xander smiled back, pulling his brother into a brief hug. "I'm here to bid you farewell."

"You're still determined?" Xavier asked, unable to erase the slight disappointment in his tone.

I slipped my hand into his and squeezed. He would miss his twin, of course, but we would see him again.

"I am," Xander said. "I leave early in the morning to head north. The latest rumors suggest she's in Northhelm, so I'm accompanying Prince William and Princess Celeste when they return."

I didn't have to ask who *she* was. Princess Daisy. The last remaining girl missing from a delegation that had been attacked four years ago. According to Xavier, his brother had been obsessed with the idea of finding and rescuing her from the moment he first heard the story—even before the wise woman had come with her cryptic message about the missing princess.

Xander believed her to be in danger, so I couldn't blame him for wanting to find her. I didn't even blame him for prioritizing the search over fetching me some clothes, all those months ago.

"I hope you find her this time," I said, and Xander smiled warmly at me.

"It's easier to go knowing you'll be there to look after Xavier this time."

Do you think Kali is good for such a role? a curious voice asked. *She seems to get into more trouble than he does.*

"Puss! You're only supposed to say nice things on my wedding day," I said with a laugh.

Puss raised an eyebrow. *Do I ever say anything else?*

Xavier and I looked at each other, both bursting into laughter.

"Do you really have to leave?" I asked. "Won't you come back to Kuralan with us?"

Puss looked horrified. *Why would I want to go there? I can finally return home.*

"But you'll come to visit us again?" I asked, remembering the words of the wise woman who had visited only a week ago.

According to her, tonight marked the completion of Puss's assigned task. He might not be a wise woman, but apparently true love had been part of his mission regardless.

The woman—a gray haired lady with twinkling eyes and sparkling wings—had explained that after the success of Arvin's time among the kingdoms, the High King had decreed that the other creatures in his realm should also spend time here. Puss was merely the first to be assigned a task to complete—a prospect I found both thrilling and terrifying, although sadly it was likely I wouldn't be part of whatever adventures the other creatures experienced.

Puss leaped up onto the table beside us and eyed a whole fish that still lay on a platter there.

I will come again. He didn't look up from the fish at my exclamation of pleasure. *When you have children who need training. Naturally they will need my guidance.*

"Children?" Xavier asked in a choked voice, while I stared at Puss in horror.

"*You're* going to train our children?"

"Could anyone be better suited to the task?" Xander asked with a straight face, and Xavier lunged for him.

Puss ignored us all, taking several bites from the fish. He gobbled them down before suddenly freezing. His sharp cough made me step forward, my brow creasing.

"Puss? Are you all right?" It didn't sound like the usual noise he made when hacking up a fur ball.

Turning, he coughed again and spat out a shiny gold object. Xander and Xavier stopped wrestling, all three of us peering at the coin resting on the table.

"Was that inside the fish?" Xavier asked, fascinated.

The fish must have been caught from the river just outside Lanare, Puss said primly.

"The river? Why would you think that…" My voice trailed off, my eyes widening.

"Puss," I said, my voice choked. "Do you have some particular reason to think there might be gold coins in that river? Did you, perhaps, throw the gold coins in there?" My voice rose. "A whole pouch full?"

Puss tore off another piece of the fish. *I don't know why you're so upset.*

"You don't know why I'm—" My voice failed me, and I snatched at the cat.

Xavier only just pulled me back before my hands could close around him. "Leave him be," he said, laughing. "You have gold enough now."

"It's not about the gold," I said through gritted teeth. "He took everything I had and just threw it away! That flea-bitten, mangy—"

Nonsense. Puss looked up from his meal. *That wasn't all you had.* He looked at Xavier, who was still holding me around the waist. *You also had him.*

I froze, staring at Puss while Xavier laughed.

"You always were wise, Puss," he said.

"But…I didn't have you then," I spluttered, while Xavier grinned down at me.

"Of course you did. Didn't I tell you that I was chasing you from the first moment I saw you?"

All this time, Puss shook his head disapprovingly, *and you still haven't learned that I'm always right.*

I snorted. "I'm not sure you've learned the lesson the High King wanted."

Lesson? Puss gave me a superior look. *I am not Arvin. Naturally I wasn't sent here to learn a lesson. I was here to help you. And I have performed my task admirably. As I always do.*

"We bow to your superiority," Xander said solemnly, only the twinkle in his eyes giving him away.

But Puss had turned back to the fish, so the prince got away with it. Shaking my head, I also turned away.

"Do you think Puss will really come back?" I muttered. "I'm not sure I want him now."

"Of course he will." Xavier smiled down at me. "He likes you, even if he pretends he only likes himself. Just like you love him, even if you pretend to want to be rid of him."

A slow smile spread over my face. "You know me too well."

"I believe I mentioned that before also," he said, pulling me close.

Xander cleared his throat. "I'll be going, then. Congratulations to you both."

We broke apart to wish him farewell, but as soon as he disappeared into the crowd, Xavier pulled me close again.

"I thought today would never come," he murmured.

"And yet here we are." I sank against him, smiling up into his heart-stopping face. "At the start of our future together."

His arms tightened around me. "Could any adventure be more thrilling? I look forward to every twist and turn."

"As do I." I tilted my face invitingly, and he reached down and kissed me, a seal on a future I couldn't wait to meet.

Find out if Xander ever finds the missing Princess Daisy in The Abandoned Princess: A Retelling of Rapunzel.

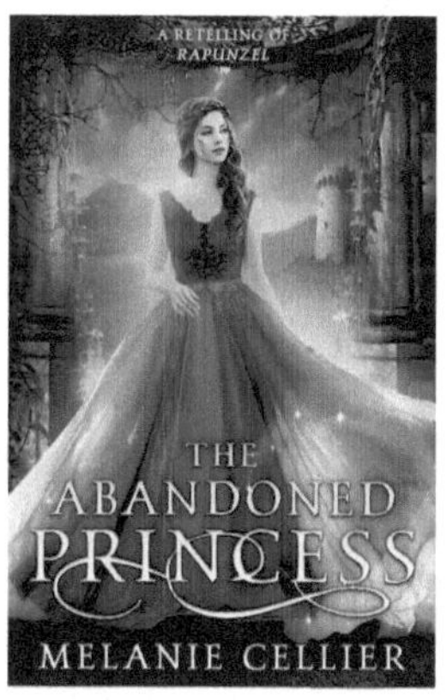

Or if you missed first meeting Kali and Xavier in Zaria and Prince Tarek's story, read The Golden Princess: A Retelling of Ali Baba and the Forty Thieves.

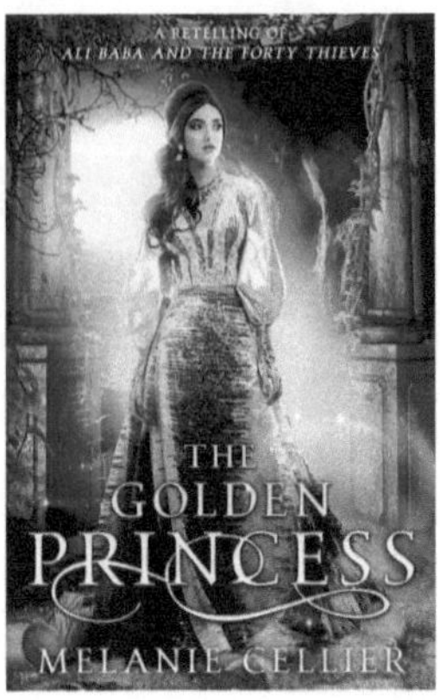

To be informed of my new releases, as well as new bonus shorts, please sign up to my mailing list at www.melaniecellier.com. At my website, you'll also find an array of free extra content in my Four Kingdoms world.

Thank you for taking the time to read my book. I hope you enjoyed it. If you did, please spread the word! You could start by leaving a review on Amazon or Goodreads or Facebook or any other social media site. Your review would be very much appreciated and would make a big difference!

ACKNOWLEDGMENTS

Kali and Xavier were a fun couple to write, and I hope they were equally fun to read. The original tale of the crafty cat who turns a miller's son into nobility definitely has Puss as the main hero, but I enjoyed turning Puss and Kali into a more equal partnership, as well as giving them more significant challenges to overcome.

And I'm excited that at long last, my next fairy tale belongs to Daisy who has had to wait years for her happily-ever-after. (Just enough years for her to grow old enough to become a romance heroine, that is ;))

However smoothly a book flows, there are always improvements to be made, and I'm grateful for my expanded team and the love and care they gave to this book. In particular to my editors: Mary, Laura, Deborah, and my dad. But also to my beta readers, in particular, Priya, Ber, and Rachel.

Thank you also to Karri for inspiring aspects of the story with the beautiful cover, and to my author friends. Kitty, Brittany, and Aya, thanks for the chats and encouragement. Cheri and Shari, thanks for entering into my excitement as I discovered the world of kdramas—it's been so much more fun thanks to you. And thanks Marina for keeping me focused with writing sprints—I know I got more words in each day thanks to your presence, even if it was only virtual.

To my delightful children and husband—thanks for fueling me with hugs and love, and thank you to God for being the foundation that everything else is built on.

ABOUT THE AUTHOR

Melanie Cellier grew up on a staple diet of books, books and more books. And although she got older, she never stopped loving children's and young adult novels.

She always wanted to write one herself, but it took three careers and three different continents before she actually managed it.

She now feels incredibly fortunate to spend her time writing from her home in Adelaide, Australia where she keeps an eye out for koalas in her backyard. Her staple diet hasn't changed much, although she's added choc mint Rooibos tea and Chicken Crimpies to the list.

She writes young adult fantasy including books in her *Spoken Mage* world, her *Mage's Influence* world, and her various *Four Kingdoms* and *Kingdoms of Legacy* series that are made up of linked stand-alone stories that retell classic fairy tales.

www.ingramcontent.com/pod-product-compliance
Lightning Source LLC
Chambersburg PA
CBHW060750190726
48285CB00002B/377